Family Values

Other Books by Michael J. Bugeja

POETRY:

What We Do For Music
The Visionary
Platonic Love
After Oz
Flight from Valhalla
Talk

FICTION:

Little Dragons

NONFICTION:

Guide to Writing Magazine Nonfiction
Poet's Guide
Living Ethics
Academic Socialism
The Art & Craft of Poetry
Culture's Sleeping Beauty
The How-To Newswriter

Family Values

Michael J. Bugeja

SLIGO PRESS
P.O. BOX 523
BEND, OREGON 97709

Published in the United States of America by:
Sligo Press
P.O. Box 523
Bend, Oregon 97709

Publisher's Cataloging-in-Publication Data

Bugeja, Michael
    Family Values / by Michael Bugeja
      p. cm.
    ISBN 0-9651213-4-8
    I. Title
    1997
    LCCN 96-70656

Printed on acid-free paper
Manufactured in the United States of America

First Edition
10 9 8 7 6 5 4 3 2 1

In memory of Ann Howland

This book was completed with the help of a grant from the National Endowment for the Arts, a federal agency.

1

No News Is Good News

Mylo Thrump was waiting at the curb when the taxi pulled up to take him to work. He was the editor of the morning newspaper in a nameless Midwest city. On his way downtown, particularly on a Monday, he liked to watch the city and its inhabitants as a monarch might, noting every pothole, detour, siren, billboard, and building site. It calmed him to behold the usual monuments of civilized man—the Andover Court condoplex, the White Castle and Burger King, the Tutor Park mall, and finally his stop outside the Little Prince Book Palace below the Chronicle Building.

Nothing remarkable occurred today on that route. Mylo felt no pothole into which the cab lurched. Traffic, in fact, flowed smoothly. Several police and state patrol cars were parked at fast-food restaurants. The city was calm enough for a coffee break. Mylo saw no racy or outrageous billboards about Colt 45 or abortion, and construction work at building sites—a new hospital wing, a larger homeless shelter—was progressing on schedule.

Normally such sights would rile an editor looking for a story, but no news was good news for Mylo Thrump. It meant that he could invent some, and invented news was always more interesting or dramatic than *real* news. The talk and tabloid shows had proved that, and it was about time staid newspapers caught on; their newsrooms were electric now as any broadcasting booth—replete with e- and voice-mail, digital imaging, and Internet—but cronies still missed their Royal manual typewriters.

Mylo was going to raise cain and circulation today.

The cabby pulled up in front of the newspaper building. The driver had to double-park alongside a minivan with a mother inside consoling her son in the baby seat.

"Five sixty-five," the cabby said. Mylo studied him for the first time since entering the cab. Sometimes, he knew, a news story was under your nose—literally. The cabby was Arab-looking but spoke without an accent. He seemed too intelligent for the job, a sign of the times. For all Mylo knew, the man could be an unemployed schoolteacher or engineer.

A terrorist maybe.

"I haven't got all day, mister," the cabby said, waiting for his fare.

Mylo nodded. He took a crisp five from his wallet, using his thumb and forefinger, and then dug in his suit pants for exact change. The cabby took the money palm out, and the coins rolled off the cash, falling under the gas pedal and causing the driver to shut off the engine to collect them. "*Jesus*," he said.

"No Arab," Mylo muttered, thinking "*Allah*." He wanged the cab door against the minivan's side panel and startled the mother, who swung around and unrolled her window to address the cabby. "Did you bump my car?"

"What? Where'd he go? Listen, lady—"

"No, *you* listen," she said, and the two began to bicker, car to car.

Mylo strolled around the woman's vehicle and peered into the van on the passenger side, waving at a crying boy in the car seat. His arm was caught in the strap. The baby stopped wailing and froze upon seeing Mylo, a concerned look on his infant brow.

Bingo. Mylo imagined a story. He turned on his heel and looked up at the Chronicle Building, whose marble-work glistened in sunlight.

It was another glorious day.

* * *

Mylo's wife Wendy had left him. Granted, it took a while for him to notice as they had stopped living according to any schedule. They were married for eight years, much of it spent apart from each other in the final months. Wendy had been a top-flight reporter for the *Herald*, the cross-town rival, and began working nights while Mylo worked days. They could not share weekends; Wendy had Mondays and Tuesdays off, Mylo's busiest time. He planned stories then for the week. So it was not always like this, Mylo was starting to realize. For much of their marriage, Wendy had nurtured her husband and moti-vated him, offering her good judgment—steering him past newsroom politics—until Mylo reached the top. She should have been happy for him but instead put her energy into her own work, taking the night shift, she said, so that she could have more time to develop stories. Worse, she seemed to like her new-found freedom and grew resentful when Mylo revamped the *Chronicle*, changing it from a respected publication into a tabloid with sensational stories. Wendy stopped communicat-ing. She stopped keeping house. When she left six months ago, she didn't even compose a note for fear, he supposed, that he would overlook it amid the general disarray of their country club split-level home. Instead he received a business letter—she had the gall to use a colon after the salutation—informing him that she had been promoted to editor of the *Herald*. "I just can't live with a competitor," she wrote. "It wouldn't be right."

Mylo had not heard from her since, although Claude Turner—Mylo's publisher—mentioned recently that Wendy was planning to refocus the *Herald* so that it could compete bet-ter with the *Chronicle*. As of late, though, the newspaper under Wendy's editorship still clung to its old format of safe commu-nity news. Her so-called changes in format might be gossip to keep him on guard, Mylo thought. At any rate, he could have phoned her and inquired, pretending to be a disgruntled reader. Disguised his voice.

But Mylo was in no hurry to contact Wendy. He figured she would sue for divorce soon enough. That was all right. Mylo felt married to the *Chronicle* anyway. Wendy left while he was suf-fering a rare form of midlife crisis. It began simply enough about a year ago. Mylo would stop outside the Little Prince Book Palace window display where the front pages of the

Chronicle and the *Herald* were tacked to a bulletin board along-side the likes of the *Globe*, the *Star*, the *Weekly World News,* and, of course, the *National Enquirer.* He would admire the colorful banner headlines of the sensational tabloids—"Pygmies Shrink Alien's Head" or "Preacher Explodes During Sermon"—and compare them to the staid conservative titles of the *Chronicle* and its competitor: "Mayor to Announce Reelection Bid" or "Private Donations Rise at City Campus." When Mylo com-pared the tabloid world to that of the *Chronicle* and *Herald,* the scandal sheets seemed as alluring as models in *Victoria's Secret.*

Something sluttish was born within him. His outlook, usu-ally bleak, began to brighten along with his newspaper's front page. He ordered up a menu of bizarre stories that allowed for absurdity—something the tabloids knew and the legitimate newspapers did not. The old world of the *Chronicle* was a con-trolled world; mayors and judges were reelected, civic projects always improved, doctors always cured patients, cops always caught robbers, bank and college presidents received awards, schools got funded, sports got praised, and murders and rapes got buried with bankruptcies and obituaries. The new world of the *Chronicle* did not rule anything out, even aliens. (Readers who close-encountered were given free subscriptions, if they told their tales on the *Chronicle's* website [http:www.mylo.com] or editorial pages.)

Mylo questioned everything: how police could rule as sui-cide the demise of a man with thirty-two hammer blows to the head (the coroner was on vacation). No one was spared, not even the husband who lost his thumb while working on the Lawnboy near the doghouse in his yard (Rover ate the digit). Nothing was sacred, especially sports and religion. The *Chroni-cle* reported that the college football team had abandoned chapel services in the locker room because the players, when they lost, assumed it was God's will. (When the coach complained, Mylo focused on the marching band and blew up a photo of the sax player mooning opposing fans.)

The readers loved it. He brought out the worst in them. The more cynical they became about their city, the harder Mylo worked to uncover the macabre. When there was a rape, he bannered it. When there was a murder, he splashed the headline with red ink.

Of course, at first there was opposition. Claude at one point during the transition threatened to fire Mylo. The publisher was a Forbes-like flat-tax millionaire whose image meant nearly as much as his money. Mylo persuaded Claude to focus on the latter. As circulation increased and the *Herald* lost ground—to the point of layoffs—Claude gave his editor the green light.

Mylo covered the basics. To begin with, he allowed older reporters to protect their reputations at city hall, the police station, and the college. Their upbeat stories made the wilder ones stand out with a hypocritical vengeance. Mylo, for instance, would postpone the FBI story announcing lower crime statistics and then publish it on a bad day, when a bank was robbed or a bystander wounded in a shootout. The annual hospital fund-drive appeared above an article about malpractice in the emergency room. When a senior reporter profiled the city planner as a family man and churchgoer, Mylo ran it alongside a scoop about bid-rigging with the planner's *Goodfella* relatives in the plumbing business.

Mylo knew the system. As long as ad revenue and circulation kept rising, along with Claude's profits and prestige at the Gentry Club, where he jet-setted, Mylo could do as he pleased. And he did. The editor transformed the publication as if from the grave. The newspaper thought like Mylo. He was its creator and bodyguard. He daydreamed when seasoned reporters confronted him about his ethics, knowing they could not jump ship and join the failing *Herald*.

He had to admit, it felt good to destroy his runaway wife's old newspaper. It felt better to rely largely on women to do his dirty work at the *Chronicle*—underlings like Laurel Eby and Kimberly Spears—who watched him warily from their computer terminals, wondering what Mylo had concocted on his way to work.

"Kimberly, come with me. Bring the overnight file," Mylo said as he entered the newsroom that morning. The "overnight" was a list of wire stories sent in the wee hours, combined with e-mail messages to the home page or calls to the 1-900 line. Usually Laurel brought the file to Mylo in the morning, but he wanted to keep his ace off balance—in the holy name of competition. So he went with Kimberly today. She was a cutthroat reporter whose methods reminded Mylo of his estranged wife. She had the same kind of nose for news, which wasn't necessarily an asset these days at the *Chronicle*. Mylo often had to help her taint a story, highlight its sensational aspects. He didn't mind. It pleased him to work alongside Kimberly, although he never let on. He sensed that she was eager to blame any man who admired her.

Mylo waited for Kimberly to fetch the file and her notebook and pen while Laurel eyed her with suspicion. They sat at facing desks—Mylo's idea—so each knew what the other was working on. Laurel had just finished an offbeat story about a moose in love with a cow and was temporarily idle. She was eager to get another story and another step on Kimberly, whose role was to balance Laurel's sex/sensational stories with her bizarre/gruesome ones. This way, the newspaper was a combination of "Ricki Lake" and "Rescue 911."

Mylo headed toward his office.

"What about me?" he heard Laurel ask.

"Just Kimberly," he replied.

Mylo liked to undermine women the way Wendy had undermined him. Sometimes, just to taunt the gals, he would ask Kimberly and Laurel to cover the same story and then use the "better" written version, which meant the more flamboyant one for the *Chronicle*. He hired them as stars of rival state journalism schools. He bannered their stories when they obeyed him and buried them when they did not. In sum, he had created two brides for Frankenstein, and he depended on each of them to come up with an odd or bewildering account of life as Mylo knew it.

Kimberly entered his office. She closed the glass door and took a seat, looking smug. Mylo sat down at his desk and gave her a slight but respectful nod. He did not like smug in anybody but himself. Yet he tolerated it in Kimberly. He did not care much for her appearance, though. She didn't wear makeup. Sometimes she didn't even shave her legs but wore dark blue stockings (as if he couldn't tell). And she never did up her hair as neatly as Laurel. When it frizzed, as it did today, Kimberly would unroll the rubber band of a newspaper—everyone knew that she did this—and twist her strawberry-blond hair into a ponytail that resembled a Shetland's. She also was a large woman, not fat but big-boned, and did not fit well in skirts. She adjusted the one she was wearing—Mylo enjoyed her uneasiness—and poised herself, ready to read from the overnight file. "Not much here," she said.

"Anything on that list about babies?" Mylo asked.

Kimberly scanned the yellow printout and looked up, surprised. "Why, yes. Someone called in on 1-900 to complain about daycare in the city."

Mylo waited. "That's all?" He asked if the caller mentioned a specific facility or some kind of abuse. It was about time for another daycare scandal story.

"Nope," Kimberly replied. "Seems the woman is unemployed. Single parent. She says she can't look for a job because she has two kids under five." Kimberly handed him a printout of the call to the main computer's answering machine, transcribed automatically. Mylo immediately put it in the trash. Kimberly sighed and continued, "The woman wants to get off welfare and find work, but she has no one to watch her sons." She shrugged. "Good human interest?"

Mylo shook his head. "Let the *Herald* have it." He reached for a pencil and tapped it on the desk like Morse code, a nervous newsroom habit. "Did you check the e-mail?" Last year Mylo had begun a *Chronicle* discussion group on the Internet— "No News Is Good News"—inviting on-liners to suggest stories they would like to read and he could invent.

"Nothing on Inter*nerd*," Kimberly replied. "Usual close-encounter stuff."

"Any mention on that list of yours about cab drivers?"

Kimberly sighed and scanned the overnight again. Then she glanced at Mylo. "Were you in here earlier? Did you go over the file already?" Her eyes narrowed. "Is this some kind of test? Because if it is," she warned, ready to threaten her regular discrimination suit—but caught herself. "Well, *did* you?"

Kimberly wanted to report Mylo because he favored Laurel Eby, a beautiful snitch. Mylo was on to this. Newsroom gossip was that Kimberly wouldn't implicate another woman to get back at a man. Sisterhood.

Mylo pointed the pencil at Kimberly as a teacher does a ruler to make an impression. "What are you talking about, some kind of test? You don't study to pass my kind of test. You know it. It's called 'The News.' " He eased back in his chair and tapped the pencil again as if sending an SOS. "What do have on the cabby?"

Kimberly shook her head and consulted the overnight again. "Nothing on a cabby. But the union may go on strike because of layoffs."

Mylo snickered. "Give it to one of the old-timers on the city desk." As Kimberly read the rest of the overnight, Mylo began to doubt himself. He blamed Wendy for scooping his manhood and legitimate news. The only way to beat her was to go manic on the newsbeat. Deep down he knew he was heading for a crash like an IBM clone with a virus. If Wendy really loved him, he reasoned, she would stop him from committing professional suicide. A few years ago he would have been fired for his antics, but the world had gotten proportionately *weirder* with Murdochs and Newts. He was bringing the Big Apple/Beltway to the Bible belt, and that required imagination. A few minutes ago, standing at curbside by that van, Mylo was sure he had a story about mothers, babies, or cabbies. Mothers. Babies. Cabbies. Then he put it all together: people were either looking for or losing jobs. That explained the quick ride in to work today. Freeways were clear because rush hours were lighter these days. Billboards weren't controversial because they were blank. And the construction projects—the hospital wing, the homeless shelter—were on schedule because they were funded by the feds *before* their blasted "balanced budgets." Okay, there were no potholes to speak of, but the city was going to pot. He explained this to Kimberly.

"An unemployment story?" she inquired. "How mundane."

"Not just any old unemployment story. The mother of all unemployment stories!" Mylo put down his pencil and grabbed the telephone book, holding it like a Bible. It *was* his Bible. "I want you to call every psychic in the city. Astrologers, too. I want prophecies. Doom. Gloom. Then call up the mayor and the city commissioners. Get their usual responses. They'll say that psychics are crazy, but our readers will know who's on the ball."

"As in 'crystal,' I presume," Kimberly quipped.

Mylo gave her the phone book. "Call up a few gypsies while you're at it."

She put the overnight file on the phone book, stood up, and flipped her notebook shut. "Mother of unemployment stories," she mocked, as if foreseeing Mylo on a jobless line.

His phone rang. "Look into it," he said as she exited.

"Right."

It was Claude Turner. The publisher seldom called so early. "Good morning," Mylo said. "What can I do for you?"

"I'm not certain you already have," Claude said. The voice was as high-toned and melodic as ever, bordering on the phony side. But not quite. "Good news."

"Not in *my* newsroom? You know the motto," Mylo said, listening for a chuckle or sign of approval. There was none. Mylo reminded him anyway. "No news is good news at the *Chronicle*."

"The matter is ad revenue," Claude replied. "Receipts are in, and up another 3 percent. Of course, I have to tally expenses. We'll do books later in the week. But as ads go, so go profits. Wonderful!" You could hear the computer printout rustling on the other end. "Three. Symbol of our success."

"Well, then, this *is* a good morning," Mylo said. He took some pleasure in giving the readers what they deserved.

"My thanks." Claude paused for emphasis. Then he coughed, an indication he was going to get serious. "Mylo, I know people

in media don't exactly appreciate your—how shall I put it?—
concept. But we at corporate do." Claude coughed again. This
could be serious, Mylo thought. A two-cough conversation
could lead to anything. Another Yale flunky on the copydesk.
Maybe a special project, a Red Cross blood drive to undercut
the vampire image. "After all," Claude was noting, "the *Chronicle is* a business. We are businessmen. First and foremost."

"I understand that."

"I knew you would," Claude said. "I also know that *as* a
businessman, you appreciate that people of our caliber, well, we
hesitate"—he even said the word slowly, almost condescendingly—"to ask a favor. In a word, when it comes to such matters, we are unschooled. Unaccustomed. As my grandfather
used to say, ask a favor, and the grantee expects quid pro quo."

Quid pro quo? "No doubt," Mylo said. "Quid and more."

"You get my drift. Here it is," Claude said. "My family has
dealt with the Effingtons—you know, as in Values Inc., the
department store people?—for, oh, some two generations, and"—

"Effington? As in Luke, the D.A.?"

"Precisely."

Mylo began to worry. Effington used to be a stand-up guy
until his sister Elizabeth got religion and ruined him. As far as
Mylo was concerned, the D.A. now was a slime who deserved
everything Kimberly leveled at him in the *Chronicle*. Once, on
his sister's advice, the guy locked up a battered wife—obstruction of justice—because she refused to testify against her husband. That was when Mylo nicknamed him "Lock'em'up," and
it stuck. He couldn't believe Claude wanted special treatment
for such a character. "You don't mean Lock'em'up, do you?"

"The same," Claude said. Cough. Mylo was making him
work. Claude continued, "Ever since Laslo the father died, I

have taken it upon myself to counsel, as it were, the daughter Elizabeth, who has been so *active* in the church. And she has made a request, which—reluctantly, mind you—I feel obliged to pass along. Elizabeth asks that we cover her brother Luke at Rotary Club. He is giving a speech and getting a public award. As you may know, Luke has political aspirations."

"Can't do."

Cough. "Give it some thought. A blurb in Club News?"

Mylo eased up. He could handle that. "A few inches then. Remember our motto," he said. "No news"—he paused to let Claude finish the phrase, but the publisher didn't—"is good news."

"Of course. But know this," Claude said in a breathy, gossipy tone. Mylo had to struggle to hear him, as if the publisher had put a hand over the receiver. "Elizabeth tells me that Luke not only will announce for City Commission. He also will discuss the Buchanan hot-button issue of 'family values' "—Claude snickered—"unrelated, naturally, to the registered trademark of his business concern."

"So what?"

"Luke will focus on values of community leaders," Claude said, "especially ones that his sister believes have, well, *gay* tendencies."

This was getting interesting. Mylo told that to Claude.

Encouraged, the publisher added, "I find it remarkable— perhaps *ironic* is a better word—that Luke would discuss family values when his wife Allie, I hear, may be having an affair."

"Perfect."

Claude loosened up. "We understand each other." He spoke in his regular melodic twang. "The *Chronicle* does such important work in this area. I knew you might be, um, *intrigued*. And let us be frank on the type of coverage I am requesting."

"Yes?"

"I don't care how you play it up. Not a jot. I promised, simply, that a representative of our newspaper will be present at the function tonight. In actuality, we shall endorse another candidate, but that of course will occur at the appropriate time."

"We'll get right on it."

"Thank you, Mylo Thrump." Mylo listened for the click on the other end but it did not come. Instead he heard the computer printout rustle again, only louder, as if the publisher was holding the receiver closer to the machine.

Mylo hung up the phone and buzzed Laurel. Kimberly was telling her something, waving a file folder under her nose. Good. Laurel lifted the intercom. "Stop pouting. Get in here," he said.

Laurel entered quietly, as if it were not an office but a sanctuary, and sat down without taking her eyes off Mylo. She looked snappy in a pink slit skirt and white silk blouse. But she was still pouting. "Did you like my moose story? Kimberly says it has holes."

"I saw you two out there," Mylo said. He lowered his voice and let his face go slack, feigning compassion. "Kimberly told me about it." He shook his head in mock sadness.

Laurel saw the opening and took it. "She called me a bimbo. I wouldn't mind if she said something like you are a bad speller, because I am at times, or you are a tease. Of course I am a tease. I have the best network of sources in the newsroom. How else?" She composed herself, flipping her short-cropped auburn hair from the collar of her blouse. "If men are in high places, then someone"—she crossed her legs, as if punctuating her sentence—"let's say, for the record, *me*, has to tame them."

"I thought the moose story had holes," Mylo said.

"Holes?" She brought a hand to her heart, then let it drop to her side. She sat up, smug as a Kimberly. "Name one."

Mylo felt the pressure in him rise. Images of Wendy flipped through his head like an unstoppable slide show. He focused on Laurel testing him. She did not wear smug as well as a skirt. Mylo felt a twinge and tried to concentrate. One day, he knew, thoughts about women and skirts would get him in trouble, but now they melded with visions of moose-cow intercourse. "Can a moose actually, well, you know"—

"Copulate with a cow?"

"You have yet to mention that. You have been covering this story from the start—I even sent you to Maine—and you allude like heck that they can, no, that they *have*. But you never tell us or explain. This, I think, is a hole. A legitimate hole. The common everyday Joe and Josephine want to know, in this order"— he held up one finger—"first, if it can be accomplished." Mylo held up another finger. "Second, if the bull of the herd will mind."

Laurel fixed her eyes upon Mylo as if in a trance. Then she patted her chin and came to. "A small but important point. You see, these were milk cows. Guernseys, to be exact. If they were, say, Angus—you know, as in black *beef* Angus—there might have been a bull in the herd. The bull would have been worth mentioning, because—antlers or no antlers—he would have made a Big Mac out of Mr. Moose. As it happened, this herd was milk cows *sans* bull." Laurel cocked her head—Mylo noticed the high cheekbones—and pressed on. "As for the copulation, I think the common Joe and Josephine realize"—she held up one finger— "first, it can be accomplished." She held up another finger. "Second, only a *bimbo* would explain it."

She stood up to leave.

"You're off the moose follow-up. I have a story right up your alley." He told her about the D.A.'s political aspirations and his "family values" speech. Then he enhanced Claude's gossip about Allie Effington, the mistress wife. "Word is that she has more than one lover. But we'll be conservative for the moment. Just get the goods on one of them."

Laurel grinned. "Just my kind of story," she said. "Apart from the gay angle, I mean." She brought her finger to her cheek and tapped it, as if in deep contemplation. "Who do you think she's sleeping with? Any candidates?"

"Nobody else has declared."

Laurel blushed. "*Male* candidates. As in paramour."

"Look into it," Mylo said, shuffling papers on his desk.

Laurel didn't take the hint. "Sorry about the moose story—I mean, my attitude about it," she said, contrite. Then she beamed. "I just love scandals." She smiled at Mylo as if they were privy to a secret that Kimberly couldn't share.

That made him nervous. Mylo thought again about a discrimination suit, half-welcoming and half-fearing one. That might stop the madness, but Wendy wouldn't be impressed or sympathetic. "Kim's on a hot story," he said, trying to get Laurel on the defensive.

"I know, I know," Laurel breathed. She stood there being pretty, knowing the effect she was having on him. She refused to take the bait. "Sex and politics. Can't beat it," Laurel said, lifting a well-shaped leg to untuck the slit of her skirt. It had folded under, revealing more tease than the moment required. She looked like some kind of flamingo, all pink and white. She put her foot down and continued. "Unemployment stories, no matter how maternal, are 'out.' " She rocked her shoulders and said in a singsong voice, "Anyway, I know who got the best assignment." She smiled again and became self-conscious about doing it. She straightened up—"bye-bye"—and closed the door behind her as gently as she had opened it.

Mylo rose from his swivel chair and went to the window overlooking the city, his domain. From here, this vantage point, he stood stories above city hall, the cluster of downtown build-ings, the park, the homeless shelters, the interstate clovers, the country club, the suburbs, and the mall. It was a heady feeling. Then he spied the Herald Building in the distance and thought of Wendy, his gutsy wife.

Relax, relax, he reassured himself. He had scored a success. Kimberly and Laurel were competing again. The publisher was pleased with the "concept" for the *Chronicle*, which meant more freedom to become racier on the front page. A calm flooded his being. This was a spiritual moment. A mission. Indeed, it *was* a glorious day! You could feel big things were about to happen: a plane crash, missile crisis, assassination. Events fell into place, if you let them. Wendy had never learned that lesson. Ha! If she could see him now! His face—a fleshy, smooth, Celtic one with Brezhnev eyebrows—became ominously placid. He envisioned tomorrow's banner headlines, brighter than tabloid ones on dis-play in the bookstore window:

Psychics Say City on the Verge of Collapse!
Cuckold Candidate: Values Begin in Boudoir!

2

Another Bovine Romance

Across town, in a subdivision not far from the Country Club where Mylo lived, but more posh, Allie Effington retrieved the morning paper from the portico of her minimansion. She undid the rubber band and, on a whim, stretched it from the tip of her forefinger to the trigger finger of her thumb. She uncocked her thumb and the rubber band struck the nearest column, falling limply to the concrete. "Bang," she said. "Double bang." She smoothed her full-length nightgown, tracing her slim figure, and felt a little achy and stiff. What timing. She groaned and returned to the kitchen.

Luke was late for work—they had made love last night—and
that meant Allie could not be alone with her thoughts for at least
another hour. She heard him flush the toilet upstairs at the same
time Mr. Coffee sputtered and steamed on the counter. She
poured herself a cup of coffee, sat at the kitchen table, and spread
out the *Chronicle*. Her mind wandered. What was he doing? She
glanced at the wall clock, a gaudy thing Luke had bought for her
in Switzerland during their honeymoon four years ago. Cuckoo,
of course. In a few minutes a miniature hausfrau in a dirndl
would swing out of a balsa chateau, and the bird in the belfry
would cackle nine times. Some mornings she would catch herself
silently mouthing the cuckoo sound, counting the hour on her
fingers. *One, two, three, four. . . .* Allie hated that clock. It had
come to represent life with Luke, Mr. Precision. No, the *Chronicle* had a better name—Lock'em'up. How he loathed that newspaper! So Allie subscribed, and her husband—district attorney—
couldn't resist reading it to see what was said about him each day.

Allie scanned the front page. The banner, "Lovelorn Moose
Loses Antlers & Interest in Cow," appeared above a picture of a
Guernsey gazing at trees, presumably where Bullwinkle had
fled. Typical, Allie thought. She followed the story whenever
the *Chronicle* carried it. At first she identified with the cow—
wasn't she as domesticated?—and took heart that the Guernsey
had enough spunk to attract something wild. Then she identified with the moose—wasn't she as gullible?—and forgave herself for being fooled somehow by fate. Now she didn't know
what to think. The moose reminded her of Luke losing antlers
and interest. Once her husband had fascinated her. He was
ambitious, too. She had imagined that the energy he put into
his career would bring them a joyous, bustling life. And it did,
for a while. Then he was converted by his sister Elizabeth to a

born-again faith, which killed their marriage (along with his passion and her patience).

Allie recalled their lovemaking the night before. She saw herself below him in the dark—fancied him with horns, with eyes that bulged larger than Bullwinkle's, with mooselike whiskers on her lips. . . . The clock began to cuckoo and Allie, in a daze, began to mouth the count. *One, two, three, four, five, six, seven, eight, nine.*

That's about all it took.

"Morning, hon," Luke said, sitting across from her at the table. He already had poured his cup. "Big day, big day." He was grinning at her, condescendingly, she thought.

"What?" she asked.

"Nothing," Luke said. His grin waned.

Allie pretended not to care what was on his mind. *She* used to fill his mind, but now politics did. Also religion. Not so long ago, *rapture* symbolized their relationship; now, it symbolized some second coming that had nothing to do with sex. To protect herself, Allie feigned disinterest. Maybe then he would leave quicker for work.

No chance.

"Okay," Luke said, "I'll tell you. I sat down here, and you were in a haze." He took a sip of coffee. "As if"—he was wishing more than guessing—"you were praying."

"Praying?"

"What of it?" Luke asked. "I pray each day now when I get up. It's good meditation." He reached for her hand, but she didn't let go of the *Chronicle.* So he shrugged and added, "The world would be a whole lot safer with a psalm or two at the table." Then he got sincere, preachy almost. "Pray together, stay together. Is that how the saying goes?"

Allie was uptight. Luke had a way of coming on hunky-dory the morning after intercourse. "Pray together, stay together"— she wanted to say *lay* together, but thought better of it—"Yes. That's right." She went back to reading the *Chronicle*, putting distance between them. "I wasn't praying, though. In case you're interested."

"Could've fooled me," Luke said, pausing until she raised her eyes from the page.

"I *did* fool you."

"Yep." He reached under the table and patted her thigh. "Thought you were praying, say"—he put his finger on his chin, in mock contemplation—"for more time with me," he said, grinning. Then he became sincere. "Had a great time with you last night, hon."

"You're late," Allie said abruptly, referring to his spending more time with her.

Luke looked at his watch. "You're right."

Allie was stone-faced.

Luke said he had a meeting with his sister Elizabeth. "Talk about praying," he said, as if remembering something bothersome. He clasped his hands, hard, so that the fingertips whitened. "You know, I could be like my father, wasting my life at the store, wondering what to put on special. Playtex? Press-On Nails?"

"Instead you're wondering, usually, about something else." *And it's not me*, Allie thought.

"Yep."

She fought the urge to smack him and then the urge to cry, focusing on his forehead because she couldn't look him in the eye. Luke was telling her about plans for his upcoming primary campaign for City Commission. He and Elizabeth were supposed to map out strategy in his office. "Big day, big day," he said. "Anything to eat?"

Allie got up and went to the cupboard, dreading the weeks that she would have to spend in her role as a candidate's wife. She also would be seeing more of Elizabeth, Luke's campaign manager. Allie took a box of Sugar Frosted Flakes from the cupboard and put it before him—"Here you go, Tiger," she said—along with a bowl, spoon, and more sugar. She poured the cereal for him and it came out in a rush, spilling over the rim and onto the table. She sat down again and looked at the Guernsey on the front page. "Oh, yeah," she said. "We're out of milk."

Luke stared at the bowl. "Oh," he said. "No problem. I'll get a bite on the way in."

"Sorry." Allie looked up from the paper, trying to distract herself. Change the topic. "Remember this story, the moose who fell in love with that cow?"—Luke was shaking his head, no; he was peeved about something. "Well, he dumped her," Allie said. "It doesn't matter."

"I don't know why you read that rag." He took another sip of coffee and cocked his head to the side to cipher the news upside down. "What else? Anything in it about me?"

Allie sneered. She pushed the newspaper across the table. "Take a look at that moose story. You might like it."

"Don't have time for 'mooses'—is that right?—or is it like 'deer,' no plural?" He scooped a spoon of dry flakes and chewed a long time before swallowing. "Anyway, gotta go." He gulped some coffee, swishing it like mouthwash. Then he swirled his tongue over his teeth. "Speaking of Liz, did I tell you she planned this Rotary thing for us tonight?"

"Rotary?" Allie glared at him. Rotary was big in this city, one of the largest chapters in the country, where car dealers, shopkeepers, and idle developers wiled away evenings with their wives. "No. Not tonight, Luke. I got dance class on Monday nights. You remember."

"Big day," he said again. "I'm supposed to get an award. Civic Servant of the Year." He seemed skeptical about something—gears were turning in his head—and remarked, "The primary's around the corner, Al." He addressed her like a voter: "I need your support."

Allie was silent. She had made plans and had not expected this.

"Be a sport. We get a homemade Rotary-Ann dinner. Steak, salad bar—the works." He flicked a flake off his sleeve. "You can't eat like that at that place you go—where is it?— Dominique's. Listen," he said, irked, "I have to give the speech. Just sit at the head table and smile."

"I can't believe this. *Smile?* How come I'm hearing it just now?" She grabbed the *Chronicle* and hid behind it. "Uh-uh. Not going. It's my night out," she said. "Dance class."

"What's more important?" he asked. "Politics or class?"

She spared him the bloodsport of a reply.

He pulled down the newspaper and stared at her as he would a suspect—she had seen him do that once as D.A.—and inquired: "All this over aerobics?"

"Dance. Modern dance," she said. "Not aerobics."

He was scrutinizing her still—"You ought to be happy"— and leaned back in his chair, as if trying to uncover a motive. "You know," he said, "sometimes you're a million miles away, even though you're right in front of me." He paused for impact. "What gives?"

She shook her head and sighed. How could Allie tell him that she was punishing him and he was supposed to realize it? Apologize? Make amends? "I'm not myself this morning, okay?"

She ran her hand through her shoulder-length hair and pulled a long strand of it around to her eyes so she could inspect the ends. "Have to do something with this, then, don't I?" She needed toner, maybe some honey-blond highlights. She would try to get in on short notice at Hair Today downtown. "Rotary, huh?" She twirled the strand with a finger as if it were a curler and let it wisp on her forehead. "What time's this thing, anyway?"

"Seven, I think." He was lightening up, satisfied that Allie would accompany him. "Liz'll know. This is spur of the moment, hon. The guy who was supposed to get the award was nailed last week. Drunk driving. Too bad," he said. "We had to lock him up."

Allie laughed, then became aloof again before he could notice. She remembered reading about the man in the *Chronicle.* "Wasn't he a nutritionist or something?"

"Health inspector," Luke said.

She hid behind the newspaper again and suppressed a giggle.

"Plan on seven," Luke said. "Am-Vets Building, first floor."

Allie waited until he got up and left, slamming the front door. Then she put the paper down and went to the bedroom picture window to watch Luke disappear down the street in his double-barrel Firebird, a new toy. The nerve of him. Rotary Club! Civic Servant of the Year! How did she get into this mess? One day she was smoking pot at Mount Holyoke, a clothier's daughter with a fabulous SAT, and the next she was enthroned here with Luke Effington—a Harvard grad—with a bottomless inheritance and a strange middle-class taste.

She thought again of the cuckoo. That was a sign. She could picture herself in a dirndl—wouldn't Luke love that?— serving him Saint Pauli beer on one of those Woolworth trays you can spread across your lap while you watch TV in a La-Z-Boy. *Nirvana a la Effington.* She could imagine how he would have decorated the house, had she let him. He was into the weirdest decor, a kind of Naugahyde and Formica motif. *You can't get that stuff at the place you shop—where is it?—Boussac's,* she could hear him saying. It was simple. The man had no taste. You could grow up as he did in a family with a coat of arms and a controlling share of a minor conglomerate and prefer Big Macs to Beef Wellington, Corningware to Waterford Crystal, Firebird to Ferrari. She wrung her hands. Thank God that Luke let her furnish the place. It had become her prison. It might as well look pretty.

Allie recalled moving here after the honeymoon. Luke was worming his way up the D.A. ladder, busy as usual. She had time to do the house up right. And she enjoyed every phase of it, especially the shopping sprees at some of the classiest places in town—Clarence House, Casa Bella, the Emporium, and yes, Boussac's. The salesmen knew her by name, took her to lunch at Dominique's, sent their catalogues whose slick paper smelled like herbal tea. Ah, such innocence! She had a huge, lonely, half-empty house and a fistful of credit cards, not to mention a flair for interior design. She even liked waiting for the delivery trucks, little caravans of them arriving mid-morning and late afternoon. She grew particularly fond of the workers who filed through the rooms in their sweat shirts and buttonfly jeans. *Lovely.* Then, the commotion was over. The bills paid. The job done.

She sat at the edge of the bed and surveyed the room. Savonnerie rug, custom woven. Crepe de chine lounge chair and hand-painted ottoman. Even a stone-sheathed, bedside pedestal—what possessed her to buy that?—and a seascape lithograph above an Art Deco console and canopy bed. It was classy, all right. You could not fart in it, let alone host a lover here.

She walked to the marble-top vanity and picked up her wedding picture, examining it like an artifact. Luke was a sure thing when they met—oh, a bit pudgy, perhaps—but blond, tall, and blue-blooded. A catch. What went wrong? Every time she asked that question, she thought about Elizabeth and her motto: "Do Unto Others Before They Do Unto You." It didn't seem particularly Christian. Almost Buchananesque. The question was, why did Luke listen to his sister instead of his spouse?

Allie tried to pinpoint the root cause of her unhappiness. It wasn't as if Luke had changed much since college or as if Allie had been duped into marrying him. The alternative to marriage was social work or an advanced degree at a state school like Wisconsin or Oregon. Ivy League was out of the question—she had squeaked by at Mount Holyoke—and living in the loft above her father's clothing store in Vermont was, well, an impossibility.

Allie disliked her father. When she was still in grade school, her mother succumbed to double pneumonia after weeks of the walking kind, managing Albert & Edie Browne's "Fine Washables" through another winter. Allie did her best in the years after her mother's death, trying to replace her, for Albert's sake. She persuaded her father to rename the store The Clothes Hanger, carry Junior Miss sizes, and franchise tuxedo and formal wear (just in time for the prom, as luck would have it). Business picked up. She felt good about herself. Yet all the while she wished that Albert would remarry and rediscover love; instead, he reclused and rediscovered alcohol. So, in the end, Allie had failed twice: once with Albert, once with Luke.

She put the picture back on the vanity. *Vermont.* Talk about cuckoo! Your only hope was to marry into maple syrup and pray that the four-wheel drive got you into town and back for the January white sale at the Montgomery Ward's. Small wonder she welcomed society life. But what about career? She had made the obligatory contacts. There was always a job if she wanted one because she was Luke's wife and people owed him favors. She doubted that she could find work on her own, given the downturn in the economy.

Why did she feel empty? She was luckier than anyone she knew. Allie tried to focus, uncover motives for her recent behavior.

Maybe she needed a cause. A sense of purpose. She had thought about employment only as a means to make money—don't most people?—and when Luke inherited more than both could spend, Allie forgot about a career. She kept her own hours during the day. She did what she wanted. Read, wrote, saw a play now and then or an art show. Freedom. Independence. Wasn't this the dream?

Something was eating at Allie, something that only now was beginning to dawn on her. Was it a phase? Would it pass like adolescence, this fear of failure? This wretched idleness? She was torn. On the one hand, she still loved Luke (but hated her marriage). On the other hand, why should she end her marriage if she loved her husband? She could tolerate Luke but he bored her. Stiff. Was that reason to divorce? Allie was twenty-eight and on the verge of self-discovery. She wanted to feel *separate* rather than single, *functional* rather than free. Luke wouldn't allow it with Elizabeth calling the shots. He didn't know how to stand up to her. Worse, he expected Allie to be a cheerleader at Rotary Club, a loyal wife who understood small talk at head tables. He didn't have the foggiest notion about her newfound essence, or else, Allie reasoned, he would have assigned her a function. She could write publicity maybe or schedule his talks. Communicate with him on a higher plane. Walk alongside him instead of lying underneath.

Who was she kidding? The most she could hope for was time to endure Luke while she found herself. That was all right. She was making progress. She was seeing a new side, a beautiful side of herself. After she left Vermont, she became independent, rejecting lovers who needed too much care or tenderness. She couldn't bear to hurt a man who might demand more than she could give emotionally. Neither did she want to humiliate herself by needing as much in return. So she went from one mediocre relationship to another, following the path of least resistance that led to Luke's castle. Now she felt differently. She was no longer afraid to feel, even to suffer for love, if only life could have meaning again. Allie was coming in touch with the depth of her soul and saw, to her surprise, that she had a well of untapped emotion.

It was bound to happen. She had met a man, Eddie Ray Bok, a year ago at the Museum of Art. Allie knew about men. She was a connoisseur of the lower types. Yet she had fallen for him at first sight. He was about ten years older than Luke but in better shape, wearing a khaki shirt tucked tightly into jet-black jeans which, in turn, were tucked into calf-high cowboy boots. His belt was too thick and leathery to be stylish, but he wore the buckle on the side and attached a key chain to the loop. It caught her eye. When he walked, the keys jangled and lured her. He had long, curly brown hair and a clean-shaven face—she had expected a beard—and he took notes, of all things, in a delicate brown diarylike notebook at a photo show about Vietnam.

She spent the afternoon with him. He explained each photograph without the confusing Southeast Asian names or the military jargon one might expect from a disillusioned veteran. No. He approached each picture as a poet might, or maybe Frances Ford Coppola envisioning *Apocalypse Now*, with a surreal viewpoint that dazzled her. He spoke dreamily, eyes closed, as if he did not occupy the space he was set in. Afterward, Allie felt as if she had entered some of the photographs and participated somehow in the war. She was *born* during the Vietnam conflict and felt like a child when she followed him to his apartment— her eighteen-karat wedding band did not deter their karma— and had heady all-out sex that reminded her, strangely, of a life that could have been. Pre–Mount Holyoke. Pre–Lock'em'up Luke. Pre–crepe de chine.

But it wasn't the sex that kept her seeing Eddie Ray. She returned to him infrequently at first, trying to protect the emotions she knew were brewing within. Then she began to think about him so often that nothing else mattered. Money, comfort, time. Time, in fact, was becoming a major problem these days. Allie had begun to define it in two ways: Time With Eddie Ray, Time Without Eddie Ray. Finally, she had to schedule him every Monday night, her "dance" class. She wished that she could spend an afternoon or two each week with her lover, but he liked his freedom and she respected that. Also, she had to be careful with Luke always in the public eye. Eddie Ray was her secret. His past was now a shared one. He had killed a man, he claimed, in hand-to-hand combat and in every way was different than Luke: harder, rougher, darker, and miraculously sensitive. He was showing her another side of the psyche, changing her with stories about boys who became men in the jungle. Who never forgot the jungle. He *needed* her, and happily she could respond! She was helping a hero express himself as only a man could, in the arms of a woman who cared about his pain.

How she missed Eddie Ray! It was so unfair. After Luke last night, she wanted desperately to hear her lover's voice in the blackness of his bedroom and his memory, to hold him tenderly at her breast and console him. Instead she would be eating red meat with Rotary-Anns and smiling a lot between bites of coleslaw and lettuce.

She decided to call Eddie Ray and break the news. He was indifferent, distant. Cold. That meant he was hurting. "Eddie Ray, there's nothing I can do about it," she whispered into the phone. "You have to believe me. I take no pleasure in Rotary Club."

His voice had a sudden slur to it, instead of the usual drawl. He was from Tulsa, which she related more with Texas than Oklahoma. "Call," he said. "Get to a phone. Check on me. In case something comes up. Know what I mean? Like I miss you and freak."

Allie was worried about Eddie Ray's flashbacks. He had some kind of stress syndrome that she didn't want to aggravate. "Okay, darling. Promise," she said. She knew how important her visits were, a kind of social work in which Eddie Ray could participate again in mainstream American life. He had abandoned most of his bad habits, still smoking marijuana but at least no more crack. Doing it for her. Because of her. "I love you," she told him. She knew that she was so good for him. Allie calmed him. Encouraged him. Opened up her body, soul, and MasterCard to his recovery and well-being. "I love you, Eddie Ray," she said again. "Eddie Ray?"

He had already hung up the phone.

3

The Science of
One First Name/
Two First Names

When Allie phoned, Eddie Ray was dividing the world into two camps, and they weren't men and women. They were people who used one first name—Melissa, Bradford, Chloe—and people who used two first names: Bobbi Sue, Billy Mack, Missy Lee. Eddie Ray had learned long ago not to split the cosmos according to broad categories: Young/Old, Rich/Poor, Black/White, Gay/Straight, Cat-lover/Dog-lover, Republican/Democrat, Capitalist/Communist, Occident/Orient. Too risky. You could have a young poor black man who was gay, owned a cat, belonged to the Republican Party, and believed in Hong Kong capitalism. Or an old rich white woman who was straight, owned a dog, belonged to the Democratic Party, and believed in Vietnamese communism. No. He was discovering a simpler science— One First Name/Two First Names—when Allie interrupted. He was ticked that she had phoned, but the call had a purpose beyond the fake flashback. She confirmed his theory with her plaintive—"Eddie Ray?"—and was in his power now . . . the power a man with two first names has over a woman with one.

Allie Effington had become *predictable*.

He smiled. So the world gave up its secrets subtly. Intimately. What was more intimate than a first name? You lived up to it or didn't, and when you didn't, you changed it to fit the new image of yourself. He took another hit from the Lizard of Oz bong that looked like an alligator, hollowed out. He settled back in the bean bag on the carpet, burrowing his head in the vinyl like a man who has fallen a great distance. Who has made an impact.

First names. Take people with just one. These were Northerners, mostly. They hardly ever changed their one first name to two. Oh, a minuscule percentage of pilots did—"This is your captain, Eddie Ray Bok, wishing you a pleasant stay in Atlanta"—and also a few of your truckers with CB handles like "Eddie Ray Gun" or "Eddie X Ray." Not to mention football players, NASCAR drivers, and country-western stars, along with your average go-go dancers, gymnasts, and waitresses at chili-dog restaurants. These were the professions that favored two first names. He had to admit, though, that people with such names—Southerners like himself—were more apt to change their two names to one. He was not sure why. Betty Lou would awake one day hating hominy and cornbread and start calling herself Bethany. Or Jimmie Jeff would get transferred to the Mason side of the Dixie line and start calling himself Jefferson. Either way, the transformation was complete. So it didn't really matter whether a person changed his or her first name. The real problem of the new science was deciphering the *Madelyns* from the *Madie Lynns* and the *Ed Wrays* from the *Eddie Rays*.

He snorted. Hee-hawed. Yucked it up. Maybe he could get one of them federal grants and publish con*clu*sions. Maybe he could predict things. How a person who calls herself Bethany beholds an antelope on virgin prairie and proclaims belief again in marriage and the Almighty. Then again, how a person who calls herself Betty Lou beholds the scene and proclaims: "Pull over, Billie Mack. Unhitch the shotgun, slip me some ammo. We're grillin' to-*night!*"

Eddie Ray had time to kill. He put the Lizard of Oz bong and his stash behind the bean bag and wondered how to spend the day. He was on unemployment compensation, thirty-fourth week. Checks should be in. A way to pass the morning. With Allie busy tonight, maybe he could arrange something with that comely Puerto Rican who distributes the moola. They had a thing, sort of. He would wait in her line every week while she ran through the same questions as if they were in a play, rehearsing.

"Did you look for a job this week?"

"Uh-huh."

"Where did you look?"

"Wait a sec. Let me see"—he would pull out the classified section of the *Chronicle* and hold it before her—"Here, sugar. I looked here."

She'd whisper, "You can't do that." Then she would fork over the check and shoo him along with a more personal comment like "keep cool" or "be good" or "if you can't be good, be good at it."

Money in the bank. Yes, ma'am. He would go downtown today. Grab a *Chronicle* for the ad section and make his move on the Puerto Rican. First, though, there was the important matter of getting off the floor.

He stretched his legs and did a sit-up, falling back on the bean bag for momentum and then rearing forward to his feet in one semiagile movement. "Steady, landlubber," he said to himself as he headed for the door of his apartment. He opened it, looked both ways—all he wore was Fruit of the Loom boxers with a hole under the stretchband—and sidled across the hall for Mrs. Minelli's newspaper. He bent down to snatch it, became woozy, lost his balance, and fell across her door. "*She*-it," he said. He got on all fours, trying too quickly to scurry back across the hall, and fell once more, sprawling belly-down on the linoleum. He ran a hand through his hair. No sense looking like a dork. He struck his best Burt Reynolds pose and waited for Mrs. Minelli to open 4-E, clutching her rosary beads against her bazookas, gasping that a near-naked man had been delivered instead of her newspaper . . . inviting him in for espresso. Espresso, all right. He could hear footsteps—no, more like slippers padding toward him—stopping, thinking better of it, padding away again. Too bad. Eddie Ray stood up and returned to his apartment.

He went into the kitchen. A cockroach was scurrying across the metal table, and he snapped the newspaper at it, once, twice, three times before it lay there amid the cheddar crumbs and bacon bits. He knitted his eyebrows together. He got solemn. He walked around the table as if examining the angle of a pool shot. "Okay, Fats. Eight ball, corner pocket." He hunkered down, gauged the distance from the bug to the waste basket, and made a circle with the thumb and forefinger of his right hand. "Bam," he said, flicking the cockroach across the tabletop and—"right on, Eddie Ray!"—into the trash.

He unrolled the newspaper and thumbed to the Help Wanted section. A boxed ad there caught his eye: "Got a Tip? Got an Ax to Grind? Call Mylo Thrump, Editor, 555-2222. Be Somebody." Eddie Ray liked that ad. He wondered what it would feel like to be a journalist. He imagined himself in such a role: Clark Kent. He snapped the waistband of his undies and said the name aloud: "Clark Kent." Now there was a name that could fit into either category. Same with Lois Lane. One first name or two? Hmmm. Eddie Ray had a few holes to patch in his science if he expected to reap the rewards. You got by in life by preying on weaknesses of others. To do that, you had to figure them out and respond accordingly. You became one type of person—more serious and sincere—when dealing with a One First Name individual. You became another type of person— more fun-loving and loose—when dealing with a Two First Name individual. He thought about the Puerto Rican woman, whether the science applied to Jose Migels and Juanita Maries. Well, at least with Juanitas, he knew a more exact and universal language.

He turned the paper to the front page and read the moose story, laughing about Bullwinkle losing antlers and interest. This was his kind of saga. He saw the photo of the cow gazing at her mooseless future and remembered Allie—a good lay, not the best. In her mind she was, and that counted for something. So did her shiny blue and gold NastyCard when he needed cash at one of the automatic tellers. Sure enough. Here was a woman who tried to humor herself uptown, downtown, midtown, and mall, buying this and that, browsing here and there, taking in humanity from the air-conditioned side of a cafe window, experiencing the mystery of life in a museum, and Eddie Ray—will wonders ever cease?—had the good fortune to meet her.

Allison Effington. One loaded lady. Lord, can you believe that name? Okay, exclude the Slavic *ski*like names and the German *ich* ones. Any WASP with that many syllables on her driver's license needs a Jim Bob, Billie Mack, or Eddie Ray Bok to set her straight, and she needs him *badly*.

He went to the fridge and got a half-empty Budweiser, opening his throat so the flat liquid poured in and cleared a path. He had the role down, pat. Everyone bought it—the Puerto Rican at unemployment, Mrs. Minelli across the hall—but nobody, man-oh-man nobody, hook-line-and-sinkered it like Allie.

Vietnam? Uh-huh. He was in Tulsa for the duration. Out of high school, out of work. Lots of free time, just as he liked it. *Free time*. He thought about Juanita and the unemployment check. He would have to get dressed. He went around the room, picking an outfit off the floor, and stopped suddenly, deep in thought.

He stroked his hairy chest—with any luck Juanita would sprawl there tonight—and imagined bullet holes, bayonet wounds, gaps, missing parts. He had no right to drink Bud in a roach-invested apartment or snap the stretchband of Fruit of the Loom boxer shorts or hee-haw about a Guernsey in love with a moose. Nope. He ought to be at half-mast, pushing up poppies in Okieland.

He lay down on the bean bag with his clothes and pondered death, the great One First Name/Two First Names equalizer. You couldn't outsmart the Big "D." You couldn't use science—not even deep-freeze technology—to save your holy hide. The Big "D" had your number. These days you didn't fool with needles or crack because of AIDS and ODs. You got by with a condom, a bong, a baggy of weed. You kept yourself free of women and work: that double-trouble "W." To enjoy life, you needed a modus operandi, a cover, a silver tongue. But most of all you needed luck.

Eddie Ray slipped on his socks. He knew about luck—not everyday Wheel of Fortune luck—but incredible strokes of chance that change you like a new first name. Take a Betty Lou, down and out, forgetting to put gas in the Mercury Montego and running empty near a station where Billie Mack the mechanic works. They hit it off, marry, buy a shotgun. Barbecue. But she ought not to have met him. She ought to have whizzed right by him on Interstate 35 on her way to Wichita to go-go at a honky tonk. Every so often she imagines how seedy her life would have been had she remembered to fill up the Merc at the Sunoco. She feels a little guilty. She has no right to enjoy herself in his trailer with the Sony TV and flush toilet. But that is how it turned out. Or take a Jefferson getting stuck on Highway 11 behind a lopsided flatbed full of hay on his way to Will Rogers International Airport and missing his plane, whose cargo door falls off midtrip. He thinks about that cargo door occasionally and feels a little guilty about boarding the next available flight to Cleveland. He ought not to have gotten there. He ought to be part of a cornfield in Indiana. Instead, he is still part of a major American corporation. That is how it turned out.

Eddie Ray finished dressing, assessing how things turned out for him. Taking stock. You didn't stand much chance getting out of his neck of Tulsa. He lived in one of those square little hutlike houses by the stockyards that weren't part of the city proper when he was growing up. So you were thankful somebody was at home half-sober—Mother'd run off with that roughneck named Richardson—and could tolerate being raised by Grandma on your dear departed Daddy's side. You learned to fend for yourself, to take what was rightfully yours and what rightfully wasn't. You were in and out of foster homes, usually with an heirloom or two, and stayed in high school to dodge the oil rigs that dot the landscape like so many erector sets. You graduated, ready or not. You could sign on with Kerr-McGee or Uncle Sam, with about equal life expectancy at the time. Then something happened to Eddie Ray—an incredible stroke of chance—thanks to a man with two first names: Cee Jay. Sergeant Cee Jay Arnold, predictable as a Billie Mack or a Jefferson. This was before the science of One First Name/Two First Names, but it applied anyway. Eddie Ray could see that now. He got the picture.

Cee Jay saw dozens of boys with Eddie Ray's problem—a low draft number—and signed them up for two extra years by promising them language school, where they could learn German or Greek. Lots of interesting foreign tongues. You studied one and usually were assigned to that country. Cee Jay knew where everyone— including Eddie Ray at the time—was going to end up. He didn't say anything about body bags arriving at Will Rogers Airport. He thought about his commissions. He thought about them so much that when a boy had three outs against him—out of high school, out of work, and out of luck—Cee Jay would do a little forgery. Get the paperwork to headquarters. *Expedite.* But Eddie Ray wanted what was rightfully his . . . and what rightfully wasn't. The sergeant showed him color brochures of alpine bases and Mediterranean lagoons. It went on for weeks. Finally, Cee Jay fessed up. Eddie Ray was going to language school as promised, so would he please sign that line, right there, on the bottom below the fine print that

italicized *Introduction to Vietnamese.* Eddie Ray walked out—
Cee Jay hollered something about an oral agreement—and
waited for the draft notice that, mysteriously, never came.

It changed his life. It got him philosophical. It got him out
of Tulsa on instinct—no sense bumping into Cee Jay, right?—
and into gen-u-ine mainstream Yankee city life. People here
actually got *welfare.* The men made maximum *wage.* Women
used *birth* control, doggone it. There were all sorts of pluses.

Meanwhile, the war was winding up like Eddie Ray, slightly
less than honorable. No homecomings. No ticker tapes.
Nobody wanted to talk about Vietnam or admit anything. People got touchy about the whole blain subject. Eddie Ray saw
job-related opportunities in this. He could tap into some enti-
tlements and reap the benefits that veterans were afforded from
time to time. There was that and more. Guilt and fear, in particular. You said the word "Vietnam" and people would react a certain way. You could gauge the response and decide how to use
it. In fact, guilt and fear were powerful emotions that got people
to do what they ordinarily would not do for you. Take a
Scrooge-*oid* businessman with a patriotic pang; he might end
up paying you workman's comp or unemployment. You screwed
up on the job like anybody else, but you said the word "Vietnam." You could have yelled "nark!" or "incest!" or "porn!"—
any number of words—and Scrooge-*oid* would have bounced
you on your hiney out the factory gate. But you said "Vietnam"—sans exclamation point—and the company was downright happy to see you leave, happier even that you spared the
coworkers your brand of craziness. They saw you returning with
submachine guns, blasting secretaries out of closets, seriously
fucking up executive lunches. So the company covered for you
at Job Service. You got a weekly check from the same govern-

ment that would have taught you Introduction to Vietnamese.

Eddie Ray wanted that unemployment check today. Allie wouldn't be by, so he could not coax her to the Bucks in the Box automatic teller to score cash for some grass. He needed it more than ever, now that he had given up the harder stuff (which he seldom had money for anyway). No doubt. Allie made life easier. The woman *provided*. She swallowed his "My Lie Alibi"—without drugs, he would commit unpardonable acts—believing the toke of Colombian Gold or the line of Bolivian White was, well, *medicinal*. Uh-huh. Like Grandma Bok's recipe for rheumatism—two parts alcohol/one part Lipton. Tulsa *tea*. He could go for a swig of that right now. No wonder the old hag spent half her life rocking on the rickety porch beside a bucket; she was two parts crocked!

Eddie Ray reminisced. He was waxing downright sentimental. Grandma would appreciate his science of One First Name/Two First Names, her own being Ida May. She was what Allie called a "role model." Her spirit could guide him in troubled times, Allie said. Cure a flashback. Eddie Ray got down on a knee beside the bean bag and did an Al Jolson. "Ida May *Help* Me"—his face got sinister, as if he remembered something unpardonable from his youth—"Then again, Ida May Not."

These thoughts about his past unsettled him. Oklahoma was behind him. Juanita awaited. He got the *Chronicle* from the kitchen, tucked it under his arm, and opened the apartment door.

Mrs. Minelli was on the other side. She was not smiling. She did not have any rosary beads. "You took my newspaper," she said.

"No I didn't," he replied, a reflex action, as if she were Grandma Bok. *Mrs. Minelli*. He started again—"This one is mine. Really. I just started taking it."

"So you admit it? You are taking my newspaper?"

"No, I mean I just started *taking* it—you know—having it delivered."

She pushed up against him—knocking him an inch or so back with her Playtex Living Warheads—and grabbed his cheeks between her pudgy palms. "We're neighbors, no? Stop thinking all the time about yourself." She yanked his face to the side with one hand and reclaimed the *Chronicle* with the other. "All you had to do was ask. When I'm done reading it, I'll leave it at your door." She turned and walked to 4-E. As she opened her door, she said, "Behave, Mr. Bok." She faced him again. "Or you will lose your lady friend."

"Now, Mrs. Minelli," he said. "How do you know about lady friends?"

"I'll bring you some cookies later. You give her some for dessert."

Mrs. Minelli did bake a mean batch of anisette cookies.

"I appreciate you," Eddie Ray said, talking to her bosom. "I do. But are you spying on me, ma'am?"

"Oh, no, Mr. Bok. I just got ears."

"That's not all you got, Mrs. Minelli. You got a lot of nerve. I didn't swipe your newspaper"—she was entering her apartment now, waving him off like a bad boy—"for the life of me, I didn't." He stood up on his toes and pointed a finger at her. She snapped her head to the side and stopped, waiting for him to continue. He added, "There's a moose story you might like in there. Check it out."

She slammed her door.

"Damn," Eddie Ray said. What was she doing, eavesdropping on Allie? She was too good a thing for a gossipy Mama Mia to screw up. He didn't know what Allie would do if her husband found out about her "dance class." That much was not predictable. The guy had what Allie called "high visibility." Eddie Ray imagined clear skies and 20/20 blue eyes that saw everything, but he knew what she meant: her husband was district attorney. Some kind of Newt Republican, meaner than Marcia Clark and as public a figure. You could count on somebody recognizing Allie because of that and word getting back to Lock'em'up. So they had to keep this affair quiet, spending as much time as possible in his apartment. Maybe a quick trip to the liquor store or automatic teller. That was fine. Eddie Ray wasn't the restaurant type. When he went bar-hopping he did it alone, in case some One First Name multisyllabic WASP woman needed his services.

Tonight he wanted to tango, so to speak. No sense worrying about Allie. Maybe Mrs. Minelli would glimpse a bit of Juanita later and become confused. Maybe Mrs. Minelli would drop off a batch of those anisette cookies that weren't half bad after a little Lizard of Oz. You got a sugar attack and gobbled them up. He decided to go back to the bean bag and get out the alligator bong for one more hit before walking downtown to Job Service. Get the day in perspective.

* * *

Juanita was nowhere to be found. Eddie Ray even had sprung for a *Chronicle* at the corner newsstand, ready to improvise on their little spiel. Line number 1 was her usual station. But a blue-haired woman who wore bifocals on the tip of her nose sat there on a stool behind the Plexiglas counter with the half-moon cutout window, where they slipped you the check. Eddie Ray scanned the place for the Puerto Rican. The unemployment office was like a rundown bank with high ceilings and scummy marbly floors. The lines—there were six of them—were long and unruly, not straight like real bank lines, and the customers, all making withdrawals, were not like real bank customers. They did not wear One First Name–type outfits or carry One First Name–type attaché cases. You couldn't picture Allie in this place with her big black leather purse and her open-toe spike heels. The people here wore Two First Name–type polyester and a few carried Two First Name–type shopping bags or lunch pails. The latter gave them away as Northerners. Their shopping and lunch-pail days were over, at least temporarily, but they couldn't shake the habit; they just had to tote some worklike souvenir out the front door.

Prideful, prideful.

He checked each station—four homely women, various ages—and one black man behind the Plexiglas. Where was Juanita Marie? Instinct told Eddie Ray to cut into (a) the shortest line, (b) the homeliest line, or (c) the token minority line, but at no cost the blue-haired/bifocal line. The woman had English teacher written all over her powder-puff face. Unfortunately, there was a sign above her station: A-G. Also, there was that check in the "B" file with his name on it. Maybe Juanita was on break.

He decided to double-check. He walked alongside the line that formed at A-G and stepped closer to the Plexiglas to get a gander of The Teach. It was worse than he thought. Commas for eyebrows, upside-down semicolon for a snout. The mouth—he was watching it move—came up dashes and question marks like a pinball Jezebel on tilt. Worse, the pupils of her eyes were periods that would end all arguments. Add *finality* to a sentence. Case in point. The man she was addressing held out his hand in a woeful, pitiful plea. The Teach did not slip him a check. She was pointing to an office by the back lobby, and the man sulked there. Opened the door. Disappeared.

"You there. You with the pants in your boots. Are you waiting in line or just lost? You. Can you hear me? Hey, *John Lennon*! Are you deaf or just dumb? Sir"—Eddie Ray realized The Teach was addressing him in slow, steady, simpleton tones— "step up to the glass or go to the end of the line."

A Puerto Rican man wearing a Minnesota Twins baseball cap—maybe he knew Juanita?—backpedaled and said to Eddie Ray, "Here, my man. Step right up. Lady wants *you*." He made a big show of it, bowing so that the cap fell off his head and showed a bald spot like a bull's-eye.

This was happening too quickly for Eddie Ray. This was *Yankee* speed. He picked up the cap. He could handle it. He was hip. You had to slow these One First Name–types down, was all. "Here you go, José," Eddie Ray said. "Or is it José Migel?"

The man furrowed his brow in disbelief—*José Migel?*— and swiped the cap, dusting it off as if Eddie Ray's fingers had tainted it.

The Teach cleared her throat. She was making an effort to be ever-so-patient, in a mocking sort of way, drumming her stubby red-painted fingers on the counter. Yawning with a pat, pat, pat of her chin, chin, chin. "May I help you?"

Eddie Ray smiled, careful to turn up the left side of his cheek that Grandma Bok said was lazy and made bad impressions. "Edward Raymond Bok. B as in *Beautiful*"—he struck a manly pose. "O as in *Outrageous*"—he fluffed the curls on his head. "K as in *Kisser*"—he blew her one. "Bok. B-O-K." Eddie Ray heard the Puerto Rican hee-hawing behind him. *What was happening?*

He'd rehearsed that spiel for Juanita Marie, not—damn-nation!—for The Teach. He straightened up. Cleared his mind. Autopilot. "Here to pick up my check."

"Did you look for a job this week?"

"Uh-huh."

"Where did you look?"

"Wait a sec. Let me see"—he pulled out the ad section of the *Chronicle* from his back pocket and held it before her— "Here, sugar. I looked here."

The Teach got off her stool. She pushed a button that buzzed like an intercom somewhere in an office that Eddie Ray could not see. In a few moments, a man in a western shirt with snap buttons and rolled-up sleeves appeared on Eddie Ray's side of the Plexiglas.

"Come with me, sir."

Eddie Ray felt his pockets. No grass, in case this was a bust.

"It's okay, sir"—he extended his hand—"I'm Tim Bert Russell. I'd like to ask you a few questions."

Eddie Ray couldn't believe his luck. An incredible stroke of chance! He calmed down. He wanted to make sure. "Tim *Bert?*" he asked, shaking hands. "As in Timothy Bertram Russell?"

"You betcha. Follow me."

* * *

Eddie Ray was exhausted. Old Tim Bert there had grilled him the better part of an hour. He would not let up. Why can you provide no names of employers who interviewed you? Why can you provide no personal references? Why have you filed for extended benefits? *Why? Why? Why?*

Eddie Ray was bewildered. He had called upon the canons of One First Name/Two First Names, but Tim Bert—from

Tuscaloosa, no less—was blowing the science to smithereens. So Eddie Ray went for broke and unleashed the secret weapon: "Vietnam." He said the word, and a soft, forgiving glow came over the pale blue eyes of the interrogator.

Tim Bert put aside his pad on which he had listed a litany of Eddie Ray's sins and settled back in his leather chair. "Let's talk about it," he said.

Eddie Ray waited for him to say more, reveal a little of his psyche, but Tim Bert just trained those Once Hard/Now Soft eyes at him and grew, if anything, more patient. Eddie Ray cleared his nasal passages, as if preparing to spill his guts. He was stalling. He could not get a clear fix. Guilt? Fear? And what about that hazy-eyed look? Nostalgia?

"Let's talk about it," Tim Bert repeated.

Eddie Ray smiled, forgetting to turn up his lazy cheek. "I bet you read *Soldier of Fortune*," he said, staring squarely into those pale Baby Blues to gauge Tim Bert's response.

The interrogator bolted upright in his chair—so did Eddie Ray on reflex action—and then both men caught themselves, relaxing again, covering up.

Eddie Ray was on to something. He stared at Tim Bert again, and his Two First Name cousin made small circles with his hand, as if helping to park a plane. *Autopilot.*

"Out with it," Tim Bert said.

"Hell," Eddie Ray said, laying the drawl on thick. "I seen worse than most. Man *or* magazine, for that matter. Whole lot of trouble, Tim Bert"—he paused for emphasis—"Tet."

The interrogator bolted again in his chair, as if the dadburn thing was plugged into a 220 socket, and then grimaced before settling back again. He took a deep breath. He relaxed. "Continue," he said.

Eddie Ray didn't know if he wanted to. It was obvious that Tim Bert had been there during the Tet Offensive—when the fuck was that year?—and Eddie Ray needed a moment or two to do some quick ciphering in his head. He felt like a boy being carded for a case of Bud. Then he came up with the year: 1968. Was that right? *She*-it. He was sixteen in 1968. Not to worry, not to worry. Change the topic. Get philosophical. "Miss it. Yes, sir. If you was there, you know what I mean, Tim Bert." *Ida May* Help *Me*. "Got me an ear. Gook"—why was the interrogator balling fists?—"Gook ear." Eddie Ray let his head drop back and studied the slow-moving fan on the light fixture overhead. *Think, boy, think.* You got a science. You jot down facts about the war in that notebook of yours. You got the role down, pat. Why can't you recall anything? Why is that ceiling fan hovering like a helicopter? Why is Tim Bert standing over you all of a sudden? *Leaping Lizard of Oz!*

4

Double Shotgun Edition

Mylo Thrump needed a progress report from reporters Laurel and Kimberly. He knew that Laurel would come through tonight at Rotary Club. Luke and Elizabeth Effington were bound to make a gaffe (and hence, news). But Kimberly would have to rely on luck to earn her psychic unemployment story about the city near collapse. There were other problems. Laurel could invent news as well as any writer on the *Weekly World News*. But Kimberly still couldn't. She had that impulse to report the facts of a story. Thus, she missed important truths—how, for instance, readers planned their days according to syndicated horoscopes. Indeed, it *was* a fact that most people believed now in astrology, UFOs, ghosts, angels, demons, soulmates, and, yes, psychics. They replaced their best friends with psychic ones at $3.99 per minute. But facts, like statistics, made cold news and concerned the outer "reality" (from which people usually sought escape). Truths, like beliefs, made hot stories; they concerned the inner "reality" (where people sought asylum). Yes, one person's truth could be another person's falsehood; but if a skillful reporter could get both sides of a hot story, they would combust like matter and antimatter on the front page. This was the type of news that Mylo longed to feature tomorrow in the *Chronicle.*

"What's keeping them?" Mylo said aloud at his desk, waiting for Laurel and Kimberly. He looked at his watch. They were seven minutes late and not in the newsroom, which meant they could be commiserating or arguing in the lavatory, he assumed. He tapped a pencil on a "dummy" sheet, a piece of paper on which an editor sketched how the front page would look the next day. Mylo did not know whether the word "dummy" referred to the reader or to the editor. In any case, he already had designed the page so that Laurel's Rotary story would run down the left side and Kimberly's psychic one down the right. This was known as a "shotgun," because the banner headlines resembled a double barrel and struck the reader between the eyes. To augment that, Mylo usually put accompanying photos in full color, casting both headlines in red ink like blood.

Red was bright. It seduced the mind, particularly against a white and black background. Advertisers knew that. So did tabloid editors. The news of late had been too dull: Middle East Talks, Eastern Europe Talks, Hong Kong Talks, Newt Talks, Arms Talks, Summit Talks, OJ Talks, Newt Talks, Baseball Talks, Trade Talks, NAFTA Talks, Newt Talks; these, too, were invented news stories, fabricated by sources instead of editors. The common Joe and Josephine understood that much, but they usually did not understand that brand of news. It appealed more to business people and politicians: the gross national product, the national debt. Joe and Josephine weren't interested in that. They worked menial jobs—their parents had worked menial jobs, and their children would likely as well. Oh, they may have voted in a primary for a particular presidential candidate, maybe even Patrick Buchanan or Ross Perot, but only because he seemed like someone they knew (or wished they knew). It didn't matter who occupied the Oval Office; nothing changed except the hairdos and one-liners. Joe's loan officer at Liberty Federal and Josephine's alcoholic husband at home wielded much more power than the White House or the Congress. Forget the Supreme Court. These people's lives were dull. Stressful. They were half-dead already at the breakfast table, barely able to face each other, let alone another day. So Mylo aimed at them with a double-barrel shotgun. He wanted to assault their taste—zap life into them—give Joe and Josephine something sensational to ponder between brake linings and coffee breaks. Make the eggs go down easier. Or come up again! Editors at the *Herald* thought mealtime was a communal affair: omelet a la Sistine Chapel. Mylo wanted Joe to spew his V-8 Juice and Josephine to gag on her Poptarts, confronting each other bleary-eyed across the kitchen table, reading each other bizarre or sensational stories. Mylo brought together husband and wife and saved their marriage one more day, even though, it seemed certain, he could not save his own. *I cannot save my own,* he whispered, folding his arms on the desk and burrowing his head in them. *I cannot save my own,* he repeated, over and over, welcoming the darkness.

Then looked up.

Laurel and Kimberly were at his door, observing him. They seemed cautious. Concerned. "Come in, come in," he said, balling the dummy sheet in a wad and flinging it in the corner waste basket. He had committed the design to memory and waited until the women sat in adjacent chairs across from his desk.

Laurel was trying to smile. But Kimberly was upset, confirming his fears about the psychic unemployment story. Mylo studied them. By the blank looks on their faces, he would have to inspire them. He straightened up and said, "This is how I see it, ladies"—he spread his hands as if holding a newspaper—a pontifical pose. "Kimberly," he said, furrowing his bushy brows, "imagine this on the front page—'Psychics Say City On The Verge Of Collapse!' " He looked at Laurel. "How about this— 'Cuckold Candidate: Values Begin In Boudoir'?" Then he let his hands drop palm-up on the desk and spoke matter-of-factly. "Time for an update. Did you contact any of those psychics?" he asked Kimberly. "Any leads on those paramours?" he asked Laurel.

They both spoke at the same time, Kimberly blurting— "Well, I'm having a hard"—and Laurel interjecting, "Have I got news for you!" The reporters eyed each other, annoyed.

"Go ahead," Mylo said, nodding at Laurel. "Good news first. No news later."

Kimberly winced.

Laurel leaned forward and put her elbows on her knees, turning the toe of one shoe toward the other in a classic innocent pose. "Dyn-o-mite," she whispered. "I just talked to my sources at the Gentry Club who say that Allie seems distant these days when in the company of her husband." She opened her notebook to a quote from a socialite and explained that the woman breakfasts every morning at the club. "Basically," Laurel said, "she hears gossip from the night before and puts a new sheen on it the next day. Listen to this—quoting now—'Why wouldn't Allie step out on Luke? His father made him what he is today, leaving him all that wonderful cash. I just hope he realizes that his wife is cheating on him because, if she is, maybe I, too, can marry into his family. Lucky girl.' "

"Great quote," Mylo said.

Laurel smiled. "I knew you would be pleased."

"What do you mean, 'great quote'?" Kimberly asked. "It's gossip. The woman who talked to Laurel has no idea if Luke's wife is having an affair."

Mylo sighed. "There you go again," he complained, explaining to Kimberly that Laurel would use the quote "out of context." That meant she would print only tantalizing parts of it and place them at a key juncture in the story, maybe after a denial by Luke or Allie herself. He took Laurel's notebook. "Now listen to the quote: 'Why wouldn't Allie step out on Luke? I just hope he realizes that his wife is cheating on him.' " Mylo handed the notebook to Laurel. "As I said, great quote."

"But you changed it," Kimberly complained. "It's not the truth."

"Whose truth?" Mylo asked, becoming angry. "What gives you the right to decide what is and what isn't truth?"

Kimberly seemed confused. "That's not what I mean."

"Yes it is," Laurel piped in.

Kimberly swung around. "Shut up."

"You see? This is how she speaks to me."

"Look," Mylo said to Kimberly. "You of all people know about Lock'em'up." He cited the investigative stories Kim did

about the D.A.'s office, including the one in which Luke jailed a
battered wife because she refused to testify against her husband.
"You know Allie, too," he reminded her. "You saw her with him
and Elizabeth during his last campaign." Mylo picked up his
pencil and pointed it at her again. "Now *you* tell the truth. Do
you or do you not suspect that Allie is having an affair?"

Kimberly shifted in her seat, nervous. "I don't know."

"Oh," Mylo said. "Nice. I hate people who say 'I don't
know' in Gallup polls. I think"—

"Spare me," Kimberly hissed.

—"they're ignorant. Uninformed."

"Are you calling me ignorant?"

"You answer my question first."

"Okay," Kimberly replied. "I think she's having an affair.
But I could be wrong."

Mylo had her now. "Who cares if you are wrong? You're not
ignorant," he added, "but you're not important, either." Mylo
had a special talent, misapplying media tenets. "When thousands of readers believe as you do, who are we to question
them? Facts don't count."

"Here's a fact," Kimberly said. "Your psychics don't want to
go on record. So I have no quotes."

"Come on," Mylo said. "There must be two dozen psychics
listed in the phone book. Not one of them will speak to you?"

"Oh, they'll speak, all right. On 1-900 numbers at $6.99 a
minute."

Laurel glanced at Kimberly. "My psychic friend doesn't
charge that much. Would you like her number?"

Kimberly bit her lower lip. Then she told Mylo that psychics
and astrologers have regular city numbers but their assistants
answer the phone, providing the 1-900 listings. "I'll be glad to

call them," she said, "but it's going to cost you. And I don't like paying for fabricated news." She tugged her skirt down hard when she said this, uneasy in her chair. "Unethical."

Mylo didn't know whether she was referring to him or to the coverage. It didn't matter. At any rate, he didn't want to pay the 1-900 rates for psychic sources, either. "That's robbery," he told Kimberly. "We only charge $5 a minute for people who call in with a gripe on our newsline."

"True," Kimberly replied. "We ask readers for their opinions. They call and pay us to listen to their opinions. Then they pay us for a newspaper to read their own opinions." She was smug again. "Did I miss anything?"

"Okay, okay. We give readers what they want. Now you give me what I want," Mylo said. "Research the rates for cheaper psychics, including Laurel's. Call and interview *them*." He rubbed his temples. "Don't dawdle."

"It's your budget," Kimberly said.

"We need the story for the front page," Mylo replied. He was worried because Kimberly's assignment might not meet his midnight deadline. She and Laurel would have to work overtime, and Mylo hated those rates even more than 1-900 ones. "You're to stay here until your stories are finished," he said.

Kimberly was pissed. "I have plans for tonight."

"Cancel them," Mylo said.

"I already canceled mine," Laurel added, sucking up.

"Good girl."

Kimberly cringed, crossing her legs so a calf flattened out and stretched her blue stocking, showing the stubble beneath. She looked at Laurel and then at Mylo, making a connection. "Tell you what," she said, half serious. "Let me whip up a tearjerker. You know, telephone the ASPCA about cruelty to animals?

Cow, moose. Bull. I know," she taunted. "How about *pit* bulls? They're always hot. Bet one mauled a psychic."

"You wish," Laurel said, noting that the USDA would be the proper source to speak about cruelty to cattle. "Not the ASPCA, you cow."

"Bimbo."

"Frig you."

"You, too."

"Shut up," Mylo said, realizing he was responsible for the backbiting. You could undermine their confidence. Make them rely on you instead of each other. Mold them. But he disliked bickering that didn't involve competition. "When I taught both of you to go for the jugular," he said, "I didn't mean each other."

The women stared straight ahead, angry. Silent.

This was hardly a pep talk, Mylo thought. He concentrated on Kimberly and imagined Wendy smirking at him. He saw the resemblance, and it had nothing to do with looks—Wendy was small-hipped and black-haired—but with attitude. Taste (in the traditional sense). Wendy also would cop out when it came to the bizarre. Sic her on a murder, and she would track the killer. Sic her on an extortion, and she would follow the money trail like a bloodhound. Nose for news in the classic sense. But sic her on psychics, and you would have to coax the story out of her, word for word. The same thing was happening to Kimberly, and Mylo thought that he had the remedy. He smiled at Laurel. "I think you'd better help Kimberly with her story," he said.

"Sure," Laurel replied.

"I *don't need* help," Kimberly said, frustrated. "I need a real assignment." The only solution, she told Mylo, was for her to go the Job Service office and interview some of the officials there. "Like it or not, unemployment is on the rise. I'll interview that mother, too, who called on the 1-900 line about daycare for women on welfare."

"That's a start," Mylo remarked.

"If it were my story," Laurel said, letting her neck loll back, seemingly conscious of the effect it was having on Mylo, "I'd visit those psychics in person instead of trying to reach them on the phone. If you show up at their door, they might be more inclined to give you a quote."

"Good girl," Mylo said again.

Kimberly covered her eyes and groaned. "You're both crazy," she sighed. "I am working with crazy people."

The telephone rang. Bad timing. Mylo had to inspire Kimberly or else she would come back with an ordinary unemployment story, quoting statistics. "Get that for me, will you?" he asked Laurel, contemplating his next move.

Laurel rose slowly from her chair and answered the phone on the fifth ring, letting the caller and Mylo wait. Another distraction. He gathered his thoughts and refocused on Kimberly. "Stop trying to control the news. Let it control you."

"I don't know what you mean."

He took a softer approach. "You're trying too hard. Don't define the problem. Don't say—'psychics have no news value'—or you come away with no story. Don't ask yourself—'how am I going to believe a psychic?'—because then you won't. Go about things differently, Kim. Show up at places. Go with the flow. Keep your eyes open, sure. But keep an open mind." He paused. "Are you reading the *National Enquirer?*"

"Please," Kimberly said.

"How can you write for a tabloid if you don't read tabloids?"

"Excuse me," Laurel interrupted. "Would you like me to put this gentleman on hold?"

"What?" Mylo asked.

"Vietnam vet. In the lobby," Laurel said.

"Tell him to come back Memorial Day," Mylo replied, focusing on Kim again. "Try harder," he told her.

Laurel interrupted again. "Seems he was punched out or something this morning"—

"Have him call 1-900 like everyone else."

—"at *Job Service.*"

Mylo and Kimberly stared at Laurel. "Poor dear has a gripe," Laurel whined. "He wants to be somebody."

Kimberly opened her notebook and waited for Laurel to hand her the phone.

Laurel turned her back on her. "Call 1-900 like"—

"Give me the phone," Kimberly commanded.

—"everyone else."

Laurel turned around again. "Poor dear can't afford our 1-900 rates," she told Mylo.

He took the phone before Kimberly could. Laurel sashayed to her seat, proud of herself. "Please hold," Mylo told the man. He pressed a button and intercommed Hong, the newsroom photographer. "Get to the lobby and take a picture of a man at the pay phone. Tell him to wait there until we can send down a reporter." Hong was on his way. Mylo addressed the women. "Laurel, head out to the D.A.'s office and interview Luke or Elizabeth. See if you can get an advance copy of his speech." Laurel was on her way. "Kimberly, head down to the lobby and check this guy out. Get him to say that nobody cares about the unemployed in the city. Then go to Job Service and grill the guy who intimidated him." Kimberly was on her way. "And phone those damn psychics!" Mylo called after her. Then he pushed the release button to talk to the man with an ax to grind. "Sir?" he asked, wanting to take down the correct spelling of his name.

Some kind of commotion was going on. "Stop taking my picture!" Mylo heard the caller say. Hong must have arrived in the lobby.

"Sir?" Mylo asked, trying to get the man's attention.

"Take my picture again, gook, and I'll nuke your Nikon," the man was saying.

"Sir? Talk to me, please," Mylo shouted into the receiver.

The man got on the line. "Tell him now to stop taking my picture, hear?"

Mylo asked him his name. "None of your goddamn business. Just get your butt down to Job Service and talk to a guy there named Tim Bert Russell."

Mylo could hear Kimberly trying to interview the man, but he cursed her and wouldn't hang up the phone. "That's one of our reporters," Mylo told him. "Why don't you speak to her about what happened to you at Job Service?"

"Because," the man said, "I'm like tattling on this guy Tim Bert. Leave me out of it."

"Put the reporter on the line," Mylo said, "and I'll tell her that."

The man obeyed.

"Kim," Mylo said, "tell Hong to get back upstairs and print the guy's picture. Tell him you're going to Job Service to check out this story about a Tim Bert Russell. But the guy in the lobby is hiding something. Find out what."

"It's Eddie Ray, but I'm not sure of the spelling—R or W. Anyway," Kim continued, "he doesn't want us to use it."

"I'll decide that," Mylo said and hung up, easing back in his chair, on track again—on to Kimberly and Laurel, Lock'em'up and Allie, Eddie Ray and Tim Bert—the whole untold tabloid universe.

5

Spic, Span, and Spiritual

When Luke Effington arrived at his office in the county courthouse, he approached his secretary to ask whether his sister had phoned. But he knew without asking as his secretary pointed to his door that Elizabeth was already inside, waiting to map out campaign strategy.

"She's been here since eight o'clock," his secretary, Janice, noted.

Luke huffed. "Thanks for the warning," he said, grimacing. He opened the door quietly and saw Elizabeth in his chair, making notations in a yellow legal pad. Luke stood there a moment, marveling at the presence she made behind the oak desk with the state and U.S. flags to each side of her, complementing her bright red hair, white skin, and large body. She was six feet in stockings but appeared taller than Luke's six-two frame. Today she was wearing a red business suit, which made her appear even larger. If Luke were a suspect brought to her for questioning, he would confess at once, just to leave the room.

"Good morning," Elizabeth said without looking up.

Her husky voice gave Luke an eerie feeling.

"You can have your desk back in a second," she said, putting the legal pad aside and editing a typed document. "Where were you? I phoned the house about twenty minutes ago, but the line was busy."

"That's strange," Luke said, more to himself. He had left the house about a half hour ago and wondered who had called Allie so early.

"Nothing strange about calling a public official who is more than two hours late to work," Elizabeth said, counting the pages of the document and making another notation in the legal pad.

"Sorry," Luke said. He had anticipated a sermon. Elizabeth liked to preach at him and probably should have become a minister—the church was ordaining women when she had the call—but Laslo, their father, wouldn't allow it. Unladylike, he said. Elizabeth never recovered her teenage sense of humor—she'd wear his rugby uniforms to formal dinners—or her spiritual calling. Instead, she gravitated toward the Religious Right whose leaders were all men, as if to justify her father's pronouncement. So Luke tolerated her moral musings, but only when he could spare the time. Right now he wanted her to move from his chair so he could review what she had been working on—probably last-minute changes in the Rotary speech.

Elizabeth stood up, as if sensing his impatience. "I needed to pencil in a few changes in your speech," she said. "A reporter from the *Chronicle* called this morning while you were"—she scowled—"doing whatever you were doing."

Luke maneuvered behind her and eased into his chair. He decided to ignore Elizabeth's remark. She didn't like Allie and would be upset to learn that he was late because he wanted to show his wife some much-needed attention. The campaign ahead would take its usual toll on his relationship. "What's the reporter's name?" he asked, wary whenever someone from the *Chronicle* came to his office. "Not Kimberly Spears, I hope?" Luke would never forgive that reporter and her editor Mylo Thrump for giving him the nickname Lock'em'up, although he did take pleasure in imprisoning criminals. He felt it was his God-given mission, something he did well to serve others.

"No," Elizabeth replied, sitting in the chair next to his desk, "Laurel Eby. This one writes of late about moose."

"Moose," Luke repeated, smiling and thinking about his talk at breakfast with Allie. So the word *was* like "deer" in the plural. Luke needed more coffee. He buzzed his secretary, asking her to bring some.

"Anyway," Elizabeth continued, "she wants a copy of the speech. I'll give her this one." She laid it on his desk. "I've edited out passages that refer to Claude Turner, her publisher. No sense giving advance info to the enemy. If he wants to hear the speech, let him show up like everyone else."

Luke nodded.

"Here's another unabridged copy," she said, taking back the

edited one. "I'll have Janice white-out the edited passages on my copy and stick it in a media kit for the reporter."

"Thanks," Luke said. As much as he disliked his sister's tactics, he knew he needed her, at least until the election was over. Elections could be ruthless. But one day, for the sake of his marriage and his morals, he would have to break away from Elizabeth and assert himself. He understood that. But he didn't understand why the *Chronicle* wanted to cover the speech. Rotary was small potatoes. "It doesn't make sense," he said.

"You underestimate me," Elizabeth replied, informing him that it was her job as campaign manager to manipulate the media. "I'm good at it. That's why a reporter is coming."

The secretary came in with an elephant-gray mug that read "Draft Bush," Elizabeth's product, which most people assumed was for beer and Anheuser Busch—crates of which were manufactured and donated to the GOP by Values, Inc. You couldn't give them away. "Thanks," Luke said to Janice, taking the coffee.

Elizabeth gave the secretary a copy of the edited speech and told her to white-out the penciled passages.

"Release it to the reporter *after* she visits with me," Luke told Janice. This way he could pry to see why her newspaper was covering his speech.

Janice nodded and left.

"You *do* underestimate me," Elizabeth remarked, knowing what Luke was up to. "If you must know why the *Chronicle* is interested, I'll tell you."

Luke didn't encourage her. The more he knew about her brand of public relations, the less he liked it.

"I talked to Claude last night," Elizabeth disclosed. "He and Daddy were such good friends—why, I'll never know—and made the arrangements."

"What about the *Herald*?" Luke said. He appreciated that newspaper's objective and honest approach to news. "Did you speak to Margaret, too?" Margaret Hopkins was publisher of that paper.

"Yes, I spoke to Margaret," Elizabeth mimicked. She made another notation in the yellow pad, not offering any details.

"Okay," Luke wheezed, "what happened with Margaret?"

She stared at him angrily, as if Luke somehow was to blame. "She turned us down. So did the TV stations. Radio, too."

"Nice," Luke replied, burring his lips, disappointed. He did not want to rely on the *Chronicle* to report word of his candidacy, no matter what his sister assumed, but he had to, apparently. It was the biggest outlet in town. He took a sip of his coffee, lukewarm and sour without sugar. He buzzed Janice again. "Yes?" the secretary responded.

"The coffee maker on the blink?" Luke asked, punning the words "coffee maker" so they referred to Janice and his discount machine.

Janice replied, but Luke couldn't understand it because of static on the intercom set, a portable attachment gizmo that could hook into any phone. Another cut-rate product from Values, Inc. He tapped the set gently. Then harder. Then slapped it with an open palm.

The static disappeared. "Would you like another cup?" Janice was asking.

"No. Buzz me when the reporter arrives," Luke said, glancing at Elizabeth. "Where were we?"

"Media coverage," she reminded him. "I hated to ask Claude for special treatment in the *Chronicle*. After all, *he* is one of our targets."

Luke knew what Elizabeth meant, and he found that part of

the campaign particularly vicious. His sister and several members of the Religious Right had persuaded him to take a stand against homosexuals. In essence, they believed that the same-sex relationships were morally wrong, corrupting society and even invoking God's wrath with sexually transmitted diseases like AIDS. In precampaign meetings last month, Elizabeth and her supporters wanted him to resurrect that old theme about AIDS, but he refused, knowing it would offend many voters, especially those whose lives had been afflicted. This was an immune system disease, he had argued, noting that intercourse was only a means of transmission. Elizabeth finally relented. But in the end, he agreed to harp on the ills of homosexuality, compromising his values to gain votes.

"Everyone suspects that Claude is gay," Elizabeth commented. "Maybe if he hears our views on his illness, he won't be inclined to challenge you in the primaries."

"Do you know for a fact that Claude is gay?"

Elizabeth shrugged.

"Then you're spreading gossip."

"At least I'm not spreading"—

"Don't even say it, Elizabeth."

—"AIDS."

"You know how I feel about that."

"The body is sacred. A temple. He who runs for public office has to be pure," she said, as if reciting scripture. "Spic, span. Spiritual."

"You seem to be saying this for my benefit," Luke noted.

"Keep an eye on your wife."

Luke tensed and kept quiet. Apparently Elizabeth had noticed Allie's recent detached behavior.

"Whom do you think she was calling so early in the morning?"

Elizabeth asked, raising an eyebrow and his suspicions. "I take it, of course, that you already had left for work."

"Maybe somebody was calling *her*," Luke replied.

Elizabeth smiled.

"Point taken." Luke thought about Allie. She was odd again this morning—every Monday, it seemed—eager to send him to the office, as if she were annoyed with him. That was why he had made love last night and lingered at breakfast. He wanted to show her that he desired her after four-plus years of marriage. "Allie's lonely. That's all," he reassured Elizabeth.

"Pray for her," she replied.

"I'll pray for her," Luke repeated, thinking, *and you, too.*

"Let's talk politics," Elizabeth said, reviewing her notes in the pad. She looked up. "I don't think we should deviate much from the first campaign. We had a good strategy then, and we won. All we need to do in this one is adjust our message to suit the times." Elizabeth argued that people had been fed up with crime in the last election, and now they felt the same about the family unit. "Or the breakup thereof." The more corrupt society became, the more people longed for limits—on sex, on spending—and Luke could offer them that, she told him. "So," she added, "I think we should keep the same slogan." She walked to the corner of the room where she had set up an easel and pulled off a pillowcase to unveil the poster from the previous campaign:

Vote For Luke Effington, D.A.,
And Clean Up Crime In Our City

"Good message," Luke said. "We kept our promise, too."

Elizabeth lifted up the old poster, behind which was the new one with this slogan:

Vote For Luke Effington, GOP,
Clean Up Our City Commission

Luke stared at the poster, unimpressed. It sounded as if he were running for the Sanitation Department, not the City Commission. "I'm running for the Commission, not Sanitation," he said.

"Trust me," she told him. "The new slogan will make sense after you read your speech."

Maybe he ought to run for Sanitation, Luke thought, dreading the speech. He'd be slinging garbage soon enough if he followed Elizabeth's instincts. *Do unto others before they do unto you.* "All right," he agreed. "Let's go with the poster."

"I already ordered them. They're in boxes at my house. Today volunteers will start putting them up throughout the city."

Luke threw up his hands. "If they're being posted, why did you ask me to approve the slogan?"

"Because," she sneered, "you've been spending too much time at home and on casework at the office. Somebody has to make these decisions."

He sighed. "Point taken."

She stalked to the chair by his desk.

Luke watched her with concern. He *had* to trust Elizabeth's judgment. After all, it was her idea during the first campaign to attach "crime stickers" to the posters and place them at popular sites: street corners, arcade stores, bowling alleys, bars, automatic tellers. The stickers described various crimes—from vandalizing a pop machine to robbing a bank—along with the classification and punishment: misdemeanor, felony, federal. One year, five years, ten years. Back then Elizabeth said she wanted to create awareness and she did. Citizens actually read the stickers and became more familiar with the penal code. "I appreciate you, Liz. But I need to be in the loop. Next time let me know, okay?"

She didn't answer him. She opened her purse and took out a pack of stickers. "We'll be putting these on posters, too," she said.

Luke's stomach sank when he reviewed them. Each sticker contained one of the Ten Commandments, boxed like a baseball card. Some were reprinted verbatim out of Exodus—"You shall not murder" or "You shall not commit adultery"—with statistics about killings or divorce. But other stickers were edited for public consumption. For instance, the first commandment about other gods was rewritten to rebuke astrologers, psychic healers, and palm readers. The second about false idols condemned the artists, hard rockers, and movie stars. The third outlawed heavy-metal lyrics and obscenity in general. You could tell that Elizabeth had struggled rewriting part of the last one. The original read, "Do not covet your neighbor's ox or donkey," but she had changed the wording to "van" or "Jeep," citing car-theft statistics.

"Well?" Elizabeth questioned.

"You're stretching it, frankly. Worse, these stickers may conflict with church-state laws."

"Only if we use party funds," she interjected. "We're as rich as Forbes. And have the same constitutional rights as the poor. She cocked her face as if to make a moral pronouncement. "We can stick whatever we please where we want."

"We'll have the ACLU down our backs."

"Good publicity."

"And the media, too."

"Even better."

Luke sighed. "Point taken. Put 'em up."

Elizabeth handed him a copy of the speech. "Go ahead. Give it a whirl."

He reviewed the text and read in a monotone voice, as if at college again: *"We live in an age of rampant sin. We live in an age of sexually transmitted diseases and loose morals. It is one thing when our neighbor succumbs to temptation. Yes, he may divorce. Yes, he may"*—

"Put some feeling into it, man."

—*"Take lovers. He may be young or old, rich or poor, gay or lesbian."* Luke stopped. "Now that's really awkward," he said, putting some feeling into it. "He may be gay or lesbian?"

"I know what you mean. But I don't like that 'he/she' construction."

"Damn it," Luke yelled, standing up. "I'm not talking grammar. I'm talking content."

"You just broke your own sticker," Elizabeth said, pointing to one on his desk about cursing. She stood up and scrutinized him. "You promised. You said if we lost the AIDS argument, we could focus on homosexuality."

"I know, I know." Luke sat down, took a breath, and continued reading: *"But when our community leaders divorce, take lovers—especially gay ones—the community suffers. This is not homophobia but fact"*—"I'm really uncomfortable with this," Luke whined, without looking up from the page—*"All one needs to do,"* he continued, *"is read our local newspapers. The city seems on the brink like Sodom or Gomorrah. Why not? When certain politicians and publishers set such examples, people follow. In the process, the exodus to sin has destroyed the family unit. We need to recall our values. That's why I have put stickers around town"*—his voice trailed off—*"urging. . . ."*

"Go on," Elizabeth prodded. "It sounds fine."

Luke put the speech in his "out" basket. "I'll read it later."

Before Elizabeth could object, the intercom buzzed. Static. Then Janice's voice: "Miss Eby has arrived."

"Send her in."

"What did you say?" Janice asked. "I can't hear you. There's static."

Luke slapped the intercom and tried again. This time when the secretary spoke, her voice was drowned by static. Luke pressed another button. "Janice? Janice?" he called.

Elizabeth gathered her things. "I've got to coordinate the volunteers. We've got posters to put up."

Luke was fiddling with the intercom.

"I'll send in the reporter," Elizabeth said.

"Thanks," Luke replied. "See you later at Rotary."

Laurel entered.

Elizabeth greeted her warily. "When you're through here, see the secretary for a press kit. I'll put a copy of Mr. Effington's speech in it for you." She trained her eyes on the reporter's slit skirt and slowly raised her head until the women were staring at each other. "One more thing," Elizabeth warned. "This is a serious campaign. Remember that when you write about it."

"I can be very serious," Laurel replied.

"You'll be in attendance tonight then?" Elizabeth inquired.

"Wouldn't miss it."

Elizabeth turned to Luke. "Buzz me if you need me. Remember, we have TV coverage to arrange."

"I thought you said"—

She cut him off and smiled at Laurel. "We're very busy. Let me know if I can be of help." She went to the door—"Radio coverage, too," she lied, breaking another sticker commandment.

"TV coverage? Radio, too?" Laurel asked, sitting in the chair Elizabeth had vacated and crossing her legs.

Luke noticed.

"Nice mug," Laurel said, noticing the "Draft Bush" logo. She rose in her seat a tad as if to ascertain what Luke was drinking.

"Excuse me?" he asked.

Laurel sat back down and reached into her purse. She took out a pen and pad and then studied him, making a mental picture. "What do you have against sex?"

Luke was taken aback. He anticipated such questions *after* she had read his speech, not before. "I have nothing against it," he replied, "as long as the man and woman consent and especially if they are married."

Laurel didn't record the quote in her pad. "What about gays and lesbians?" she asked.

Luke choked. He was still wondering whether to edit from his speech Elizabeth's homophobic references, to avoid such questions from the media. Now he didn't know what to say. "No comment. You'll have to attend the speech like everyone else."

Laurel smiled and put the pen in the corner of her mouth, gently biting the tip. "Let's make this simple, Mr. Effington. May I call you Luke?" She didn't wait for his approval. "You're going to say mean things about homosexuals like all born-again Christians do. Personally," she said, "I don't care what you think. But the public might."

Luke was not smiling. "Look," he told her, "I am a born-again Christian. I'm not going to deny that. But let's be honest. What you care about is a quote."

"Now you're being mean to me," Laurel said, pouting. "Let's talk about your wife."

"My wife?"

"Let me rephrase that."

"You'd better."

"How do you feel about adultery?"

Luke shook his head. "I have no idea what you're implying. Clue me."

"How do you feel about monogamy?"

"I'm a firm believer in marriage. Monogamy," Luke said, wondering why the reporter was quoting him now in her pad. This was a boring, safe reply. He added, "Couples who pray together, stay together."

The reporter jotted down that, too. "If you ever learned that your wife was having an affair, what would you do?" Laurel asked.

Luke leaned forward and stared at her. "Why this focus on my wife? Do you know her?"

"Just from talk at the country club."

"Oh. That explains it. Gossip." Luke checked his watch. "If my wife were having an affair, I would not discuss it with you. One of the goals in our family values campaign is to restore a sense of privacy." Luke sat back in his chair, pleased with his response.

But Laurel did not take down this quote, either.

"Privacy," Luke repeated. "One of our goals."

"Well," Laurel said, "this is all hypothetical, right? Your wife isn't having an affair, right?"

"Affirmative."

"So privacy is not an issue."

"I guess not."

"What would you do if you learned that your wife was having an affair?" Laurel asked again.

Luke thought about Allie. For all he knew, given his hours, she could be having an affair. "I would keep the matter private. I would pray. Hey," he said, annoyed, "why didn't you write that down?"

"You would hide the fact of your wife's infidelity?"

Luke was confused. "It would be none of your business."

"If that's the case," Laurel asked, "why is it *your* business when it comes to sexual preferences? Family values?"

"Because," Luke said, "family values is a general term. We can discuss values as citizens without invading anyone's privacy. My wife's infidelity is personal. We cannot discuss it."

The reporter wrote the last two sentences in her pad.

Luke deciphered them upside down. "Listen, Miss"—he forgot her last name but remembered the moose on the front page—"ah . . ."

"Eby."

"Right. Listen, Miss Eby, I'm not sure what you want me to say, or why you want me to say it. Especially as it pertains to my wife."

"Are you worried about your wife?"

"Maybe," Luke said, watching her jot down that word. "Maybe, for today, I mean"—he wrung his hands—"you had better rely on my speech." He reminded her that his secretary had a press kit for the *Chronicle*. He glanced at his watch again. "Sorry to cut you off."

"I can take a hint," Laurel said, sliding off the chair and standing. She put her pen and pad away and slung her purse on her shoulder, then sidled to the door.

Luke didn't like her tactics. "Miss Eby," he called. She stopped and faced him. "I have something to clarify"—he had heard Elizabeth use that phrase—"in fact, you can play it up." He had heard that, too.

"Go on."

Luke paused, pretending to admire her. She really was quite beautiful. Playful, pert, petite. Quite a combination, almost as good as spic, span. Spiritual. But he owed it to himself and Allie to get this on the record. "I have yet to meet a woman who can sway me from my morals," he said.

"That's a new one. I haven't heard that one before."

"Well, I mean it."

Laurel walked up to him and leaned over his desk. Got in his space. He could smell her perfume—he had a nose for it—Obsession, by Calvin Klein. Her blouse was partly unbuttoned, revealing the slope of her breasts. He tried to keep eye contact but looked down and away, embarrassed. She laughed and swayed to the door. "We'll see about that," she said.

6

Better At Me
Than A Puddle

Allie arrived by cab outside the Am-Vets Building where Rotary Club met Monday nights. She paid the cabby, tipped him generously as was her custom, and stepped to the sidewalk. She had decided to dress down—not by price tag, because the Nilani blouse and skirt were ordered special through her regular boutique (which didn't carry the line)—but by occasion; the women who sat at the head table were wives of bankers and brokers mostly, and they would don the usual loose-fitting designer dresses to hide their bulk, upon which would hang slender, delicate accessories. Allie did the opposite: tight-fitting skirt, blouse with two buttons undone, bulky pearl necklace and large, heart-shaped earrings, along with half-spike pumps whose heels clicked when she walked. It was a small revenge for having to attend tonight and forego her rendezvous with Eddie Ray. Luke would be delivering the speech, but his wife would be turning the heads.

Allie slowed her pace. A woman outside the Am-Vets Building was watching her and did not seem the type to be intimidated by anyone's appearance, however svelte. She had near-punk auburn hair and wore a pink slit skirt and lacy white silk blouse with *three* undone buttons. She was not a Rotary Ann. Allie clicked closer, smoothing her newly highlighted hair—at least she outdid the woman in that category, having visited the salon—and stared back, trying to strike a little terror. She did not succeed.

"Laurel Eby, the *Chronicle*," the woman said outside the entrance.

Allie stopped. "Excuse me?"

"I'm a reporter. You're Mrs. Effington, right?"

"I know you," Allie replied, associating the name Laurel Eby with the moose/cow love story. "I read your articles all the time. I don't know what I'd do in the morning without my *Chronicle*." She thought again of Luke; his speech was scheduled at seven, and it was already quarter past. Allie smiled at the reporter, hoping to spark a conversation and an excuse for being late. "I just loved what you did up in Maine with that Guernsey cow."

The reporter accepted the compliment and paused, waiting for another one.

"An honor," Allie said. "Really." She wanted to ask her whether the animals mated and could produce offspring, and what Laurel would call them in the newspaper—*coose* or *mows?*—but decided not to. Somehow it seemed silly at this hour. Instead Allie inquired, "Do you usually cover awards?"

"Depends on what's being announced," Laurel said and launched into an on-the-street interview, catching Allie off-guard: "Do you share your husband's view about—quoting now—'The Unnatural Tendencies of Community Leaders'?" When Allie didn't answer, Laurel shrugged. "Personally," she said, "I think your guy's a little hung up on sex."

Zing. Allie played with an earring. "Sex?"

Laurel nodded. "What is your position on adultery?"

Double zing. "Position?" She pulled at her necklace—it seemed to tighten around her throat—and then shifted on her heels. The reporter had touched a nerve and was smirking. Allie gave her the once-over again, focusing on the auburn hair that seemed purpler in the harsh light of the street lamp. "I'm not going to answer that," she said, clutching the strap of her purse and pivoting away. Allie clicked inside the building—good, there was a pay phone by the exit—and swept past the women's restroom and vestibule, through the open double doors that led into the main hall.

Allie was fuming. What a blow, she thought. Especially after a compliment. She vowed never to read another word by that woman, even if the *Chronicle* carried a moose/cow hybrid story. Nonetheless, Laurel Eby had pressed two of Allie's buttons: Luke being hung up on sex, and she on adultery. Why was she asking such questions? Allie wondered whether Luke put the reporter up to this, trying to send his wife a message? No, she decided. He'd use a cop. Allie pushed the encounter out of her mind and stopped inside the hall, searching for Luke or Elizabeth. Then she spied Laurel entering behind her. What gall.

What nerve. What *was* her position on adultery? It was okay, Allie reassured herself. There was nothing wrong about her relationship with Eddie Ray. In fact, if the truth be known about sexual shortcomings, Luke would be a prophet—no, an apostle—boring, quick. Clinical almost. Not like Eddie Ray, who made it exciting. Long. Something like a fever: hot.

"You're late," Luke said, coming up alongside her and taking her arm so that it appeared they had entered the hall together. "I said seven, Al. Not twenty after." He escorted her toward the head table, nodding at Rotarians along the way. Reviewing the crowd. Assessing it for opportunities. He seemed a bit jumpy, jittery with adrenaline, the way he always did before a speech. He stopped. Recognized somebody. "Darn," he said, "Claude Turner. What's he doing here?"

"Who's Claude?"

"Publisher of the *Chronicle.*"

Allie gently pulled her arm from his grasp. "I just met one of his reporters. Laurel Eby."

"Would you believe she made a pass at me today?" he told Allie without slowing his pace.

"Huh?" Allie cast him a look, unsure whether she had heard him correctly. "A pass?" she asked. "At *you?*"

"Thanks," he quipped. "Good confidence-builder."

Allie felt a twinge of jealousy but somehow didn't connect it with her husband. She thought about Eddie Ray and shivered, anxious. After her father became an alcoholic, she had a history of panic attacks. But even they had abated after her affair with Eddie Ray, as if she could lose herself in passion and her phobias, too.

Suddenly Elizabeth appeared on her other side and fell into step with Luke, a double escort. Her sister-in-law spoke to Luke as if Allie did not exist between them. "Claude's here," she said. "I don't know why. Play it safe. Acknowledge him in the audience."

The three of them stopped at the head table and dispersed, taking assigned places, again with Luke on one side of Allie toward the podium and Elizabeth on the other side of her toward the end. Various dignitaries approached now and made the usual small talk, during which Allie donned her plastic smile—the only thing about her that was cheap—and prepared to phase out reality. Elizabeth prevented that. Instead of partaking in the banter as campaign manager, she was staring grimly at Allie, disapproving already.

Dinner was being served.

Allie glanced down at her empty plate. It reflected the pearls of her necklace and made them seem like grade A eggs. She'd like to crack a few shells right now—smack, dab—on her sister-in-law. Elizabeth was still keeping vigil, as if Allie was capable at any moment of embarrassing Luke. During such public occasions, ensnared by the Values, Inc. duo, she could not help but long for Eddie Ray. Tonight would be difficult. She needed his touch to undo Luke's last night. *Position on adultery,* she mused. If Allie ever got to talking about that topic, she would never stop, recounting the glories of Eddie Ray's bed. Luke made her feel like a Barbie doll, something he could warehouse or stock. She had to be crazy to come here. She ought to be entering Eddie Ray's door at this hour in her flashy aerobics outfit—she corrected herself—*modern dance.*

Elizabeth nudged her with an elbow and motioned at the emcee. "You're in public," she said. "Wake up."

Allie sat straighter. "Sorry." Dinner already had been put in front of her, a bloody, half-done scar of Kansas City strip. Ugh. She focused on the emcee, a horn-rimmed, semibald broker type who was in the middle of a "Norwegian" joke. No wonder she was in another world—Eddie Ray's world, where nothing had meaning except bed, where they would talk for hours on end. She loved his sense of humor and forgave his sense of pain that caused him on occasion to withdraw when he needed her most. Poor man. She brought out his best, once a week. That was hardly enough. She longed for him now like a fix.

Elizabeth nudged her again.

"Okay, okay." Allie rubbed her ear, trying to focus on the emcee, who was saying—"Knock, knock. Who's there? Sven. Sven who? Sven you're ready, I'll tell you!"—and then groaned, lapsing into another dreamlike state, pasting a half-baked smile to match the half-baked potato on her plate.

Luke touched her arm and she recoiled, startled. "Here goes, Al," he said. "Wish me luck."

"Huh?"

"Go ahead," Elizabeth prompted. "Remember Claude."

The emcee was looking their way. "Sven ever you're ready, Mr. Effington," he said and turned to the audience, about a hundred or so people eating and watching the head table as if it were Hollywood Squares. Luke got up and stood beside him. "Let me tell you a bit about our special guest," the emcee said. "Mr. Effington is receiving our Civic Award for many reasons. Now I know it wasn't properly announced. In fact, you could say it was sort of hasty. But we were going to honor him anyway. Right, Rotarians?" He clapped his hands, evoking some applause.

Luke made a move toward the microphone, but the emcee wasn't finished yet. "In his three-plus years in office," the man said, "Mr. Effington has doubled the conviction rate of his predecessor. He keeps our streets clean. He keeps my jokes clean.

Ladies and gentlemen, let me introduce the next 'Clean-Up Commissioner,' Luke Effington."

Scattered applause. People were too busy sawing the KC strip. Some clanged their forks against water goblets.

"Thank you," Luke said, reaching out to accept the lacquered wood plaque that the emcee held like a carrot. They posed, anticipating the flash of a photographer. But there was none.

"I hereby present you with our coveted award," the emcee said, transferring the plaque with one hand and shaking Luke's hand with the other. Again, they posed. Nobody took pictures.

The emcee sat down next to the podium. Luke put the plaque behind him on the table and adjusted the microphone an inch higher. "Testing, testing." He cleared his voice and glanced at Allie, who immediately turned her head toward Elizabeth because Luke seldom acknowledged his wife in public. Allie didn't want him to begin doing that tonight. His sister gave him the go-ahead sign, bobbing a finger at the side of her plate, making a swirl, and then aiming it at someone in the crowd.

"Thank you," Luke said. The room was silent. You could almost hear people chew. "I want to acknowledge some VIPs in the audience before delivering my speech. First, we have a leading citizen with us. Claude Turner, publisher of the *Chronicle*." Several people in the audience moaned, probably Elizabeth's cohorts. Luke pointed at a man in a black suit by the side exit. The crowd turned just as the publisher stepped out of view, into the hall. "Don't be shy, Claude," Luke said. "I know your newspaper and I don't see eye-to-eye on the issues, but that's all right." Claude returned and nodded solemnly. Luke pointed now at Allie, who looked at Elizabeth for guidance. "I also want to acknowledge my wife and sister, who also serves as my campaign manager."

Allie remained seated while Elizabeth rose for a faint round of applause.

Luke readjusted the microphone. "Testing."

Allie slumped in her seat. Why does he keep testing, testing, she wondered, as if the microphone were malfunctioning? It wasn't. She wanted him to get on with it.

"Testing." He smoothed his double-breasted navy-blue suit and stared at a spot in the back of the room, undoubtedly something he was told once to do in a campus play and had never forgotten. "As you heard from our master of ceremonies," he said, "I intend to run for City Commission. The primary is weeks away, I realize. But the work ahead is important. The issues are complex. The one I will address tonight is controversial. I know that"—he looked at the head table again just as Allie, mechanically, was cutting into her steak, and continued— "I do not shy from controversy. I confront it. In that spirit, let me proceed with my talk."

"He's improvising," Elizabeth said quietly to herself. "He doesn't appreciate me."

These were Allie's feelings exactly. But why was Elizabeth articulating them?

Luke picked up the speech and read from it. *"We live in an age of rampant sin,"* he said. *"We live in an age of loose morals."*

"He's edited my copy," Elizabeth fumed.

Allie started listening to the speech.

". . . take lovers," Luke was saying.

Allie choked on the meat—Elizabeth immediately patted her on the back—and swallowed, turning her head slowly to gawk at her sister-in-law, spooked by her lightning-bolt reflex.

Elizabeth was trying to smile at Luke, showing teeth. Focusing. Setting an example for Allie.

Allie put her fork down and did the same. She came here tonight hoping to attract attention away from Luke and now wished that she had not been so spiteful. A few men in the audience were gawking at her. A fat one smiled. Allie wanted to fade into the background and reappear at Eddie Ray's apartment, gently rapping on his door. *Knock, knock,* she fantasized. *Who's there? Allie. Allie who? Allie needs is love,* she thought, so her name sounded like "All he": *All he needs is love.* Love. Sin. Sex. Her husband was expounding on these concepts, explaining his position, boring her as he did in bed. She drifted off. Imagined what Eddie Ray was doing at this moment—conjured him in the haze of her semiconsciousness—and saw him opening the door of his apartment. Letting someone inside. She sat up straight. Letting *who* inside? Knock, knock: someone *else.*

"Wake up."

Allie felt the urge to choke again but fixed her eyes even harder on Luke until they watered: a kind of penance. He was still staring at that invisible spot in the back of the room—reading in his monotone voice—*"I'm a strong believer in marriage and monogamy. . . ."* It put her in a daze again, an eerie state of uneasiness. What was she feeling? Why was her stomach contracting as if stricken suddenly with salmonella? She glanced at her plate. Was it the rubbery steak? The lettuce? The yellow wax beans? The lime Jell-O that jiggled in the cup? At once she knew the answer: jealousy. It had never occurred to her that Eddie Ray saw other women on nights they did not meet. Allie had lived monogamously for so long with Luke that she assumed Eddie Ray was hers alone. That she satisfied him every week, once a week. And that was enough—for a husband, maybe. But what if it wasn't for a bachelor? What if Eddie Ray had, say, an *urge?* Allie spotted Laurel Eby in the crowd, ogling Luke. What if Eddie Ray knew women—this was difficult—as sexy as the moose/cow reporter, slim enough for slit skirts and open blouses? Her stomach heaved. At once she knew the answer: *he would sleep with them.*

* * *

Allie was standing up. There must have been a blank, for when she came to, she was standing up and Elizabeth was hissing, "What are you doing?"

God, how embarrassing! "Powder room," she said—the first thing that came into her mind—"got to go." Allie tiptoed around her chair.

Elizabeth pushed back her chair and blocked her. "People are staring."

"Better at me than a puddle."

Elizabeth stood up, smiling, and let her by.

"Pardon me," Allie said. She waltzed around the head table and led the way to the woman's room with her sister-in-law in tow, tailgating her, nodding at Rotary members as if this were the most normal thing to do during a speech.

Luke's voice began to crack. *"The thing about family values is the sense of well-being it instills in those who embrace them,"* he was saying. "Enough said, um, about that. *I want to, to,* uh, *stop*—huh?—yes, *the moral decline. . . ."*

As soon as the women reached the exit and were safe, Allie broke into a run. Elizabeth's flat shoes slapped the floor and kept pace with the click of her pumps. "I told you I had to go!" Allie yelled, ducking into the loo.

The door slammed on Elizabeth. But she burst in a second later and exclaimed, "What on earth? Lord, woman! Couldn't it wait?"

Allie reddened—"Sorry"—and headed for a stall.

"Come back here," Elizabeth said. "I said come back here!"

Allie locked the door. She heard the door of an adjacent stall open—*God!*, how embarrassing—and latch shut. Nobody else was in the restroom. "Jesus," she whispered. It had to be Elizabeth.

"What did you say?"

"Nothing." Allie braced herself. She had been rebuked before. She knew what was coming.

"What's going on?" Elizabeth hissed on the opposite side of the wall. "What are you doing?"

Allie was spacing out, a habit of hers when life got complex. She contemplated the graffiti on the wall and wished she had a pen. Somebody had written: **My Mother Made Me A Lesbian**. She wanted to reply: **If I Send Her The Yarn, Will She Knit Me One Too?**

"I don't hear you peeing," Elizabeth said. "If you had to go so bad, how come I can't hear you?"

In desperation, Allie pulled down her lined panties and sat. She wanted Elizabeth to witness a rush of water. No such luck. Too tense. Allie tried to will it out but got nowhere. Groaned. It was the last day of her period.

"I still can't hear you."

Allie bent forward and peeked under the stall. Elizabeth was seated, too, long cotton underwear dangling around the ankles. "As long as I'm here," she heard her say. "You've got me so nervous, I, well"—

"Jesus," Allie said again, sitting up.

"What did you say?"

Allie would never live this down. She needed an excuse. An alibi. One that would get her off the hook so that she could get off the pot and on the line with Eddie Ray. He would know what to do. This was a crisis of immense personal importance. Her sex life hung in the balance. Allie was spacing out again, reading the writing on the wall:

Jumping Jack Flashed Me
Dexter Creighton Gave Me Crabs
Newt Is My Personal Savior

Fuck Me, Rape Me, Pick Up
My Kids At The Babysitter—
Go Ahead, Make My Day

The muse struck Allie where it had others in her position. What an inspiration! If there was one thing she could rely on, it was her sister-in-law's innate response to sex. Allie spoke with a quaver in her voice. Feigned distress. "Liz"—she used her nickname—"I'm in trouble. A man in the audience was staring at me. *Assaulting* me . . . with his eyes. And I"—she wanted to puke—"couldn't let Luke see it. Not in public." She listened—Elizabeth was all ears—and continued: "I was afraid he would follow me here. Did you see him?"

"No."

"Liz, I'm scared."

"Shush. Don't make a sound."

"Oh, no!" Allie hiked up her panties and straightened her clothes, carefully unlatching the stall. "My God," she moaned, slipping out.

"What? What?"

Allie pushed the restroom door open so it squeaked as if someone were opening it.

"Who's there?" Elizabeth asked, her usual husky voice up an octave.

"Get out!" Allie shouted, pretending a man had entered. "Leave me alone!" She scruffed her heels on the floor. "No! No!"

Elizabeth let go a rush of water.

Allie ducked out of the women's room. The coast was clear. Everyone was listening to the speech. She walked toward the pay phone by the exit, trying to contain herself. Allie was elated. Floating. High. She had gotten her sister-in-law back for some of the crap she had had to endure in her marriage to Luke. She'd tell her husband it was a practical joke, and she didn't care whether he believed her. Maybe then Luke wouldn't ask her to attend such functions on her dance night. Maybe he would learn his lesson. Stop underestimating her. Her body shook: an adrenaline rush. Allie had played a prank, and like the prankster was reveling in the moment.

She couldn't wait to tell Eddie Ray. He was always getting on her case for not laying back. Letting go. Well now she had, and she felt great about it. She reached into her purse and dug out a quarter. Dialed. "Eddie Ray, it's me. You won't believe what happened. Smack dab in the middle of Luke's speech, I"— she paused, listening; something was not right—"Eddie Ray? Are you all right?" She listened again—labored breathing. "Oh no," she said, fearing he was drunk or smoking crack again— not that. "What's wrong?"

It began slowly, a series of coughs that grew into gasps and blossomed into wails, groans. Crashing things.

"Say something!" She pressed the receiver tightly against her ear. "Eddie Ray?"

Silence.

"What's going on?" Allie asked.

Silence.

"Are you having a . . ." Her voice trailed off, hearing Luke's echoing in the hall—*"Position on adultery,"* he was saying. Allie spaced out, not knowing where or who she was or with whom she was speaking on the telephone.

"Flashback," Eddie Ray said.

The receiver slipped from her hand, and she watched it swing like a pendulum on its metal line, his voice growing tinier as he repeated the word. A dial tone followed, and then the clickety click of her heels heading out of the hall.

7

Another Nightmarish Installment

Luke had regained his rhythm at the podium. He was as much embarrassed about his bumbling the speech as about his family's sudden disappearance. Elizabeth, he hoped, would have things in hand and would cover for him afterward. Perhaps Allie was feeling ill or misbehaving. Up to new tricks. Sad. He wished that she would enjoy events like this and be proud of him but figured that she must have gotten bored. Took a powder. He would discuss it with her later. For the moment, he was holding the crowd's attention for the first time in his career, and it exhilarated him, as accidents do when they lead to new discoveries.

This one happened subtly, so much so that Luke only now was realizing the effects. When Allie and Elizabeth stalked off, he abandoned the invisible spot in the back of the hall and searched the audience to decipher the problem. He actually made *eye contact*. With Elizabeth gone, he relaxed. Better still, while he was contemplating his predicament, he unconsciously lengthened the natural breaks between sentences. The effect was surprising: the Rotarians soon forgot the interruption. The eye contact engaged them and the slower pace emphasized the import of his topic, making him sound sincere. Concerned. Passionate. (Or so he consoled himself.)

"The values of our leaders set our agendas more than their politics do. We often have heard the cry—'back to basics'—but have long since forgotten what those basics are, especially as they relate to relationships within the family. Within a marriage," Luke said, resting his eyes upon Laurel. She was under his spell, watching him intently from the side aisle, away from the tables. Encouraged, he launched with new vigor into the conclusion of his speech. *"A new era of morality and service is upon us,"* he said. *"Doors of opportunity will open when our hearts do. Either our community leaders will allow more citizens to enter those doors"*—Elizabeth was entering the hall without Allie—*"or they will close them. Business as usual."* Then he saw Laurel veer around and look at Elizabeth moving more awkwardly than usual, as if she had lost her way. *"Fellow Rotarians,"* Luke bellowed, trying to impress his sister with his sudden oratory prowess, *"you know me as your D.A. and as a local businessman. But you don't know me as a family man committed to values that promote the common good."* He stopped. His voice cracked again—Elizabeth was closer now, visibly shaken—bug-eyed and staggering toward the podium sans Allie. "Testing," Luke said hoarsely into the

microphone, stalling to assess the situation. The faces in the crowd—swayed by momentum, as if following a tennis match—swept toward Elizabeth. Luke fidgeted with the mike as his sister stood at attention by her assigned place at the head table. "Liz?" he whispered, but the microphone picked up his voice and the faces in the crowd swayed back again, wondering what Luke planned to do. When it appeared he would do nothing, they turned toward Elizabeth, who was trying to communicate something, opening and closing her mouth like a carp on a hook.

The crowd began to buzz. What was happening? Luke spotted Claude Turner in the opposite aisle. He was wending slowly toward the head table. Did he say something critical to Elizabeth or Allie? Where *was* Allie? Did she insult someone significant and storm off, throwing caution to the wind? Throwing a tantrum? Was it something he had said in the speech? "Where's my wife?" he asked Elizabeth.

His sister remained mute. Now Laurel and Claude were both treading stealthily up the aisles on each side of the hall.

Luke decided to end the speech quickly and come to his sister's aid. *"As I was saying, uh, excuse me, pardon me"*—Luke tapped the microphone, causing it to squeal. Now, when the faces in the crowd swayed toward him, they were grimacing. *"Ah,"* he said, *"Yes. I seem to have lost my place."* He glanced furtively at his sister. She was lifting her head, rolling her eyes, apparently praying for guidance. Luke stared at the back of the hall again. He was on his own and would have to ad-lib: *"You know me. You also know my record. A vote for me is a vote for family values. Thank you for your support."*

The Rotarians were murmuring in earnest. Nobody applauded. Luke stepped quickly from the podium and bumped into the emcee. "Watch out," he said, trying to squeeze by him.

But the emcee moved the wrong way and blocked him again. "For Pete's sake." Luke pushed him aside, upset that his own campaign manager had embarrassed him while he was at the podium and his own wife had left while he was discussing marriage and monogamy.

"Is everything all right?" the emcee asked, readjusting the microphone lower.

Luke ignored the question and returned to his seat.

"Knock, knock," the emcee said, trying to bait the crowd with another joke—"Who's there? Lena. Lena who? Lena little closer, and I'll tell you"—but the audience leaned that-a-way, observing Luke and Elizabeth.

"What's happening?" Luke asked without looking at his sister, assuming that if he sat down, so would Elizabeth. But she didn't. Meanwhile, Claude and Laurel were stalking them like prey. They stood as near to the head table as possible on both sides of the hall. Claude had a quizzical look. Laurel was poised with a note pad, ready to pounce with a question.

This was a bonafide media problem. But Elizabeth could not solve it in her current state. Neither could Luke without knowing the nature of the problem. He was beginning to acknowledge that. Beginning to see the ramifications. This was a nightmare, and he would have to deal with it as such, hoping he would feel better in the morning.

The emcee took mercy and stopped telling jokes. "Remember," he said, "Saturday is Civic Day at Riverside Park. Potluck picnic afterward. Don't everyone bring salad! That's all, folks. Drive home safely." People stood up hastily, but the emcee interrupted again, causing the mike to squeal. "Wait," he said, extending the misery. "I forgot something." He held up a handful of blue-and-silver aluminum-wrapped packets. "Help yourself to some packs of salted peanuts on the way out, compliments of Values, Inc." He turned toward Luke and Elizabeth. "Good night."

As soon as the function officially ended, the VIPs at the head table fled, not wanting to be associated with the unraveling faux pas. The rest of the crowd mingled, milled, and mulled over what they had witnessed, but like Luke seemed uncertain of what that was, exactly. They wanted to have precise stories for the grapevine, so they lingered, keeping a respectable distance but dispatching a few adventuresome souls—a hefty dark-haired woman in a tent dress and a scrawny old man in a blazer—within earshot. The old man kept popping complimentary peanuts in his mouth, skeptical but curious.

Luke got out of his chair and confronted his sister. "Elizabeth," he pleaded, *"what is wrong?"* But she seemed semicatatonic. He yanked her by the arm—"Let's get out of here"—and led her around the table.

Claude, Laurel, and the emcee were waiting for them. The hefty woman and scrawny man stood off to the side of the greeting party, slowly drawing nearer.

"Where's Allie?" Luke whispered as they walked. Elizabeth shook her head, no, and stopped so abruptly that he swung around as if on a rope and faced her. She was swallowing hard, trying to speak. He hoped she would not faint. She would hit the floor like a ton of Bibles.

Claude, Laurel, the emcee, the hefty woman, and the scrawny man inched closer, surrounding Luke and Elizabeth.

Luke stood in front of her. "Claude. Miss Eby," he said. He tried the emcee. "Thanks for the award." Oops. *The award.* Luke had forgotten it on the table behind the podium and froze on the spot. This was a new predicament. Another nightmarish installment. His dreams were often like this. Some red-tag item—a fuzzy pink stuffed rabbit, say, made in Hong Kong—would become life-size and life-threatening, pursuing him (a la *The Shining*) in the maze of Values, Inc. aisles before realizing it could leap. That's when the fun began: the thing went aisle-hopping, "Toys" to "Automotive," making him cower finally on the scuffed hard-wax floor, awaiting the unlucky rabbit's foot that would land, *kaboom!*, on his head. It recurred so often the year that Laslo died and his mother remarried that Luke read up on the phenomenon: "small items harmless in the waking world cause trauma in the dream one." He remembered that quotation. As D.A., he prided himself on memory. At the moment, though, he had forgotten the award.

Luke glanced over his shoulder. He had two options: haul the frightened Elizabeth back to retrieve it or leave her with Laurel and Claude. Then he realized what he was doing and told the emcee, "Forget about the plaque." He had to get Elizabeth out of here.

"There it is!" the emcee said. "On the table. By the podium."

Laurel smiled knowingly at Luke.

"No comment," he said. He wanted to drag his sister to the exit but instead remained rigidly beside her, focusing on the invisible spot in the back of the hall.

"Not to worry," the emcee said, trying to ease the tension accumulating like a halo around Elizabeth. "I'll get it. And my joke book, too. Okay?"

"Okay," Luke said, using the moment to gather his thoughts and plan a getaway. The night was not yet a total disaster, he reminded himself. In fact, the more he looked at that invisible spot, the less anxious he became. Things happened for a reason. If Elizabeth or Allie ruined his candidacy, so be it. He would have more time with his wife. Then his stomach sank. Suddenly he sensed that Allie was responsible somehow for his sister's condition. "Have you seen my wife?" he asked Laurel.

"Well," the reporter said, "I was the last one to talk to her. Sure would like to talk to her now, though."

Claude addressed Elizabeth. "What's troubling you, dear?" he asked. "Stars. You look positively *ashen*."

She nodded.

Luke felt terrible for Elizabeth. She was a strong woman who would feel stabs of embarrassment because of her behavior, unless, of course, her behavior was appropriate for the occasion. Now he felt a stab of fear as if something terrible had happened to his wife. He shook Elizabeth by the shoulders. "Did something happen to Allie?" he asked.

Elizabeth nodded.

Luke let his arms drop to his sides. "What happened to her?" he asked again.

The emcee returned with the joke book and award. He gave the latter to Luke, assuming his hands—palms out in frustration—were meant to receive the plaque, and then leafed through the book, ignoring the tension.

The hefty woman and scrawny man, munching peanuts, edged in and added to the suspense.

The emcee found the page he wanted. "Bust a gut," he intoned. "This one's a *killer*."

Elizabeth sucked air.

The emcee grinned at her as he would an admirer, misreading her raised eyebrows and ga-ga expression as keen interest in whimsy. He told the joke to Elizabeth: "How many Norskis does it take to change a light bulb?"

Claude put his hand on Elizabeth's shoulder. "What is it, dear?"

She was still nodding.

The emcee looked up. "Aw. You heard it before."

"Yes," Elizabeth said. Her voice was raspy. Powerful. Her eyes darted the room and then descended on the emcee. Claude withdrew his hand. "Though one may be overpowered," she said, "two can defend themselves. A cord of three strands is not quickly broken."

"You tell him, honey," the hefty woman said.

"Well, no," the emcee whined, checking his joke book to be sure. "That's not it."

Laurel pounced on Elizabeth, waving a note pad in front of her face as if trying to coax her out of a hypnotic trance. "I saw you leave with Luke's wife. Where is Mrs. Effington?"

Luke jerked at Elizabeth's arm. "No questions." If something did indeed happen to Allie, he needed to know about it as D.A. without the media getting involved. "No comment," he said again. "We're leaving."

"Unhand me," Elizabeth hissed—a sign she was feeling better and would offer an explanation—but suddenly gazed upward, as if marveling at the huge chandelier hanging from the Am-Vets ceiling. Her arms extended outward like wings.

Luke stepped back. "Oh, boy."

The scrawny man dropped his peanuts and backed off, anticipating the outburst.

Elizabeth spread her arms, a harbinger of good news. Her face was peaceful again. "What God has joined together let man not separate," she proclaimed. Then snapped her head at Luke and donned her semisinister half-smile, seemingly knowing all along that something like this might occur, despite her efforts. Elizabeth breathed deeply. "My sister-in-law has been kidnapped!" she blurted, wild-eyed. "Praise unto the Lord!"

8

The Sub-Science of Cosmology

Eddie Ray took a hit from his Lizard of Oz bong, trying to get in touch with the Id. He knew about that word. He read up on old Sigmoid Freud during his Hip-Mo phase, after happening upon an advertisement in *Hustler* about "How To Make Women Fulfill Your Every Whim." He couldn't afford the $29.95 information packet but had a library card, forgetting in his haste the seventeen past-due books on Southeast Asia. The male librarian wanted a quarter times seventeen per day for each book and wouldn't let him check out *The Ego and the Id*—"ego" had caught his eye—or what seemed more suited to the new sub-science: *Beyond the Pleasure Principle*. So he returned with a razor blade to collect the pertinent chapters.

Eddie Ray took another pinch of MaryJane and fired up, filling his lungs with Oz. He put the bong to his side and the matches in his jeans, which were cut a wee bit tight at the crotch. He had to reach inside. Straighten. Get comfy on the bean bag and theorize. "Uh-huh." Sigmoid was right, when it came to drives. Eddie Ray had more hard drives than Apple. Ask Allie. Juanita. The dozen or so multisyllabic WASP women, "hip-moed" during the past year. Poor babes. They believed what they wanted to believe, even if the facts of his life were in their face. Literally. He felt no remorse—why should he?—and gave them what they deserved: *plenty,* which was beyond the pleasure principle of their boyfriends or mates.

Eddie Ray surveyed the room. Recalled the conquests where WASP women had fallen. He ought to put notches on the furniture and walls. Maybe apply for one of them grants and erect some historical markers. Litter the place with them; after all, this was a *conveniency* apartment: bean bag, bed, table, chairs. Dresser/Undress-her. He hee-hawed, pumping himself full of pride. Ego. Id. He didn't need *Hustler* anymore. Or Sigmoid Freud, for that matter. The bulge of his blue jeans reaffirmed the pleasure principle. He had one, all right. Along with a new sub-science to augment the study of One First Name/Two First Names: *Cosmo*logy.

The sub-science had dawned on him suddenlike a year ago. Eddie Ray had stopped reading porn magazines and started reading old women's magazines, stolen from laundromats. He especially liked *Cosmopolitan*. He missed Helen of Gurley Brown, who gave you the lingo and all manner of insight into the mysterious concepts of PMS and liposuction. *Relationships.*

Right. She was big on relationships. A couple or three back issues, and you were in the know. Wise to the wonders of women. You learned about food, fashion, feelings, beauty, health, confidence, and clear skin. You used words like "libido," "charbroiled," "taffeta," "jasmine," "massage," "antidepressant," "wellness," and "vitamin A." You pretended to listen to them, saying phrases like "Get it all out" or "Go with those feelings" or "You have to be true to yourself," and then spaced out while they jabbered, focusing on their eyes and imagining them half-closed in the throes, which occurred when they finished "emoting." Sure enough. They would collapse in your arms, ready to unleash all that pent-up libido. Satisfy those *drives.*

"Yes, indeed," Eddie Ray said. He rolled to his side on the bean bag and reached for the bong, admiring the ceramic alligator that slithered up to the mouthpiece. It reminded him of a snake, something out of Genesis, which, by the way, was all about Ego and Id. Pleasure principles. He wondered how Adam would have fared if he knew Eve's *Cosmo*logy, concepts like "More Than A Mate, Less Than A Lover" or "Luscious Low-Cal Apple Delights." He could have lent Adam a hand. Shown Eve what paradise could be in a fig leaf and rattleskin boots.

He laughed and took another hit. His spirits had picked up considerably. He was having a bad day with old Tim Bert throwing him out of Job Service—without his check. Making all sorts of threats. *Allie-gations.* For a moment, Eddie Ray thought he actually might have to look for work again and opened the classified pages of the *Chronicle* when he saw that boxed ad: "Call Mylo Thrump. Be somebody." At first he tried calling the 1-900 number from a pay phone, but Ma Bell had that figured out. He got a male operator and his quarter back. He was only a few blocks away from the newspaper and tried to see the editor in person, but the guard at the front desk wouldn't allow it. Instead, the guard gave him the newsroom number. So Eddie Ray plunked in his quarter and phoned Herr Thrump direct, planning to squeal on Tim Bert, who didn't behave according to precepts of two first names. Nobody behaved as they should. The gook photographer took his picture and the homely reporter asked her questions, petrifying Eddie Ray. He didn't need the publicity. It could be used against him by some do-gooder Yankee out to cut benefits. Worse, when he wouldn't release his name, the reporter said she would get it anyway from Job Service. "Get this," Eddie Ray said to himself, holding up his middle finger. No sense worrying about this now. Tomorrow he'd find a new place to crash in case Tim Bert & Company came looking for him. Or Thrump & Company. Eddie Ray trembled, dreading the waste of his free time. Such thoughts were spoiling his high. He had to stop goofing off and devote more study to the mother science before branching into the sub-categories. Tim Bert. Tet. It just plum didn't figure. Lucky Juanita Marie wasn't around to witness his ouster at Job Service. He wished he was with her now, nuzzling her nachos, as it were.

Eddie Ray yawned. He was fagging out. It had been a long day and wasn't over yet. He had to keep awake in case Allie showed up at his door and would lay on her a special four-star Ida-May-Help-Me attack of the Jungle Jitters. He was fairly certain that she would break free of her old man and crash here sometime tonight. Hopefully before *he* did, considering the MaryJane he had toked in his loneliness. He wanted Juanita, not Allie, and felt sorry for himself. Everyone got what they deserved except him, it seemed. He had to rely on science while others relied on their lot in life. Good fortune. Good families.

"Good riddance." He slumped on the bean bag and slipped into a luxurious half-sleep, envisioning the many-sided faces of mul- tisyllabic WASP women—Hip-moed/Cosmoed/*Ram*boed—to the max. Fulfilling his every whim. Then images of heirlooms, NastyCards, fig leafs, snakes, and paradise belly-danced in his head. One day he'd have a harem of his own. A pimpdom, per- haps. He would be happy.

* * *

Someone was knocking at his door. Eddie Ray awoke: flash- back. He got up, wobbly. Disheveled himself, pulling at his hair so that a few curls stood on end like wires. Untucked his shirt and a pant leg from one boot. Bent down, sprawled on the floor. Let go a deep Jungle Jittery moan. Shook, rattled, and rolled himself toward the door, slithering up toward the knob. Then held his breath to turn a certain shade of pale. *Lights, camera. Action!* He banged the door open with his skull—he hoped Allie was appreciating the effort that went into this—and slowly, sorrowfully, looked up to behold a plate of anisette cook- ies and then down to a thick set of Mama Minelli ankles in stiff- looking Values, Inc. shoes.

"Mr. Bok?"

He watched her stomp like a matador.

"Are you sick?"—the shoes inched forward, pounding dan- gerously close to his fingers—"No," she said above him. "You aren't sick. You're making fun of me!"

He tried to stand up and put the best mug on a touchy situ- ation. But now that he was vertical again, the MaryJane made him swoon. Mrs. Minelli was all out of proportion, a fat lady in a hall of mirrors. She sloped this-a-way/that-a-way, like a Leaning Tower. He fell against the door, tongue-tied, momentarily losing track of the Here/Now.

"You've been drinking!" he heard her say.

He glanced up with a semisick half-smile and couldn't see her face above the points of her breasts and the plate held out like a threat. The image of the plate reminded him of Grandma Bok, who had broken a few on his head. (This sobered him quick as smelling salts.) He breathed deeply, reached for the door knob. Managed to stand. "Thought you were someone else," Eddie Ray said. "Company coming."

"You're in no condition to see anyone," she replied, observing him closely. She held the plate of cookies in front of her so that they trembled when she spoke. "You've been drinking," she bellowed again.

"Hell, no," Eddie Ray said, tucking in his shirt and boot. "A couple or three beers, is all." He had to regain his cool. He wanted those cookies, their rich, liquorlike aroma filling his nostrils. "Those for me?"

"Yes," she said. She hesitated, unsure whether she should let him have goodies that were laced with anisette. "Don't eat too many. Save them for your lady friend." She surrendered the plate and pointed at him. "Make some coffee."

He hung his head and stared at the cookies while his neighbor crossed the hall. "Leave the dish at the door in the morning," Mrs. Minelli said, "and do not take my newspaper."

"You betcha"—

She slammed 4-E.

—"bitch."

Eddie Ray burped. Then he picked a plump, sugar-powdered morsel and popped it into his mouth, savoring the burst of flavor. He entered his apartment and stuffed another chunk into his mouth. And another, feeling a sugar fix coming on to add to the anisette and the buzz. Good thing he could handle his MaryJane, he thought. For no sooner was he back on the bean bag, polishing off the treat, when someone was at his door again, banging up a storm. Damn that meatball Minelli! This time he was going to ball her out, even if her cookies were hitting the spot—he crammed another one into his mouth, just in case she wanted the rest back—and pushed the plate behind the bean bag. Let her find it. He got up and went to the door. Opened it.

"Honey, angel—are you all right?"

Eddie Ray gasped and a cookie chunk lodged in his throat, sending him into first-rate believable spasms, his face turning that certain shade of pale—causing Allie to scream, "Eddie Ray! No, please. Eddie Ray!"—until he collapsed in the hall with a thud, dislodging the cookie chunk from his throat to his mouth. He chewed the evidence and swallowed. Then writhed on his back, coughing.

"Oh, my God!" Allie dropped to her knees behind him and slipped her hands under his armpits.

"Help," he whimpered.

She grunted and dragged his near-dead weight into the apartment with Eddie Ray finally aiding somewhat, walking backward while she steered him to the bed. He flopped there, part on/part off. She yanked at his boots and then unbuttoned his shirt and jeans, gently lifting his legs to the sheets. He curled in a ball and continued with more gut-wrenching coughs and hair-raising spasms.

Allie scurried across the room to close the door, losing a pump in the process. She returned in a huff—"Darling, what's wrong?"—and sat down beside him, taking his hand and checking his pulse. She kicked off her other shoe and got on the bed with him. Cradled his head.

Eddie Ray swallowed the last crumb of the cookie chunk that had been lodged behind a molar and said in a syrupy voice: "Flashback."

"Poor baby," Allie said. "Don't think of it. Put it out of your system." She stroked his hair, twirling a curl with her finger. Soothing him. Trying to free him of his demons. "It's okay now. I'm here."

Eddie Ray struggled to get his bearing. Jesus. He had nearly met the One First Name/Two First Names equalizer, the Big "D," thanks to Mama "the Cookie-Killer" Minelli. He wondered whether he should launch into some aftershock stage of the Jungle Jitters—mumbling about hooches and gooks—but decided that his semidemise sufficed for the moment. Allie's eyes were welling up with oh-so-sorriness. "Glad you made it," he told her, half meaning the words. His nerves were shot. He needed a shot. Or a toke to calm him down. "Get my bong by the bean bag, babe. Will you?"

"Not now," Allie pleaded. "You don't want to smoke, hon. You want to sleep." She kissed his forehead. "I could fix you some tea."

Tea? Eddie Ray thought of Grandma Bok—two parts crocked—and nigh about blacked out again. "Git it, git it!" he heard himself yell—surprised by the tone of voice—and pointed with both hands at the bong. "Don't give me no lip."

Allie hopped off the bed. "Easy, darling. Please."

"Stress, babe. Stress."

She returned with the bong and his bag of weed.

He dug into his jeans for the matches. Loaded and lit up. Toked.

Allie watched him. She didn't seem annoyed, but her head tilted slightly away from his, which was what women did when they didn't quite believe you. And her eyes were clear now and penetrating. "I can't stay long," she said. "You won't believe what happened."

He inhaled the smoke and settled on the bed, ready to employ the sub-science of *Cosmology.* "Nice 'do,' " he said, using women-talk. He reached out and touched her hair, stroked it. You had to time these words right—"Good texture, too"—or else they fell as flat as he did in the hall: "Ac*cen*tuates the cheekbones." He smoothed her hair gently behind an ear, noticing the expensive earring. "My-oh-my. What fine cheekbones you have, Allie." He bent over the side of the bed and put away the bong. "So what-all happened to you?"

Allie hung her head and looked up, embarrassed about something. She touched him lightly on the chin and ran her nails up his face, placing her palm on his forehead. "Are you sure you're all right?"

"Let me show you, sugar." He took her hand and put it at the nape of his neck. Pulled her down for a long, slow, anisette-flavored kiss. Closed-mouthed, at the moment. (He had to clean the remaining cookie crumbs with his tongue.) Then he opened wide and teased her.

She tried to slip away, but he moved his lips to her earlobe—the earring was in the way—and had to abandon that strategy. Instead, he went for broke and undid her blouse.

"No," she said. "I have to get back."

He wasn't listening. "Hold still." He unsnapped her bra, silk and lace. Dropped his head between her breasts. Nuzzled. Talked as he kissed, humming a lexicon of *Cosmology* about agony, love, pent-up libido. Undid the skirt and removed the panties—she was "hip-moed" already—and moved over her, about to fulfill a whim.

Allie pushed him. "Stop. Please." She reared up on her elbows and whispered, "Wait. Damn it." She undid the earrings and necklace and put them on the nightstand, an upturned Pepsi crate he had ripped off a truck.

He undressed while she took a condom from her purse and put it on him. Then she undressed herself, as she would for her husband, sensing that Eddie Ray lacked the energy.

She was wrong. He started in again, slowing the pace the way she liked it, playing the part to the hilt—a gentle, tortured, restless soul in need of a woman who cared too much. Allie cared. Right now she cared about simpler things—not the so-called *Cosmo*logy or highfalutin social graces or even the Sigmoid dreamier stuff—but about concepts like "how long?" and "when?"

She and Eddie Ray were equals now. She was at his level. He looked down at Allie in the throes of WASP-woman passion, her head whipping back and forth on the pillow. *Yes indeed.* He slumped atop her, staying hard. Closed his eyes. Imagined that Allie was Juanita Marie, her legs around him as if she were a flamenco floozy in heat, and pumped her pistonlike again. "Come on, bitch," he hissed. "Do it."

She screamed—*"Please, Eddie Ray!"*—over and over, her voice growing fainter, his body arching and then silencing hers until the only sound in the room was of sleep, regular and easy.

9

Something Must Have Happened

"Cannot disengage," the scanner above Laurel Eby's desk announced, breaking the silence of the newsroom. It was late. Past deadline. Mylo felt like a father awaiting a tardy daughter. He sat in front of Laurel's computer, rapping his pencil against the blinking screen. He already had put one story to bed—Kimberly's unemployment piece (sans psychic comment)—but was worried about the Rotary/adultery scoop that he had assumed was a shoo-in. Where was she? Laurel should have returned more than two hours ago.

"Backup unit responding," the dispatcher on the scanner said, her voice monotonous. Scratchy. "Report Unit Three."

Mylo stared at the radiolike black box whose frequencies picked up police, fire, civil defense. Emergencies. (There had been none.) He heard the cop at the scene repeat: "Cannot disengage."

Mylo debated whether he should shut off the scanner and do some serious fretting. He was impatient—weren't all editors?—and watched the black box as an anxious father might watch late-night television, to pass the time. An hour ago he had ducked into the men's room to shave a stubble of beard with an old X-acto knife, a penlike cutting tool with a razor on the tip. He had also downed two chili dogs from the all-night vendor outside the Chronicle Building. Reread the *Enquirer*, the *Star*, the *Globe*, and the *Weekly World News*. And still Laurel had not checked in.

Mylo rubbed his clean-shaven chin, removing a wedge of toilet paper he had stuck there to stopper a nick. He flicked it in the waste bin under Laurel's desk and decided to give her another fifteen minutes before replacing her story on the front page with a summary of UFO sightings, rewritten from tab magazines. (He kept it in a computer file for emergencies like this one.)

Mylo's concept—no news is good news—was failing him today. It had been a dull morning, and now it was a dull night. No murders, muggings, rapes. No big burglary. It happened on occasion. Usually after a major TV event, such as the last season installment of a sitcom like "Friends" or "Seinfeld," streets became safe. Cops became bored, and editors who listened to cops on scanners became annoyed. Following such lulls, the city would hyperventilate. The sitcom was overhyped, say, disappointing viewers. Domestic squabbles would break out. But no such finale had premiered tonight. For some reason, common Joes across town were going happily to bed instead of angrily to bars, ruining Mylo's plans. He checked Laurel's calendar: crescent moon. The worst kind. Common Josephines got romantic then. You depended on full moons for banner weeks. People got loony (the FBI could document that); maybe it had to do with the tides. Or the stars. There were signs, all right—something big was coming—but Mylo could not decipher it, and he wondered whether Jeane Dixon ever felt this way, puzzling over her emphemeris, not sure what to forecast for Gemini, which was his sign.

"Unit Three," the voice on the scanner said, reporting once more from the scene. "Cannot disengage."

Mylo sighed. The saga had gone on all night. Some Joe locked his keys in his car outside the Fifth Street coin-operated laundry and phoned police for help. They had nothing better to do. But the cops who came also could not open the vehicle—"anyone know how to unglitch a Celica?"—and thus began a series of scanner bulletins that soon degenerated into a precinct betting pool. Which patrolman could pick the lock? It had become a male thing. "Twenty says Willie can't open it with a hook," the voice said. "Twenty says he can," the dispatcher replied.

Mylo perked up. He took a piece of copy paper from the pile on Laurel's desk and tapped his pencil on it, making a crescent of dots as he contemplated a headline. This locked-car story could develop into a "brightener," one of those oddball accounts that add a little wit to the front page. **Bookie-Cops Tie Up 911.** He wrote that in block letters. But then a cop on the scene said, "Negative on bet. Wife just came with spare keys." The scanner went dead. Units began patrolling the streets again. Mylo wouldn't get to use the headline because Josephine was in a good mood under the light of a crescent moon, rescuing her Joe so they could trot happily to bed.

Mylo was miserable. The world was at peace. He wadded the copy paper and put aside his pencil, noticing Kimberly's purse by her computer. She had not gone home; her story—already type-set—was still on her screen. The corrected version was laid out in a computer file not yet sent to the press room and would be processed as soon as Laurel's story was edited for the front page.

Where was Laurel? Mylo mulled. How could a Rotary speech continue so long? Why didn't Laurel at least place a courtesy call and update him? Now he would have to edit her story in record time—the press crew was waiting downstairs—and the fore-man, Hans Auerbach (whom Mylo called "Kraut Face") raised hell when overtime depleted his budget. Mylo checked his watch. Half past midnight, and Hans had not intercommed yet to find out what was holding up the front page. That concerned Mylo. He decided to make the first move and get a jump on the foreman, who did not know that Laurel's story had yet to be written, let alone edited.

He picked up the phone. Dialed. Hans answered. "Finishing up here," Mylo told him. "We have to run down a piece of information. Shouldn't take too long."

Hans had an accent, pronouncing "V" as "W" and "W" as "V." Mylo could never figure that out. German was all "V"s and "W"s. *Volksw*agens. Yet Hans said, "You vill have it done wery soon, I hope. You are vasting waluable time."

"Don't worry"—Mylo almost said "Kraut Face," succumb-ing to a Freudian slip—"we'll send the story down in a jiff," he said, hanging up. "Damn." He didn't want to rile the foreman when he needed his cooperation.

Kimberly was watching him. Mylo swung around in Laurel's chair. "Don't sneak up on me like that," he said. "Why are you still here?"

She was smug. "Thought I would stay and reread my story. See where I went wrong."

"It's late," Mylo replied. He knew that she was waiting for Laurel and hoping for the worst. "Do it in the morning."

"Nah," Kimberly said in a mocking tone. She sat across from him and scanned her computer screen. Took out her pad and meticulously copied some of his edits, as if she were planning to use them as evidence. She glanced up. "By the way," she asked, "how long do you plan to wait for Ms. Twoshoes?"

"As long as necessary."

"Goodie," Kimberly quipped and returned to her task.

Smug-ass. Mylo got up and walked around to her desk. "What are you doing?"

"I already told you."

"Tell me again."

"Nah."

Mylo knew that she wasn't trying to learn from his edits. Kimberly had turned in poor work and argued every time that he had made changes. Her instincts were wrong. Mylo could see that now, viewing the split screen that showed her original story and his rewrite. Kimberly had not extracted good enough quotes from the ex-Marine at Job Service who had assaulted a con man named E.R. Bok; instead, Kimberly had emphasized facts, not truths. Worse, she had telephoned and interviewed psychics about the city on the verge of collapse. The story had changed, but Kimberly hadn't changed with the story. So Mylo had made her concentrate on the Job Service scuffle and transcribe her psychic quotes for Labor Day, next month.

"Go ahead," Kimberly said, acknowledging him. "Read. Mine's the better version."

Mylo didn't reply, comparing the stories:

Suspected Con Man Gets Boot
By Ex-Marine At Job Service

By Kimberly Spears

An Oklahoma man suspected of defrauding the Veterans Administration and State Unemployment Commission scuffled briefly with an official at Job Service Monday because of their views on Vietnam.

Tim Bert Russell, who served with the U.S. Marines in Hue during the 1968 Tet offensive, said a 43-year-old Tulsa man engaged him in a weird conversation about the Vietnam War. Russell, district supervisor at Job Service, had summoned the man to his office to seek answers on extended unemployment benefits.

The man's identify is being withheld pending an investigation by federal authorities.

"I understand that times are tough," said Russell, who became enraged when he thought the Oklahoma man was using Vietnam as a means to bypass rules governing unemployment compensation. He was seen escorting the suspected con man out of the Job Service building and then shoving him to the curb.

"I shouldn't have pushed him but I was angry," Russell noted. "He's always free to file a complaint with the state Commission. I'll be happy to tell officials what I know about the man," he added.

Later the man complained to the Chronicle but then refused to disclose his identity or elaborate on the confrontation.

Mylo excised this like a surgeon. Then he rewrote:

Vietnam Vet Takes Down Slacker
In Job Service 'Scuffle-Gate'

By Kimberly Spears

Tim Bert Russell, ex-Marine and bureaucrat, is fed up with phonies. When he fought in Vietnam during the terrible Tet Offensive in 1968, he thought he was defending democracy. Now he may be defending himself in court for assaulting a slacker Monday at Job Service.

The slacker, Edward Raymond Bok, also may find himself in court as a defendant, if what Russell says is true: Bok's a con man who pretends to be a veteran, cheating the system. Wasting your hard-earned tax dollars by filing false claims, extending undeserved benefits.

Russell welcomes a civil suit by Bok and has initiated a federal investigation into the 43-year-old native Tulsan. "I'll be happy to tell officials what I know about Bok," Russell said.

Bok, on the other hand, may have something to hide. He told an editor at the *Chronicle*, in an exclusive interview, "I'm like tattling on this guy Tim Bert. Leave me out of it."

It went on like this for several paragraphs. In the business, the edit was known as a "write-through." The original was so bad that Mylo had to revise it, top to bottom. Kimberly objected every pica of the way and at one point asked him to pull her byline from the story. Mylo refused. When Kimberly told him that Bok could sue for libel because the story implied that, indeed, he was a con man, Mylo said, "Let him," thinking about Wendy again. He could go out in the glory of a libel suit and get support from his editor-wife, whose vow to the First Amendment was greater than her marriage to him. Anyway, Mylo knew, Bok really was a slacker who avoided lawyers and courts. Kimberly, on the other hand, would welcome lawyers and courts. So when she mentioned that she was keeping a diary about his treatment of her, and that his behavior tonight was going to be recounted therein, Mylo told her that he had a diary of his own, called her annual review. She took down that comment on a scrap of paper and put it in her purse. Mylo knew that she was lingering in the newsroom to determine what had happened to Laurel, making her latest diary entry as complete as possible.

"Finished?" she asked him. "I'm going to make some notations and take off."

"Good," Mylo said. He had had about enough of her tonight and went back to Laurel's desk, keeping his vigil. He wondered what Wendy was doing at this hour inside her new condo by the river. Sleeping, he hoped. *Alone.* He became anxious again, uncertain if the ache in his belly was related to Wendy, Kimberly, Laurel, chili dogs, or the silence in the newsroom that was like the eye of a storm. He cleared his mind and waited. Nothing. He glanced at Kimberly, filing her personal log. Nothing. Even the telephones were quiet. "I'm going downstairs to get a Coke," he told Kim. "Cover for me."

"I'm off duty now," she replied, "but sure. Get your Coke."

Mylo walked toward the exit. Stopped. Listened. Nothing. Started again and turned around.

"Go on," Kimberly said.

"Shhh." Mylo began retracing his steps, slowly at first and then with conviction.

"I'll cover for you, I said."

"Shhh."

Kimberly watched as he went to the scanner. "Hear something? What's going on?"

The scanner lit up and buzzed: "All points, priority code. Suspect last seen Am-Vets Building, approximately twenty-hundred hours." Then the dispatcher gave the code for a hostage/assault situation.

"Yes!" Mylo yelled, scurrying to Laurel's desk. "I knew it!"

Kimberly sat stunned for a second and then said, "You don't think it's Laurel, do you?"

"Laurel?" His glee ended as reports flooded in on the scanner. Cruisers were en route all over town. "No, surely." Mylo pieced together the story: The kidnapping occurred at 8 P.M. at Am-Vets, plenty of time for Laurel to return to the newsroom. He burped, holding his stomach, feeling woozy.

Kimberly was beside him now. "This is my type of story," she said. "Hard news. You know it."

He looked at her—she reminded him of a rodeo rider in the chute, set for the second go-around—and asked, "Do you think something happened to Laurel?"

She spoke slowly, deliberately: "Just put me on it and I will find out."

"Okay," Mylo said. "Go for it."

Kimberly grabbed her purse from her desk.

"Wait."

The scanner fell silent, and another ominous lull overcame the newsroom.

"Out of the way, out of the way!"—Mylo and Kimberly swung around and saw Laurel burst into the newsroom— "What a story!"

"I don't believe it," Kimberly said, hurling her purse at her computer so the screen rocked and went blank.

"Finally," Mylo said, turning up the volume of the scanner and hurrying to Laurel's desk. "We're way past deadline, kid. Type, type, type." He watched over her shoulder as she wrote about the kidnapping of Allie Effington, the D.A.'s wife. "Mother lode!" Mylo exclaimed.

Laurel flipped open her pad and typed while she talked. "Detectives won't tell me a thing," she said. "I got most of this on my own. That's why I'm late."

"Auerbach's been hounding me," Mylo said. "Write fast."

"I followed Luke home," she said as she typed. "Do you know the guy has cherry bombs instead of mufflers on his Firebird?"

Then paused while she checked her notebook, continuing again on the keyboard as if playing an instrument. The clickety click of the keys were music to Mylo's ears. He began to feel better. "Anyway," Laurel continued, "he won't tell me a thing either. He went back to his office. Locked *himself* up."

"What about Elizabeth?"

"That's another story." Laurel stopped typing and looked at Mylo. "The woman winged out."

"Type, type!"

Clickety click.

Mylo read what Laurel had written, in perfect tabloid style.

Kimberly wandered over to read Laurel's story. "Jesus Christ," she said. "What luck."

The telephone rang in his office. Mylo punched a button on Laurel's phone and picked it up—"Let her write," he told Kimberly, holding the receiver at his side—"Don't bait her." Laurel clicked the keyboard with a steady vengeance. A voice was yelling something in a low decibel. Mylo glanced around the room, trying to isolate the sound. Then realized he had a call. "Hello?"

"Vhat are you doing? There are *trucks* outside! Vee got papers to deliwer!"

"Ten more minutes. Tops," Mylo said to Hans Auerbach.

"Vee can't vait that long." Someone was speaking in the background to the press foreman. "Mr. Turner has just arriwed. I vill speak to him."

"Give me a break, Kraut Face," Mylo said and winced.

"Vat?"

Mylo hung up the phone. "Damn, damn." His stomach hurt again. What was Claude Turner doing here at this hour? He held his head, trying to get a bearing. Then looked up and saw Kimberly hovering over Laurel's story again. "Give her space," he shouted. "She has work to do!"

Kimberly stalked off, her ponytail wagging like a tongue. She grabbed her purse from the floor and headed for the elevator.

"Frig you," Laurel whispered as Kimberly left.

Mylo took her position over Laurel's shoulder and read her copy for typos or misspellings:

D.A.'s Wife Feared Abducted at Rotary Club! Ransom or Revenge? Lock'em'up Awaits Word!

By Laurel Eby

It was supposed to be a night of speeches and Norwegian jokes, a Rotary dinner that nobody would remember much—here, a gaffe and there, a faux pas—all of it to celebrate Luke Effington, district attorney. Aka Lock'em'up. Aka Civic Servant of the Year. Aka newly announced candidate for City Commission.

Given such an affair, nobody would suspect the intruder. Some believe he arrived to avenge a too-harsh sentence. Some say he seeks a sizable ransom from the affluent Effington conglomerate whose interest Lock'em'up controls.

This much is certain. Taunting the D.A.'s wife with lecherous looks from the audience, stalking her in the women's lavatory, the intruder abducted the comely Allison Effington with the calm of a professional killer and whisked her away to an uncertain fate. . . .

Mylo told her to write another inch of copy and then file it directly to his front-page layout and then send the layout to the composing department. Then Auerbach's crew could print it up and call it a night.

The night had not ended for Mylo Thrump, however.

Claude Turner arrived in the newsroom and summoned Mylo with a finger, indicating he wanted to speak to the editor in private in the hall by the elevator.

Maybe Kimberly had said something to Claude on her way out, Mylo thought. He approached the publisher, coughing by the exit. Mylo asked if there was a problem.

"Several," the publisher said in the hall. Cough. "But we'll discuss problems later in the week." He told Mylo they would meet for lunch Thursday at the Gentry Club.

"What's on your mind?" Mylo asked, wondering why Claude wanted to speak alone.

"I helped your reporter tonight," he replied. "Put her in touch with some people. But there is one piece of information that is off the record until this—hmm, how shall we call it— *incident*, yes, is resolved. First"—cough—"some business."

"Business?"

"About your wife."

Mylo froze. "What does she have to do with Laurel's story?" he asked, knowing the *Herald* didn't hit the streets until late afternoon. He was looking forward to scooping his wife again.

"Are you on speaking terms with Wendy?" Claude asked.

"No."

"Then never mind."

"What?"

"We'll discuss it at the Gentry Club," Claude replied. "As for the piece of information," he said, pausing, appearing reluctant now to disclose it, "well, it concerns *me*."

Mylo remained silent, obsessing about Wendy.

"Are you listening?" Claude asked, a harried look on his face.

"No."

"My word!"

"You're talking about my wife," Mylo said. He asked if she was seeing someone.

The publisher's face softened. "Oh. No, my dear man. Sorry. This is a business matter, not a personal one, I assure you."

"Ah," Mylo said, understanding now. Claude probably had heard that Wendy got the green light from her publisher Margaret Hopkins to revamp the *Herald.* That would explain Claude's inviting Mylo to the Gentry Club to discuss "problems." Mylo burped. "Excuse me," he said. "I'm not feeling well."

"Perhaps tonight is not the time," Claude said.

"No, go ahead."

"It's a delicate subject."

"Well I'm not. I'm editor of your newspaper."

Claude was stalling. He pushed the button and the elevator doors opened. Then the publisher put his foot on the track so that the doors kept bumping his shoe and grinding to remain open. The sound unsettled Mylo. "Resolve this unfortunate incident concerning Mrs. Effington," Claude said. "Let an appropriate amount of time elapse until the woman's whereabouts be known." Claude held the elevator doors open with his hand now, but they ground like chili dogs in Mylo's stomach.

"Let time elapse for *what?*" Mylo asked, losing patience.

The publisher coughed again as the doors began to close. "You see," he said, stopping the doors with his foot so that they framed his aristocratic shape, "we must time this story so that it has maximum impact." The doors opened wide and began to close. "I intend to run against Lock'em'up in the primary."

10

Allie Hears
A Thump

It was a familiar thump. One that arrived at a familiar time, first light, and at a familiar place: the door. Allie awoke and, for a brief moment, did not know where she was. "Luke?" she said, sitting up and rubbing her eyes. The man who sprawled next to her on his belly was definitely not Luke, who of late hogged the bed, trying to get closer to her. This had to be a dream. The mystery man was Eddie Ray, with whom she longed to spend an entire night. She reached out to remove a curl from his ear and nibble it, whispering—"Wake up, darling"—when the horror struck. She had abandoned her husband at Rotary and fooled

Elizabeth in the loo. She had not made it back to the banquet. She had not made it home.

When she realized this, her hand was halfway to his hair. Instead of planting a nibble or a kiss on his ear, she nudged him on the shoulder a little more forcefully than she had intended. "Wake up," she said. He was out cold. She looked to the window; it was early—about 7 A.M., judging by the light and the thump—and figured he was used to sleeping late. She grabbed his arm and wiggled it; he batted at her touch, as if trying to shoo a fly. Allie patted his back—"Come on, sweetie"—making him muffle and growl on the sheets. Again he batted at her with his arm and clutched a pillow, putting it over his head.

Allie pulled away. She remembered Luke and trembled. "Please," she implored Eddie Ray. "Wake up. Don't do this."

He began to snore. She swung her legs over the bed and got out, suddenly aware of her nakedness. She touched her toes on reflex, as she did every morning upon rising. Sighed. For the first time in a week, she did not ache. They had made love last night—a more physical, aggressive love—that must have conked her out. She saw her clothes and purse in a pile on the floor, the blouse and skirt hopelessly wrinkled. Eddie Ray shifted on the bed. Allie turned toward him and asked, "Are you asleep?" No reply. "Honey angel?" she called, and he grunted. She could have been talking to the wall.

Allie dressed and assessed the problem. She had to get home. Her husband was utmost in her mind for the first time in months, and she wondered whether that was normal for a woman who slept with two men. When you were with one, you thought of the other. She was thinking that Luke would be waking soon. Mr. Precision. He would roll to his side of the bed and grope for his slippers when the cuckoo clucked eight times.

She still could sneak into the house and crawl under the crepe de chine and invent an excuse, reasonably certain that Luke would not suspect she had a lover. Neither could she, at the moment: the man on the bed was immobile. Nonresponsive.

She decided to leave him a message. She put on her heels and rummaged deep in her purse for a pen. Found one that must have lain there for ages, embossed with a familiar slogan: **Clean Up Crime, Vote Effington, D.A.** "Wonderful," she said, as if Luke were here. As if she had committed a crime, got caught, and needed cleaning up. She did, in fact. Allie considered undressing again for a quick shower but doubted she had the time. Maybe she would let Luke find her in the hot tub at home. She could say she became ill at Rotary and then fell asleep in the tub, in their labyrinth of a mansion. She glanced again at Eddie Ray, still asleep on the bed, and searched her purse once more for something to write on—the receipt from Hair Today.

Allie was confused as she went to the kitchen table and pulled out a chair. What could she tell Eddie Ray? "Thanks for a lovely night?" Not exactly. Maybe she should she just sign it "Allie" and dot the "i" with a smiley-face. Or something simpler, more direct, indicative of her dilemma—"Help!"—or something in between: "Help! I'll call. Wish me luck." That seemed okay. Eddie Ray would know that she needed a few days to unruffle Luke before she could return next week as scheduled. She sat down—the table was littered with stale bits of cupcake and foil wrappings—and found a spot. But the crumbs pushed up beneath the receipt and made her handwriting—already shaky, given her situation—fairly illegible. All she could muster was "Help!" and she had to scan the table top for a cleaner place to complete the message. A piece of cupcake moved. She rubbed her eyes to be sure. It moved again. It was crawling toward her—"Eke!"—a cockroach. She jumped up, knocking over the chair in the process.

Eddie Ray whipped the pillow from his head. "Hush. Will you? Let me sleep."

Allie scurried to the bed and nudged him hard. "Wake up," she said. "We got a problem."

"Okay, okay." He groaned and rolled on his back, rearing on his elbows. "I'm up. All right? Satisfied?"

Allie tilted her head and observed him in new light. Literally. Eddie Ray was disheveled, in need of a shave—the stubble of beard on his face made him appear ominous, *evil*—not the cool, detached, silky-smooth lover with pants in his boots. Even his apartment looked different in sunlight that was cascading on the bean bag, revealing rips. Slits. Crisscrosses of electrical tape as patches. She never noticed that before. When she would tryst here at night, the lamps cast a yellow aura that complemented the atmosphere; oh, it was still sleazy—the better the sex—but now the apartment seemed plain *dirty*. Ominous? Evil? Dirty? What was happening to the mystique? Why was he glaring at her, wanting to go back to sleep? Was he *lazy*? Somehow he had metamorphosed into another creature on that bed. So had Allie. Slowly, ever so subtly, she began to miss her mansion. Her furniture flashed in her mind as if something beautiful inside her were dying—*flash* went the Savonnerie rug, *flash* went the crepe de chine, *flash flash* went the Art Deco console and king-size canopy bed—leaving stale bits of cupcake crumbs and cockroaches in their sted.

This was weird.

"So what-all do you want to talk about," Eddie Ray asked her, "now that I'm up?" He sat on the bed, Zen-style, running his tongue over his lips and wiping his mouth on his wrist.

She related what had happened at Rotary. "I wanted to tell you last night but you were out of it. Pretty bad, too. But then you had this *miraculous* recovery." She dropped her head in her palm and felt guilty. "I didn't just walk out on him," she said. "I walked out while he was giving a big speech and didn't make it back to explain." She looked up, anticipating a little compassion. "Can't you see why I'm upset?"

"What-all do you want to do about it?" he asked. "What's done, s'done." He lapsed into a coughing fit and held up a hand until he was able to swallow and speak. "Say you got sick. Couldn't make it home. Spent the night with a friend." He yawned, feeling his beard. "Call up a couple or three girlfriends. They'll cover for you."

It occurred to Allie as she stood there despising Eddie Ray that he was her sole friend. She never got along well with women, given her looks—slender, porcelain, all-American— along with her personality, always willing to listen to a man and offer advice or consolation. Oh, nothing to undercut her female acquaintances; she wanted to help them, in fact—make their men more compatible—but ended up being compared more favorably than her pals. One day her girlfriends would invite her on a shopping spree, and Allie would gratefully go, only to be cornered in the dressing room and cut down in a triptych of mirrors. Allie had given up entirely on friends by the time she met Luke, who didn't qualify as one either. She squinted at Eddie Ray, irked at his behavior. "You're the only friend I've got," she said. "Isn't that sad?"

"I'm going back to sleep."

Allie sat down on the bed where he flopped again and debated whether she should wallop him or wallow in her disappointment. Maybe she should dally here a bit longer and invent a believable alibi. Anyway, she would never make it home before Luke arose on the eighth cluck. She thought about dance class, her usual excuse. She had met the instructor Cathy once when she had signed a six-month contract. Maybe she could call her up at the studio, explain her problem, and extend her contract, striking a deal, as women sometimes do (or don't?) in the name of sisterhood. Or maybe Allie could say she got sick—salad salmonella—and went home. Lost the key. Took a room at the Regency. It could work, as long as Elizabeth didn't spoil the scam with suspicion. *Elizabeth!* What did she tell her? Something about a pervert in the crowd, following her to the toilet? She hung her head again—"Unbelievable"—and walloped Eddie Ray.

He spun on the bed and sat up—a hand rose as if he planned to slap her—but then slithered on a pillow to massage his rump, where she had struck him.

"Listen," she said. "Goddamn it. This is a big problem. I can't leave until we figure out what to do."

The words—"can't leave" and "we"—seemed to catch his attention. One second he was half-sitting on the bed, massaging his backside, and the next he was standing, pulling on underpants. "What-all do you mean, 'can't leave'?"

"Luke. My husband. Remember him?" She balled her fists and considered using them on his face. "Come on now, think. Give me advice."

Eddie Ray's demeanor changed. "All right," he said, thinking. He stroked his beard. Calmed down. Became serious—the pensive poetic side of him that she loved—and bent down to fetch the bong on the floor. Then sauntered to the bean bag and lounged on it. Stretched. Pinched more weed from the baggy, filling up the bong. Lit it and toked, deep in contemplation.

Allie watched him, hoping. Eddie Ray had a good mind, when he put it to use. (She couldn't have misjudged him entirely.) He'd help her. He bolted upright on the bean bag, nodding with the answer. "What is Luke's middle name?" he asked.

"Huh?"

"Middle name." Eddie Ray motioned with his hand as if signaling a jetliner into the gate, indicating that she should trust him. "Well? What-all is it?"

A jetliner might be just the ticket, Allie thought. "Ekeziel," she said, playing along. "Luke *Ekeziel* Effington."

"Man-oh-man. Have you got a problem."

"*We* have a problem," Allie said. She clicked her heels to the bean bag and stood before him, arms crossed. Peeved. "You don't know him, Eddie Ray. You want a name? They call him Lock'em'up because he locks up people like you!"

"Me? I ain't got no problem." He rose to face her, their mouths only millimeters apart. Allie could smell the sour breath and smoke and turned her head, losing her bearing—*flash* went the cuckoo clock, *flash* went the Mr. Coffee, *flash flash* went the double-barrel Firebird down the drive—making her homesick for her husband. She looked at Eddie Ray again. He looked wrinkled, used. Hours ago that mouth was precious. Now he was taking her chin in his palm, hurting her.

"*You* came here last night," he said. "*You* called. *You* skipped out. Not me, babe."

"Flashback," she said—he let go of her chin and jumped away, spooked—"You were having a flashback. What did you think I would do?"

Eddie Ray shrugged. "You got the problem. Leave me out of it."

"No."

"Oh, go fuck yourself."

"Eddie Ray?" Allie said, offended. Her voice hardened. "You don't say 'fuck' to women. You don't say 'fuck' to me."

Eddie Ray smiled with one side of his face. "I say it. Do it. Hell, sugar. You should know." He drew near again. "I'm a regular Caesar," he said. "I see, I come, I conquer."

Eddie Ray was changing before her eyes. A chameleon. Cockroach. Reptile that lived under rock. "I'm not going to fight with you anymore," she said, spinning away before he could grab her chin again. She stopped at the door and turned. How could she have been so wrong? So gullible? The man had no backbone, no spine—just a horny head and lizard tail that curled between his legs. She wanted to tell him this, which she composed on the spot. She wanted to tell him that he wasn't an artist—probably not even a veteran—but a lowlife who would rather leave a woman in the lurch than come through for her in the clutch. She wanted to call him "cocksucker" and add an incestuous dig for his grandmother, whom he raved about, as if she were some sort of Okie Eleanor Roosevelt. She wanted to humiliate him, critiquing his lovemaking with precise comparisons of apparatus and technique, along with detailed tips for improvement. She opened her mouth to do that, but nothing came out. So she shook her head furiously and left the apartment.

Then tripped on something in the hall. It was a rolled-up *Chronicle* with part of a headline that read:

D.A.'s Wife . . .

"Huh?"

The flashing began again in earnest again, blurring her vision momentarily but also softening it for the blow. She bent down carefully and picked up the paper, unrolling the rubber band from the scrolly paper as she had done every morning for four years, even twining the band around her thumb and forefinger and pointing it at Eddie Ray's door. Letting it fly. Then she read the banner:

D.A.'s Wife Feared Abducted at Rotary Club! Ransom or Revenge? Lock'em'up Awaits Word!

She reentered the apartment and left the door open, for a quick getaway if she needed one. Eddie Ray had his jeans on now but was still bare-chested. The sight sickened her for some reason. He groaned and closed her purse—"You forgot this," he said—putting it on the table. "I was just coming after you"—

Allie stepped back.

—"to return it, I mean."

"Eddie Ray," she said in a low voice. "It's in the newspaper. All of it. Do you know what this means?"

"Man-oh-man," he said, rubbing his temples. He mumbled something about cosmology, which seemed odd and more in character with his poetic, sensitive side. Then he did another about-face. "I can't figure you out, woman."

She thrust out the newspaper, folded in half so the right side of it showed the abduction headline and her mug shot.

"It's too early for this."

"Read it."

"This some kind of joke?" He scratched his head and grabbed the *Chronicle*. Snapped it fully open and held it on each side. "Okay. I'm game. I got me a sense of humor."

"You'll need it."

"Right," Eddie Ray said slowly. He focused on the left side

of the front page and his mouth dropped, and his tongue went slack and slipped over his teeth, hanging out. Then he shook as he did last night in the throes of a fake flashback. "I told him 'No Picture'! I told him 'No Name'!"

Allie had no idea what he was jabbering about. The file photo of her that appeared with the story? "Of course they're using my picture and name. This was a public event." Allie was perplexed. "What do you mean, 'You told him'? What do you mean, 'No Name'?"

He seemed oblivious, holding the paper with one hand now and reading the left side of the page. The *wrong* side.

Allie swiped the paper from him—"That's the wrong story, dimwit!"—and saw his picture under a story about Job Service. She scanned the lead paragraph that disclosed his name, using the first and middle one as authorities do with prime suspects: Edward Raymond Bok.

He was smiling, first one cheek and then the other. "Now you know," he said.

Allie *did* know. And as soon as she did, she was not angry or heartbroken or even in the slightest way concerned about how he had used her. Money. Drugs. Sex. Neither was she disappointed in herself for being gullible, for when she tilted her head and studied Eddie Ray as a scientist studies a specimen, the long curly hair became swirls of marble and the face became shards of slate, and the body broke into a million pieces that she would never be able to put together again. Eddie Ray—artist, lover, war hero—had turned into stone.

"Give me the paper," he said.

"No."

"Fuck you," he told her, coming at her.

"Eddie Ray!" she screamed, glancing at the open door that led to the hall and running there.

He caught her from behind and swung her around—she screamed—and tried to yank the newspaper from her hands, as if the *Chronicle* were a wishbone. She ended up with the front page and he with the classifieds, the inside sections falling on the floor like guts. She held the full front page and saw both of their pictures, absorbing the absurdity of it all, as if for the first time. Allie laughed eerily, her mind flashing like a video on fast-forward. Then a pain rippled in her gut and she groaned, sick to her stomach. Eddie Ray was staring at her in disbelief because she, not him, was having a bonafide flashback. "Shut up," he hissed. She tried but couldn't calm down, the pressure inside her building to a crescendo. Eddie Ray dashed into the apartment. When he came out with her purse, holding the long strap as if he wanted to use it around her neck, Allie was having an anxiety attack. Her groans had turned to pitiful whimpers and then to hiccups. She was losing it, landing hard, realizing that Eddie Ray might hurt her.

He hefted her purse in one hand and hurled it at her face.

The strap struck her in the eye and she temporarily lost her balance, falling to one knee.

"Hope you learned a lesson, bitch," he said.

She was silent. She clutched her purse and watched him close and lock the apartment door. Her eyes stung with tears and pain from the strap. Through the blur, though, she could still read the banner headlines and collapsed on the floor in a heap.

Allie Effington had fallen from suburbia. Allie Effington could not go home.

11

Running Out
Of Time

Luke could not go home after
checking there to see if his
missing wife had returned. He felt responsible somehow for her
absence. So he spent the night in his office, trying to piece
together the mosaic of his wife's disappearance or abduction.

Elizabeth had been no help. His campaign manager had created a P.R. nightmare with her behavior at Rotary and a D.A.
nightmare with her allegations that someone had kidnapped her
sister-in-law. Luke doubted that scenario. To dispute it would
embarrass Elizabeth before the press in a conference scheduled
that morning.

This, again, was his sister's doing. Soon after recovering from the "incident" in the ladies' room, realizing that Allie may have been abducted, Elizabeth had become positively gleeful. She saw the abduction as a media opportunity. Editors and station managers who only hours ago would not give the Effington campaign the time of day now wanted to speak to him day and night. The more opportunity Elizabeth found in his misfortune, the less Luke believed in her judgment. The kicker occurred when she left the office at about 2 A.M. to get some sleep, telling her brother about the press conference. "We'll hold one each morning," she said, "and reap the rewards." Luke bristled. How could she call herself a Christian, he wondered, thinking such thoughts? At dawn Luke said a prayer for guidance and listened closely to the tiny voice within. The voice said: *Fire Elizabeth.*

He glanced at the wall clock: 7:50 A.M. Elizabeth would arrive in ten minutes, as was her custom. As soon as he received information on Allie's fate, he would let his sister go. Then make other tougher decisions. Should he remain as a candidate? Remain as D.A.? Remain married?

Luke sensed where the investigation was leading, especially after speaking early this morning with a detective on the case. No physical evidence of an intruder, he had told Luke. Police had learned that a few men in the audience had been gawking at Allie because she was acting rather strangely during dinner. One prominent businessman admitted to ogling her but sat with his Rotary wife for the duration. Until evidence was found to the contrary, the detective informed Luke, he suspected that Allie had left the Am-Vets Building on her own accord. In fact, he revealed, a woman matching Allie's description was seen hailing a taxi at about the same time as her reported abduction. The taxi driver who answered the call would be interviewed today at work, and police would investigate the house or apartment where Allie was last seen.

There was another jigsaw piece, however. Luke unrolled the *Chronicle* and scanned the headline about his missing wife. Apparently Allie had given an interview to Laurel Eby before the Rotary speech. Luke even remembered Allie mentioning it to explain her tardiness. As such, Miss Eby was one of the last people to speak to his wife, and that made the reporter key in the investigation: a material witness. Luke planned to question her after the press conference. If what he suspected was true, he would get a bench warrant for obstruction of justice.

Luke would lock her up.

The intercom buzzed, startling him. Janice, his secretary, asked if he needed coffee. She had come a few minutes earlier to work, she said, anticipating a busy day.

"Yes," Luke said, referring to coffee and business.

She brought in his cup.

He took it and a sip, then asked on her way out, "Janice, do you believe that my wife has been abducted?"

"I can't answer that, Mr. Effington."

"I'm not asking as your boss. I'm asking as your friend."

"I know that."

"Well?"

Janice was a professional who had served more than fifteen years in this office, working with three other D.A.s. She had seen too many bizarre cases. But she also had seen hoaxes, and Luke needed to call on her experience. He told her that.

"I would be more inclined to believe it," she said, "if your sister had not made the initial report." Janice was looking at Luke as the door behind her opened.

The secretary swung around and saw Elizabeth.

"Thanks," Luke said. "I appreciate your help."

Elizabeth was blocking the door. "I'm glad he appreciates *someone*," she said, letting the secretary escape. Elizabeth sat in the chair beside his desk and took a legal pad out of her purse. She proceeded without the usual morning prayer in which she asked the Lord to vanquish their enemies.

Luke had grown to despise such prayers. Once, when he had disagreed with her about the morals of his wife, claiming that they were none of her business, she had resorted to Job, quoting the Bible out of context: "And this is how you now treat me, terrified at the sight of me. . . . Put me right, and I shall say no more; show me where I have been at fault, fair comment can be borne without resentment, but what are your strictures aimed at?"

Right now Luke's were aimed at uncovering the truth. He stared at Elizabeth, trying to determine if she was withholding information or embellishing it.

She returned his stare.

"Did you get any sleep?" Luke asked.

"Mercifully," she replied. She looked away, reviewing her notes. "Word is out already in the *Chronicle* and on the radio," she said in a flat voice. "We're doing the press conference primarily for TV. And the *Herald*. Not that the *Herald* deserves special treatment." She looked at him again. "You know, if Margaret Hopkins had agreed to cover the ceremony—as *I* had requested, mind you—her newspaper would be sitting pretty right now." She turned to another page in her pad on which appeared a list of questions. "We need to run down what you may be asked during the conference," she said. Before he could interrupt, she rattled off her list: "One: Do you have any leads on your wife's whereabouts? Two: Have you received a ransom request? Three: Do you. . . ."

Luke tuned out Elizabeth. He used the moment to sit back in his chair, eyes closed. He hadn't slept a wink and his sister's voice was lulling him to sleep as it did when he was a boy. She used to read him fairytales and Bible passages with some emotion in her voice. This was before their father suppressed her religious aspirations. She must have known then that Luke would control the family fortunes because he was a man. "You'll be working for Luke," Laslo would tell her. "Not God." Luke should have stood up to his father and supported Elizabeth's desire to preach. But Laslo didn't want Luke working in law enforcement, either, preferring his son to head the legal arm of the family business. "You'll be working for me," Laslo would tell him. "Not the state." Luke fought his father and won. He thought of that every time he threw a criminal in the slammer, as if locking up memories of oppression. In shaping his own future, however, he had neglected and betrayed his sister's. Now he had neglected and betrayed Allie, too, putting his career and standing in the community before their marriage—just as Laslo had done. The thought sickened him. This was marital abuse, Luke acknowledged. To use his sister's phrase, he "reaped the rewards."

"Here," Elizabeth was saying, handing him some file cards. "These are the main points."

Luke snapped out of his daydream. He took the cards and tried to read them. Elizabeth had a minuscule penmanship that was neat enough but tiny, as if she did not want anyone stealing her thoughts. Perhaps it was part of her personality. His father was parsimonious by nature and had built Values, Inc. into an empire on that concept. "If the Dutch could buy Manhattan for trinkets," Laslo used to say, "then someone has to sell trinkets at discount to the Dutch." His father was proud of that phrase, proud of his wealth, proud of his accomplishments. Luke knew about pride. He and his sister had inherited it, along with the company. One criticized Elizabeth carefully—even when the matter was minor, as now—and tried to keep her on keel instead of on the defensive. So he remarked: "Can you get Janice to type these cards out for me?"

"There is nothing wrong with my penmanship."

"It's hard to read under lights. Especially TV lights."

"You're right," Elizabeth said. "But we haven't the time." She grabbed the cards. "Let me drill this into your head," she added, snarling, as if she understood the double meaning of that phrase. "It's really quite simple. Just get across these points." She snapped the first card as she read it. "One: a $10,000 reward has been posted for information leading to the whereabouts of your wife. Two"—

"That's too low."

"*Point two*"—Elizabeth waved the card to avoid a discussion—"you hereby vow to hunt down your wife's abductor. You're the D.A. You lock up people. Three: you will remain in the race, no matter what. After all," she told him, "you're the cleanup commissioner. You don't quit."

Luke reached for the cards but Elizabeth mistakenly put them in her purse and stretched. Her lanky body grew lankier as it went slack in the chair, seemingly shutting down.

Luke burred his lips in frustration. Watched her. Speculated. Elizabeth was the last person to see Allie. Along with Laurel Eby. These two women had opposite views about sex. The more opposite, Luke knew, the more alike. Each woman had something to gain via Allie's absence; Elizabeth could manipulate politics and Laurel the news. In sum, you could not believe either one of them on face value. Luke shivered with premonition. Along with Laurel, he feared, he would have to depose his sister to get to the truth.

Elizabeth had begun to snore.

"Liz," he called gently, hoping to rehash her account of the incident and forego the need for a formal interrogation. But she did not respond. Elizabeth was sitting limply in the chair, mouth open. Eyes half-open. He almost felt sorry for her, remembering the closeness of their youth, but as soon as he did, she awoke and gasped—Luke lurched forward at the sound—and yawned. "Come on," she announced, standing. "We have a press to face."

* * *

The lights were bright in the D.A.'s conference room where Luke had conducted so many plea bargains. This time it felt as if *he* were under the lamp. He watched Elizabeth seat herself alongside the lectern and yawn ever wider. Finally her face found itself again, and she gave the go-ahead to start the session.

Luke shivered anew. This reminded him of the Rotary speech. He recognized the anchor women and men and a few of the newspaper people. You could always tell broadcasters by the fancy way they dressed—scarves, ties—coordinating outfits. Good quality, too. Better than you could buy at Values, Inc., where the print people obviously shopped. The older ones squirmed in their itchy off-white shirts and polyester pants and the younger ones in their Hawaiian shirts and weak-seamed imitation Levy jeans, slightly irregular. The only newspaper person who could pass as a broadcaster was Laurel Eby from the *Chronicle*. She dressed slicker than anyone on CNN-News. Luke had been attracted to her initially, and when he recalled this now, about to speak of his missing wife, he felt a sharp pain in his belly. Laurel made him feel *guilty*—that was it!—something he associated with felonies, misdemeanors. Torts.

The fact was that Miss Eby in a blouse and miniskirt may be guilty of concealing information about Allie. Luke didn't care about the nature of that information. He'd pursue the facts of the case where they led him, even to the door of Allie's paramour. Once convinced of a person's guilt (even his own), Luke chased the culprit until justice was served. Detectives who knew this often joked that Luke would lock himself up, if the evidence warranted. That impulse, coupled with guilt, urged him now to drop out of the race and resign as D.A. But he resisted. When Luke felt the time was right, he'd make those decisions. For the moment, though, he needed the media and his official powers to help find Allie and uncover basic facts about the case.

Laurel knew some of the facts. This much was certain. Luke already had heard through the grapevine at the Gentry Club that she had been snooping there, questioning members about Allie's infidelity. And then there were her improper questions to him about his views on adultery. As he was putting all this into perspective, he noticed Laurel smirking at him. He remembered her embarrassing portrayal of him on the front page this morning. Anyone who read it would think that Luke was more concerned about image than his wife. As retribution, he planned to conduct the conference without calling on Laurel. Afterward he would summon her to his office—without Elizabeth being present—and question her. If she was really concealing information, he would get that warrant this morning and charge her with obstruction. Confiscate her files at the *Chronicle*. Yes, lock her up.

The reporters were getting impatient. It was time to start. Luke searched the conference room for an invisible spot, but the confines made that too obvious. Also, he was still learning the intricacies of eye contact. Reporters were waving their hands at him now as if he were a schoolteacher and they arrogant students who always knew the answers.

"Get on with it," someone shouted.

Luke took a breath. "Before we begin," he announced, "I want to say that I've been up all night. I hope we can keep this short. I'd rather be in my office, working on the case, than discussing it with you." The reporters put their hands down, ready to write, except for Laurel Eby, who used the momentary lull to push closer to the lectern.

He cleared his throat. "Testing," he said, although the tangle of microphones in front of him were not wired for amplification but for recording purposes. Elizabeth had not pointed that out. "Excuse me." He swallowed, realizing his mistake. He had to go through with this, no matter how weary he came across on camera. So he narrowed his eyes and stared into the minicams, saying, "I want to make three points. One, we're going to get to the bottom of this case"—he glanced at his sister, listening intently—"Two, we're going to pay a reward of ten grand to whoever helps us. And three"—

"That's cheap," Laurel heckled, breaking his concentration.

Luke forgot point three and turned to Elizabeth, confused.

Laurel persisted. "You got millions." The cameras swayed toward her. "Come on, Lock'em'up," she said, "don't you want her back?"

Elizabeth stood up, and the TV cameras swayed toward her.

"His name is Luke Effington," she said, pointing at her brother, "and *he* wants her back."

Her comment sounded as if she didn't.

Nobody picked up on the accusation. The cameras refocused on Luke.

"Yes," he added, "the reward is a little low. It is also a bit early to sensationalize the case by offering a substantial reward, particularly since there has been no ransom request." Luke stared at Laurel and then at his sister, as if each was a suspect. "What we're after is information. We aren't even sure an abduction has occurred."

"Point three?" Elizabeth asked, trying to remind him to comment about his still being a candidate for City Commission.

Luke's mind was blank. "I'll take questions now."

The reporters' hands waved wildly again.

"No you won't," his sister corrected, and the cameras swayed toward her once more.

The reporters lowered their hands, confused.

"Yes I will."

Elizabeth sat down and glared at him.

The reporters waved their hands again, and the cameras swayed back toward the lectern. This was too much for Luke, reminding him of robotic one-eyed Rotarians at a tennis match. That image sank into his subconscious, and he knew he would dream of this recurrently as he had the pink fuzzy Hong Kong rabbit with the unlucky Values, Inc. foot. Luke tapped his foot, annoyed, and pointed at an anchorwoman alongside Laurel, to rile her.

"Any leads at all?" the anchorwoman asked as her crew shined flood lamps on him. He squinted and hoped that the harsh light wouldn't show any worry lines from lack of sleep. He wanted to appear strong, especially if Allie or others were watching him.

"Yes," he replied, thinking about Laurel and Elizabeth. "But I can't discuss them. Also, I want to emphasize once more that we have no physical evidence that an abduction has occurred."

Elizabeth stood up again. "What are you talking about? You know for a fact that I heard the intruder. Are you questioning my account?"

The cameras swayed toward her again.

"Sit down," he told Elizabeth, and several reporters in the conference room obeyed. Then his sister did, too, containing her outrage as a pressure cooker contains steam. She seemed ready to explode.

"Let me clarify," Luke said. The cameras swayed and refocused. He was getting dizzy. "No one has actually *seen* an abductor. But I can understand how you may think so by reading the crap in the *Chronicle*."

"What do you mean, *crap?*" Laurel interjected. The cameras began to sway toward her now, but Elizabeth, taller and threatening—not to mention magnetic—stood up, luring the robotic eyes her way in a media tug-of-war.

"I just wanted to say. . . ." Her voice trailed off.

Luke watched his sister with growing suspicion. He knew why she was hesitating now; Elizabeth stood up to object to the word "crap," but then she realized that she would have to correct him in public. So she sat down again.

The room was abuzz. Mayhem.

"Let's continue, folks," Luke called out over the confusion, choosing Laurel's rival from the *Herald*, a dumpy balding man with a gray beard and glasses. The reporter checked his pad and asked, "Isn't it a conflict of interest for you to still be involved in the investigation?"

"Yes it is," Luke replied without missing a beat. "It conflicts with my, er, *feelings*"—Elizabeth cringed, as if Luke had sullied his hard-earned image—"that's right," he said. "Feelings. Even I have some. But when these feelings conflict with my investigation," he said, "I promise, on the record, that I will remove myself from the case."

Elizabeth stood. "No you won't."

"Yes I will."

"No you won't."

The cameras ignored her.

Luke called on an unknown—a short, husky man with long hair—who wrote for a national wire service. That meant the story was growing in interest, and Luke shuttered to think of the tabloid shows that would be calling him soon to showcase the situation on network and cable channels.

"This is a difficult question," the reporter said. He had a pained look on his face, as if he had something better to do. Luke understood. When you had as much power as this reporter, whose stories were transmitted to hundreds of newsrooms, you wanted to get on with your day. "Nobody seems to know if this is an abduction. Even your sister didn't see the suspect. She heard him"—

"That's right," Elizabeth said.

—"in the restroom."

"That's wrong," Luke said, knowing from the police report that his sister had overheard *Allie*, not her abductor. This was privileged information, however, which would be key in uncovering any antics.

"You dare to question me?" Elizabeth asked.

"Sit down," he told her.

Elizabeth stalked toward the exit, and cameras followed her until she slammed the door. No reporter followed her to the hall, though, unwilling to take her on in her current state. Moreover, they didn't need to since they had captured her tantrum on tape.

"You and your sister seem at odds today," the wire-service reporter noted.

"She's under a lot of pressure," Luke replied, as reporters took down his words. "She's trying to help me run a campaign and finds herself as the focus of a news story." He loosened the knot of his tie, thick as a noose. Luke knew that Elizabeth had forced his hand with her behavior and, although he regretted it, would have to take the emphasis off her and put it back on him and the case. "I appreciate my sister more than anyone knows"—*except Allie,* he thought, feeling a twinge of guilt—"but until this is resolved, I am putting my campaign for the City Commission on hold," he said. "It's the right thing to do."

The room buzzed again.

Luke pointed at and called on a local magazine writer, knowing her deadline was longer than that of TV stations, radios, and newspapers. Of all the media, magazine writers were the least obnoxious, Luke thought. They asked theoretical questions upon which one could expound and improvise. The writer, a middle-aged black woman in a business suit, asked, "Is it at all possible that your wife has not been abducted but simply is missing or maybe"—she paused, cringing—"how to put this?"

Luke hung his head. It was ironic that the reporter with the longest deadline was going to ask the question that would elicit the shortest answer.

The other reporters in the room sensed it, too.

"Is it possible," the woman began again, "that your wife is not missing but . . . *with* someone?"

"With a *man,*" Laurel Eby stated, solving the riddle.

"*Who?*" Luke asked Laurel.

The cameras swayed toward her as if she possessed the missing clue. They circled the reporter, threatening one of their own like the cannibals they were.

"How should I know?" Laurel responded.

Luke was pleased with himself. Once you got the hang of it, it was easy to manipulate the media. He pointed to the magazine writer. "No comment," he told her. "The press conference is over." Then he pointed at Laurel Eby. "See me in my office," he said, "immediately."

* * *

Laurel Eby was smirking at Luke in the chair beside his desk.

"This won't take long at all," he told her.

"Maybe. Maybe not," she said, trying to undermine his authority.

"Good," Luke remarked. "Then you won't miss your deadline if I decide to detain you."

Laurel pouted. "Oh."

"This won't take long," he said again, starting over.

"Thanks," Laurel replied. "I *do* have a deadline."

"Good." Luke stood up and went to the window, opening it to let in more direct light. The interrogation began. "Did you see a man abduct my wife?"

"No."

"Did you see a possible suspect at Rotary?"

"No. Just a lot of cardiovascular types," Laurel said, slowly smirking again as if she had figured out that this was a chance to interview Luke. Get an exclusive. "No suspects," she replied, "but I'll gladly trade information with you for a few quotes."

"Good," he said. "What else do you know about the case?"

Laurel took out her pad and pen, nibbling on the tip, in her element again.

Luke despised her but forced a smile, playing the role of a man who easily succumbs to temptation.

"Well," Laurel said, "I've spoken to people at the Gentry Club."

"And?"

Laurel shrugged and shook her head. "It's confidential, actually."

She was going to make him work for it.

He returned to his desk and sat down, folding his hands. "I'm not interested in their names."

"In that case," she said, leaning enticingly toward him, "I'll tell you what I know if you promise to give me regular *and* exclusive information as I require it for my stories."

Luke twiddled his thumbs, pretending to consider the request. "What do you know that I don't already?" he asked, baiting her. "Give me a hint so I can take you up on your offer."

Laurel went for broke. "I know for a fact that your wife is having an affair."

"Thank you," Luke said, buzzing his secretary and ignoring the static that ensued. He was saying this for Laurel's benefit anyway. "Janice? Please show Miss Eby out of my office."

The secretary must have heard him because she appeared at the door.

"What about our deal?" Laurel asked, standing and sensing a trap.

"Don't you have a deadline?" Luke asked her.

"This way, Miss Eby," the secretary said firmly.

Laurel was speechless.

"You'd better get back to the newsroom," Luke told her. "Time may be running out."

12

Thai Sticks
And Stones

T ime was running out for Eddie
Ray, and he knew it. One of
his talents was the sixth sense, knowing when and where to flee.
Ask Sergeant C.J. Arnold, recruiter, Tulsa, Oklahoma. Vietnam
Era. Ask Grandma Bok. Eddie Ray escaped both of them,
headed due north, and never regretted it.

Now it was time to head south, as it were.

"Fugitive," he said, liking the sound of the word. Yes,
indeed. Eddie Ray had a flight plan, filed according to the Science of One First Name/Two First Names: Tuscaloosa,
Alabama, hometown of native son Tim Bert Russell, expected
any day now to change his two first names to Timothy.

The problem was, however, that Eddie Ray couldn't afford the Greyhound ticket out of town. He had six dollars to his name plus assorted coins, fake coins. Tokens. In fact, his net worth was in the cupboard: a dozen Thai sticks and some hash, but no blow of Bolivian White. (Allie had failed to provide after her visit.)

He also had what was left of weed in the baggy by the Lizard of Oz bong.

Eddie Ray figured he had until noon to pack and leave his apartment. It would take at least that long for Job Service to procure the necessary warrants from the federal bureaucracy. This was good/bad news for a two-first-name individual. The good part about the feds was that they were woefully slow in expediting paperwork. The bad part was that they could put you in the slammer for years on account of the slightest infraction.

Eddie Ray knew a neighbor in Tulsa named Ham Bone Weaver who got ten years in the Oklahoma State Penitentiary for ripping off a Coke machine in the lobby of a U.S. Post Office. If that machine had been across the street by the liquor store, and Ham Bone had gotten caught kicking the carbonates out of it, he'd probably have spent a couple or three nights in jail. At most. When it came to crime, however, the feds had no sense of humor.

The feds wanted Eddie Ray.

This required some contemplation, he decided, slumping on the bean bag to toke the rest of the pot in the baggy. Eddie Ray wouldn't mind doing jail time in the basement of the courthouse downtown where word was that meals came from fast-food restaurants. They got a tax break donating leftovers to jails instead of homeless shelters. He could tolerate a week of pizzas, burgers, and fries. But the thought of spending five to ten in prison petrified him, especially since many of the inmates were real Vietnam vets who might hold grudges against the likes of Eddie Ray.

He poured the last of the marijuana from the baggy into the bowl of the bong, smoking mostly seeds, and dreaded what he would have to do next: get rid of the remaining drugs and paraphernalia. Eddie Ray didn't stay out of Vietnam, stay out of prison, stay free of AIDS, by being stupid; he did it out of fear of the Big "D": death. No question. He didn't have time to sell what remained of his stash on the streets, leaving a trail of informants. Or have it on his person if caught by a nark. He would even have to dump his beloved bong down a sewer on the boulevard.

"Damn," he said, nestling into the bean bag. "Yankees."

Eddie Ray had to sort things out. Allie couldn't help him anymore, that was for sure. Nor Grandma Bok in the Old Fogie Home in Okieland—ward of the state—a fate he aimed to avoid. Heap of trouble. You could take no comfort in the mother science when dealing with a man named Luke *Ezekiel* Effington, even though the initials were LEE, savior of the South and a pretty good blue-jeans maker, he had to admit. He closed his eyes and daydreamed a moment about WASP women in tight-fitting Lees, modeling topless as they were known to do in *Cosmo* ads. Redhead, brunette. Blond. Honeyblond: *Allie*. He opened his eyes and remembered his dilemma.

Allie had a lot of nerve tearing the *Chronicle* in two and leaving him with the classifieds. She ought to be home by now, pleading with Hubby-Boy to forgive and forget. "Uh-huh," he said. "I can see it." He loosened up and pretended to be Allie— spoke in a falsetto voice—"Luke, darling. Let me make it all up to you." Then he spoke with the usual drawl: "Hope you got the daylights whooped out of you."

Bitch.

He got up and went to the cupboards, taking down the sticks and hash, along with a box of Ho-Hos. He put his stash on the table and took a Ho-Ho from the box, peeling the foil from the slug of chocolate-cream cake and popping the morsel in his mouth. Then he popped another. One more. He wiped the crumbs from his hands onto the table—this was housekeeping for Eddie Ray—and headed for the bathroom, carrying the sticks and hash.

Cradling the drugs, he flushed and reflushed the toilet, watching the water swirl like a life going down the drain. He let the tank fill and flushed again, feeling high, feeling low, marveling at how the water rose and fell. Eddie Ray sighed. He broke a few Thai sticks like wishbones. "Fuck Allie," he said and broke a stick. "Fuck Luke," he said and broke another. "Fuck Tim Bert Russell"—snap—"Mylo Thrump"—snap—"The Teach at Job Service who got me into this mess." Snap. "Fuck C.J. Arnold and Vietnam." Snap, snap. Then he sprinkled the hash like green glitter over the broken wishes in the bowl.

He was stoned. "Fuck you, Grandma." Eddie Ray flushed and returned to the living room, repressing the specter of Ida May Bok that reminded him why he went astray. He read about it in *Cosmo*, articles about child and sex abuse. He realized that it was only natural for him to have pleasure principles, Ids, and libidos. His grandma *used* him in the very worst sense of the word. He wondered how he might have turned out had his mother not run off and raised him proper, taking him to watch Triple A baseball at the stadium or fireworks on the Fourth of July by the river. Maybe he would have done *home*work and attended Oral Roberts, earning a degree in cosmology, the real kind (instead of his sub-science). Yes, he could see it. He would have married a two-first-name woman, Betty Lou, and bought a pickup truck and a couple or three Harleys in the back bed: one for him and the wife, one for Eddie Ray Junior. Instead, all he owned was the shirt on his back and the slightly soiled clothes on the floor.

Eddie Ray wasn't wearing a shirt, he realized. He picked out a relatively clean black T-shirt to tuck into his frayed pair of jeans. Then rummaged through his wardrobe and found his boots under a snap-button western shirt. He heaped the rest of his clothes in a pile to make a cushion, sat down carefully, and pulled on his snakeskins.

"Steady, boy," he said, struggling to stand as the marijuana took hold and skewered his equilibrium. He needed another Ho-Ho. He went to the kitchen table and popped it. Out of habit, Eddie Ray felt for his diary about Vietnam in the right back pocket of his jeans and stuffed the ad section of the *Chronicle* in the left. Allie must have taken Mrs. Minelli's newspaper. Eddie Ray only got a glimpse of the story by Kimberly Spears and the accompanying photograph (bad angle/ lazy cheek) under which appeared the cutline: "Con man Edward Raymond Bok."

Trust a Yankee like Mylo Thrump to ruin a good two-first name.

The more Eddie Ray thought about Mylo Thrump, the angrier he became. He tried to envision what a man with a name like that looks like, but this was beyond his capability. He tried to connect a face with the voice he had heard on the telephone in the lobby of the newspaper, but this, too, eluded him. Worse, Eddie Ray realized, Mylo Thrump and the authorities had an advantage over him because they had seen his photo on the front page. They knew how *he* looked. So Eddie Ray couldn't even spy

on the editor in his office for fear that Mylo Thrump would finger him and dial 911.

"Lucky for you," Eddie Ray said to himself.

It was time to get down to business. Get out of Dodge.
Eddie Ray went to the bean bag and hefted the Lizard of Oz
bong, shedding a tear. He made an indention with his fist in the
top of the vinyl and dumped out the gray-speckled water so it
pooled like a reservoir. He wouldn't be sitting there anymore.
Then he went to the bed and yanked off a pillowcase with one
hand, caressing the bong with the fingers of his other.

He sat on the bed, putting the bong inside the pillowcase
and hanging his head. He noticed the wet spot from the previous night. Streaked, too. "Damn that woman." Allie might of
said something—he just cleaned those sheets last month. He
didn't have time to wash and dry today. It was already past 11
A.M., he figured, judging from how the sun angled in straight
down by the bedroom window.

Something glittered and caught his eye. He blinked to make
sure. There they were, all pearl and diamond-ee, refracting the
natural light—Allie's forgotten necklace and earrings—casting a
rainbow of colors on the ripped-off Pepsi crate. Another incredible stroke! It made you proclaim belief again in the Science of
One First Name/Two First Names. He had been developing bad
habits, flushing Thai sticks and hash down the toilet. Cursing
Ida May and his ancestors. This went plumb against his inbred
opportunistic nature.

Now he had redeemed himself. He stroked the gold heart
and diamonds of Allie's earrings and knew they would fetch
enough money at the pawn for him to leave town and settle in
Tuscaloosa. It was only fitting that Allie, Ms. Provider, would
leave a farewell gift. "Thank you, thank you, thank you."

Eddie Ray surveyed the room, a reflex to make sure nobody was eavesdropping on the fire escape. He held the jewelry in one hand and bent down, picking up a sour pair of boxer shorts. He put the gems in the crotch, twisting and tying the undergarment until it resembled a pouch. Then he went to the closet and pulled out the Vietnam Era duffel bag he bought for show from the Supply House and placed the wrapped jewelry on the bottom, heaping the rest of his wardrobe on top of it. Nobody would look that low for his valuables. He slung the duffel bag on his shoulder and took the pillowcased bong off the table. He would bowl it down the sewer outside his apartment house. Nobody would look that low, either.

Eddie Ray would make his getaway in middaylight. Only one-first-name criminals escaped at midnight when they stood out like America's Most Wanted to cruising cops. At noon everyone would be too blain busy hailing cabs and buses to identify him. He would lay low himself for awhile, knowing the feds would be likely to check pawns and terminals for a few hours, given the nature of his crime—fraud—but not the flophouses or shelters. The FBI had other felons to track: kidnappers, murderers, smugglers who had crossed Mason/Dixon lines.

Eddie Ray unlocked and opened the door, ready to move out (in the military sense). He wished that he had a pipe bomb with Mylo Thrump's middle name on it. That'd be nice. That'd make interesting reading.

"Uh-huh."

The hall was unusually quiet, in keeping with his good luck. For once, Meatball Minelli wasn't poking around in his business. She always had some smart-alecky remark—"Finally waking up?" or "Have fun with your lady friend last night?"—but

was deaf, dumb, and blind today. Dumbolina. She was mad at
him probably because Allie took her newspaper.

Eddie Ray remembered that he and Allie also had rough-
housed outside her door. "Hmmm." He got suspicious and put
his ear on 4-E. Strange. By now she normally would blast her
Victrola, Mario Lanza records—high-toned and melancholy—
that reminded him of a fag *I*talian in a rain shower. But Mario
was silent today. Then Eddie Ray heard the familiar patter of
her sausage feet coming toward him. Stopping. Thinking better
of it.

He smiled—everything was normal—and hoisted the duffel
bag on his other shoulder to distribute the weight. Took a step
toward the stairs. Hesitated. Something was not right. He could
feel it in his bones and went back. Eddie Ray had a bad feeling
about Mrs. Minelli—her feet had padded to the door, as they
usually did—but they did not pad away again.

So he put his ear back on 4-E, as if he were laying it on a
breast, and listened.

"Go away! Go away!" Mrs. Minelli shouted from behind the
door. "I don't want any trouble!"

13

Welcome
Home

Allie *clicked* and staggered into Saint Francis Hospital, unprepared for the mayhem that met her in the emergency room. The stagger was part of the amnesia act. She did not know all of the symptoms, nor felt compelled to look them up in the library, where she had spent most of the afternoon, reading magazines. But she feigned the most important symptom—loss of memory—and assumed that being in a daze was part of it.

Allie was good at being in a daze. She lapsed into one now, in the middle of a war zone, waiting patiently at the emergency-room entrance, hoping someone would ask if she needed help. She would say yes and ask the stranger to lead her to the admitting desk, making a dramatic entrance. But no one offered assistance. Allie was stunned, witnessing the underside of a world that existed only in TV news magazines like "20/20" and tabloid shows like "Hard Copy." She stood there absorbing the milieu: a passel of ambulance personnel, pushing a heart-attack victim on a gurney through swinging hospital doors, all sorts of gadgets monitoring him; a boy with an ice pack on his eye and bruises on his arm, crying by the entrance—where were his parents?—and wailing when an orderly led him away; a hoodlum-type with an open flap of nose and gash across his neck, lounging in a wheelchair, bleeding. . . .

Allie focused on colors instead of on people and objects, to distance herself. The predominant colors of the emergency room were red and white, she thought, hues that contrasted more than clashed: red phones, fire extinguishers, lights flashing red above hallways, even a bright red Coke machine. White walls, white front desk. Computers. Nurses and doctors in white uniforms and shoes. White gurneys. Allie breathed easier. The colors provided a temporary visual anesthesia. You could admire the various shades of cinnabar, scarlet, or rouge and the subtler ones of white: milk, snow, cirrus; and as long as you did, you could see anything you wanted (except, of course, what you were actually seeing). You didn't have to be afraid. You didn't have to feel anything.

Allie inhaled the acrid emergency-room air, ready to call attention to herself. She went into action, untucking her wrinkled blouse and hiking one side of her skirt with a smear of chocolate on the flare. "Huh?" (How did that get there?) She shook her head and messed her hair. Winged it. Tried to look disheveled (which ought to be an amnesiac symptom). In a few moments, she would be admitted. Get treatment. Let an intern pamper her a day or two and recover gradually. Persuade him to phone Luke.

This was Plan "A."

The admissions person at the front desk wore a red nametag, "Ronda"—spelled without the "h," Allie noted—and appeared super busy. Phones were ringing. Lights flashing. Patients being cleared for rooms, the hoodlum-type pretending to thumb his flap of nose at Allie (as if he knew what she was up to). She glanced away and stood at the admissions desk beside a man in a pizza uniform.

Ronda gave Allie an insurance form. "Step right up, hon. I don't bite."

"That's right. Make jokes," the pizza man said, struggling to fill out the information sheet. His right hand was ripped, a tangle of muscle, tissue, and blood. He caught Allie gawking at him. "Pit bull," he said, "pepperoni. Bad combination."

"Fill out the form, sir. We'll take care of that hand," the admissions person said. She tapped Allie's sheet. "You, too. Be right back."

"Hey, lady," the man called. He was trying to show Ronda his hand but she ignored him, going station to station—filing, typing, ordering wheelchairs—doing three persons' jobs.

The hoodlum was being carted away. "It won't work," he said to Allie—did he recognize her from her picture in the *Chronicle?*—"Not here. Mercy Med. Get you the methadone." The orderly behind him made a hand motion to Ronda, indicating that he was on break. Ronda shook her head: no. The hoodlum was speaking to Allie again. "You want more, babe? Work for Abdella, and you get it. Call him. I can fix you up." The orderly wheeled him through the swinging hospital doors.

"Huh?"

The pizza man grunted, startling Allie. He was desperately trying to fill out the form and had an elbow on the sheet to hold it down, writing with his left hand.

"Let me help you," Allie offered. She placed her palm on the paper, and a trickle of blood fell from his hand to the sheet, like a drop of red whiteout. Yuck. Allie thought of AIDS and withdrew her hand and searched for Ronda, filing forms in bins on her desk. "She'll take care of you," she told the pizza man.

He had a look of disgust that must have matched her own. "You're a good person, aren't you?" he asked in a mocking tone. "You really care."

Allie concentrated on her information sheet. Why was she worrying about a pizza man's feelings? Who cared what he thought? His hand had grossed her out, and yet she felt obligated to help. She ought to help herself and make her symptoms more believable. She studied the form. It had a warning like a pack of cigarettes:

Any person who knowingly and with intent to deceive Saint Francis Hospital to procure medication or who files a statement containing any false, incomplete or misleading information, is guilty of a felony in the third degree.

A Public Service Announcement by Luke E. Effington, District Attorney.

"Let him try," Allie said.

"I *am* trying," the pizza man complained, leering at her. "You enjoying this, lady? Let me tell you, it's not much fun."

"I wasn't talking to you."

He studied her. "You got a brain tumor or something?"

"Something."

Ronda returned to the counter. "How are we coming?" she asked.

"I don't remember my name."

"Fine." Ronda faced the pizza man. "I got time, sir. With that hand, you may not."

"Who are you, Joan Rivers?" He gave her the form. "Cutup," he said, realizing what he said.

Ronda snickered and looked at Allie. "Put Hillary Clinton," she said. "Put Jane Doe. We get a lot of Jane Does. You should see her file." She went off to another desk and came back with an identifying hospital tag—a white plastic hoop, actually—for the pizza man.

Allie watched her slip it on his good wrist. She checked her own—she wasn't wearing her bracelet—and instinctively felt her throat for her necklace and her lobes for her diamond earrings. "Oh my God!" she cried, slamming the counter with her palm as if she were demanding service. (Nobody served her.) Allie's hopes sank, realizing that Eddie Ray had the earrings and probably wouldn't return them without a blackmail threat.

"You the kind of woman gets angry at the sight of blood?" the pizza man asked, observing her.

Allie ignored him, still mourning the loss of her earrings. They were from Tiffany's, her favorite. "I don't believe it." She focused on the form, wanting to get this over with as quickly as possible:

Name:	Jane Doe
Address:	Don't know
Occupation:	Don't know
Sex:	Last night

Ronda was observing her. The pizza man looked over Allie's shoulder to see what she had written on the sheet. "Sit down, sir," Ronda said, pointing at a wheelchair by the wall. "The orderly is on his way." She waited until he obeyed. Then scrutinized Allie, who pretended to be baffled by the form. "You could make this a lot easier," Ronda told her.

"I don't remember my address."

"Listen, lady. Put anything. Put the White House."

"Where's that?" Allie asked, pleased with her improvisation.

"Amnesia," Ronda said flatly. "I get it."

"What do people in my condition usually put?"

Ronda stared at her without compassion. "Usually," she said, "they put Seton Place."

"What's that?"

Ronda's face softened. "You really don't know, do you?"

"Uh-uh." This time Allie was telling the truth.

"Homeless shelter. Flophouse, if you ask me."

Allie jotted down "Seton Place" on the proper line and asked for the address.

Ronda narrowed her eyes. "Third and Main."

Allie jotted this down, too.

"Just fill out the form." The phone rang, and Ronda sighed. "I'll be back."

The pizza man spoke behind her, sitting in the wheelchair. "You don't know much, do you?" he asked. "What's wrong with you anyway?"

"Amnesia."

"Amnesia," he said and grimaced in pain, holding his arm upright by the elbow. "A lot of my customers come down with that. They want sausage. You get there, they say anchovy. They want Canadian bacon. You get there, they say extra cheese.

Sonny Boy orders a superdeluxe. You get there, Mom sees the pineapple. Guess what? Nobody remembers ordering that. You bring pepperoni, and a pit bull attacks you." The man looked at his injury, shaking his head. "Of course, nobody owns the dog now. Nobody remembers Rover."

The orderly arrived. "You the guy with rabies?"

The pizza man showed him his wounded hand. "Dog bite, dog bite."

"Let's go," the orderly said, grasping the wheelchair and swinging him around roughly to face Allie and the double doors.

"Rabies," the man said to her. "In a coupla weeks, I could be crazy as you."

Allie didn't have to pretend anymore, nor contemplate colors, to be in a daze. She was spacing out as she had done at Rotary. But had yet to fill out the form. In the few seconds it took for the pizza man to be wheeled out, a pregnant woman stood beside her at the counter with bloodshot, bleary eyes. "My water broke," she told Allie impatiently, "and my husband's parking the car. May I go before you?"

Ronda intercepted her before Allie could reply and handed the woman some forms. "Fill these out."

The pregnant woman moaned in labor. The admissions person was unmoved. It seemed that nobody got treatment until they got past her. The woman's spasm passed, and Ronda continued with instructions. "Your husband needs to sign these, too, if the insurance is in his name." She turned to Allie again. "How we doing, Jane?"

"I don't recall having insurance."

"Okay, Hillary," Ronda quipped. "You're outta here." She reached for the form and tore it up.

"Huh?"

"We don't have to treat anyone who isn't covered, especially in a nonemergency. Hospital policy," she said. "Try Mercy Medical."

"But I have *amnesia*. I can't remember who I am."

"I know why you're here," Ronda said, patting Allie's hand. "You don't need those pills. Go home, honey. He'll come around. Give him time."

The pregnant woman moaned again, expressing Allie's feelings to a tee.

Allie left the hospital, clicking out the door without looking at anyone in the war zone. So much for amnesia. Time for Plan "B." She would spend a few days at the Regency, live off some cash with her MasterCard and automatic teller. Work up the courage to phone Luke and work out a solution. She checked her purse—twelve dollars—and walked around the hospital to the front, where a line of cabs waited to pick up or drop off visitors. She got into a taxi. "The Regency," she said, sighing as the taxi left Saint Francis.

"Looks like rain," the driver said. "Forecast says showers."

Allie's feet ached from the shoes. "Showers," she replied, trying to be polite. She glanced out the window. The morning sun had disappeared above a curtain of nimbus clouds, a perfect cap to the day. Allie couldn't wait to sink into a warm bubbly tub at the hotel. Order a light room service. The walking was making her hungry but also trimming her down. Another day of this, and she could slip into size five.

The driver seemed friendly enough. He had a ruffled copy of the *Chronicle* on the dashboard, and Allie felt a wave of déjàvu, as if she had known the cabby before because he knew about her. This must be how *Playboy* models respond on dates, realizing that any man they might meet had experienced them intimately already. Strange. She decided to test the theory. See what she was in for. "Did you read about that woman?" she asked in a blasé voice. "You know, the one kidnapped at Rotary Club?"

"How 'bout them apples?" The driver honked at a messenger on a ten-speed bike—"imbecile"—and cut him off as he turned the corner, nearly knocking him to the curb. He shook his head. "Lots of crazies in this city."

"What do you think happened to her?"

"What *didn't?*" he quipped, glancing at her. He had expressive brown eyes and an eyebrow that spanned his entire forehead, framed in the rearview mirror. "Probably got raped first. To break the ice. Tied up, tortured. The works." The cabby turned onto the freeway. "Like I said, lots of crazies in this city."

"I don't think so," Allie said, leaning forward so her face was near the wire mesh that protected the driver. There had been a series of taxi rip-offs, Luke had told her, and owners were running scared. She tapped the mesh. "I'll tell you what happened," she whispered. "The woman got bored at Rotary. Came down with a case of amnesia."

"Am-*who's*-ya? Never heard of it. That like AIDS?"

"Bad memory. Can't recall a thing."

"Roger. I read you. *Amnesia.*" He pronounced the word carefully and concentrated on freeway traffic, entering the flow. "You're pulling my leg," he said. "The woman's a goner, I'm telling you. I know this city."

"Do you really believe what you read in the paper?"

"Sometimes," the cabby said. "I don't like it when they write about the union, though. Next week we may go on strike." He passed another cab and waved. "Anyway," he said, "something bad happened to that woman. I know it for a fact."

Allie giggled. "Come on," she taunted. "You wouldn't know that woman if she rode in your cab. What do you know for a 'fact'?"

"I got inside information."

Allie laughed. "Now you're pulling *my* leg."

"No, honest," the cabby said. "I saw the cops this morning at the front office talking to one of our drivers. He picked the woman up last night at Rotary and took her to 346 Union Terrace."

Allie screamed.

The cabby put on the brakes and swerved to the right lane, avoiding traffic. "Hey, lady!"

That was Eddie Ray's address.

"What's the matter?" the driver asked her, swinging around. "You see a cockroach or what?" He looked back at the freeway and turned onto the exit. "You ain't sick? You ain't gonna puke in my cab?"

She shook her head.

"We'll be there in a minute."

Allie nodded, gazing out the window. The jig was up. If the cops had found Eddie Ray, then Luke already knew everything: the affair, the reason she abandoned him at Rotary. Her so-called dance class. Worse, the *Chronicle* would report it tomorrow, making a laughingstock out of her husband. Luke would come off as a cuckold and Elizabeth as a liar. His career and campaign would be ruined, along with the family name. Then he'd divorce her, lickety-split, with no settlement. His lawyer and judge friends would see to that! Allie's head ached now along with her feet from walking and her stomach from hunger.

Time for Plan "C."

The driver stopped. "Regency," he announced. "Five-fifty."

"Change of plans," she told him. "Take me back downtown to Liberty Bank."

The driver huffed and pulled away from the curb, mumbling under his breath. "You ain't one of them weirdos who ride taxis all over town without money, are you?"

"Not one of those."

"Because I have kids to feed."

"And I have money," Allie replied. In fact, she had access to thousands of dollars with her credit cards at the automatic teller. She didn't have to confront Luke, Elizabeth, or her accusers. She could withdraw part of her savings and take a flight somewhere. Maui, maybe. Put everything behind her. Start a new life or pick up the pieces of her old one, when the time was right.

The cabby didn't speak anymore on the ride to the bank. He stopped and told her, "Eleven even."

Allie gave him all her cash. "Keep the change."

"Dollar," he corrected. "Doesn't buy a burger these days."

She felt a hunger pang as she stepped to the curb.

The taxi moved on.

Allie entered the automatic teller booth in the outside lobby of the bank, closed in the late afternoon. She took out her wallet from her purse and then her gold MasterCard, inserting it and keyboarding her personal identification number, 2828, to withdraw the maximum daily amount. She listened to the machine whir and grew impatient as it seemed to require more time than usual to dish up the cash. Suddenly the computer screen started blinking and beeping like a shaken video game, seizing her credit card and returning a ticket:

You are using a card that has been reported stolen, which is a felony in the second degree. Thank you for using Bucks in the Box.

Public Service Announcement by Luke E. Effington, District Attorney.

"Give me back my credit card!" Allie screamed at the machine, as if addressing her husband. "Give it back!" She batted Bucks in the Box, and its computer screen stopped blinking and scrambled. She slammed it again, and the teller dished out another ticket:

> **You are vandalizing City Bank property containing bank notes and currency, a federal offense and felony in the first degree.**
>
> *Public Service Announcement by—*

She ripped the ticket out before it could complete its message and slammed the teller again, as if it were Luke. "Take that, Civic Servant of the Year. And that!"—bang—"That!"—bang—"That for Elizabeth!"—double bang. Allie panted, guilty of adultery, character assassination, and now—bang, bang, bang—*vendicide.*

Bye-bye Maui. She clicked out of the lobby and headed for the street. Soon it would be evening, and she had no place to crash. Streets downtown could be dangerous. Allie couldn't hole up at a hotel with no credit card. She had given the cabby her cash. Worse, she lacked a "Plan D."

She returned to the lobby of the bank and leaned against the malfunctioning Bucks in the Box. It was safer than loitering on the street—an offense, no doubt, in this city—and familiar, in a weird way. Allie could feel Luke's presence here. His authority. If her husband had canceled her MasterCard, he must have done the same with Visa and American Express. Her mind flashed again—*flash* went the trip to Maui, *flash* went the Regency Hideaway Suite, *flash, flash* went the hot bath and light room service—compliments of Luke E. Effington, District Attorney.

Allie took stock. Maybe she *did* have amnesia. No place to go. No husband. No lover, money, friends. Only an automatic teller whose brain she had scrambled in a wanton act of vendicide. She staggered out of the lobby, disoriented. Disheveled. Wandered down the street, wondering if she should walk back to Saint Francis and try to be readmitted when Ronda ended her shift. The woman was on to her—*Seton Place, homeless shelter*—she recalled her saying: *Third and Main.* Walking distance. "Why not," Allie said. She would check in at the flophouse and sip soup there instead of tea at Dominque's.

A light drizzle began to fall. Allie took off her heels—the wet pavement felt cool on her feet—and crossed the street, heading for Seton Place.

She arrived without incident at the dilapidated shelter scrawled with graffiti. She studied the multicolored, spray-painted lettering on the wall and assessed the degree of the crime. Vandalism. She could relate to that. Someone had sprayed a heart in yellow—*Rosie and Salvadore, forever*—another dumb *West Side Story*. Rosie would learn about Sal soon enough, just as Allie learned about Eddie Ray. The cynicism surprised her, but the red graffito above the door did not—**ENTER AT YOUR OWN RISK**—a warning. Seton Place did not look like a pleasant place.

Allie slipped on her heels and checked in. "I have amnesia," she said to the woman behind the desk. She had silver hair and a placid face and didn't wear any name tag on her burgundy smock. "I need a place to stay."

"Okay."

"I'm not filling out any forms."

"Okay."

"I don't have any money."

"Okay."

Allie got the impression that if she told the woman that she was a felon in the first degree who had just knocked over an automatic teller at Liberty Bank, she would still say "okay." Allie relaxed. At least she had a place to stay.

"You're in luck," the clerk said. "We have room tonight."

"Private room, I hope."

The clerk laughed. "Rules are simple," she said. "You can stay one night per week. No drugs, sex, alcohol."

"One night?"

"Checkout's 10 A.M.," the clerk said. She gave Allie a printed slip, listing addresses of other shelters. "Try these tomorrow. They're almost always booked, but you can stay at some of them for a week or longer."

"Why can't I stay a week here?"

"Because," the clerk explained, "this is as low as it gets in this city. Lots of homeless looking for beds in bad weather."

Allie sighed. She was too tired and afraid to walk to the other shelters at this hour.

"Do you have any belongings?" the woman asked, taking a clipboard from her desk.

"Just my purse," Allie said.

"Follow me."

The woman led her into the facility, more like an abandoned gymnasium, with row on row of bunk beds. The homeless sat or lay on them—some with children, some with shopping bags and boxes, some like Allie with nothing—and ignored or watched her as she clicked to an empty bunk.

The woman checked off the bed on a sheet on the clipboard. "My name is Gertrude," she told her, pointing to another desk at the front of the gymnasium. An empty bunk was beside it. "That's my station. I'll be there in a few minutes, after we lock up for the night. Don't leave because you can't get back in."

Allie looked around, afraid of the men in the shelter. Some of them were obvious alcoholics, reminding her of her father. "Can't I take the bunk near your desk?" she asked.

"That's where I sleep," Gertrude told her, smiling. It was the first kind gesture that Allie had seen the entire day.

"Oh."

"Don't worry. I'll be there if you need me," the woman said, returning to the front room.

Allie surveyed the facility—so many people were crammed in here that she saw mostly the backs of heads—and doubted that she would get any sleep. A woman on a bunk nearby seemed to be crying, her shoulders heaving up and down. But on closer inspection she was scratching, her skin peeling with disease. Another woman across from her with a shopping bag was staring at Allie. "Nice blouse," she said. A bearded man behind her sipped something from a brown paper bag that he had sneaked inside the room. "You're taking up space," he told her. "People could use that bed."

Allie put her purse under her arm and sat on her bunk, claiming it. She ignored the catcalls and slipped off her heels, putting them under the flat, sour pillow that was a far cry from her scented feather one at home. She swung her legs over the edge of the bunk and checked her purse, taking inventory. She didn't want anybody stealing what was hers, now that she had next to nothing.

"That's it," the drunk called to her. "Get comfy."

Allie pulled out the torn front page of the *Chronicle* and con-templated her picture, a file photo that Elizabeth undoubtedly had provided. She looked pretty but younger. Her hair was lighter than it was now and shorter than she wore it. Then she looked at the picture of Eddie Ray and quickly folded the paper again, unable to think about him without losing her temper. She dug deeper in her purse and found a compact to check her face. She was aghast. She had a light welt across her eye where the strap of her purse had struck her in the hall outside Eddie Ray's apartment. Earlier she had cried and walked in a drizzle, smearing mascara: two raccoon eyes. Great. Her lipstick had worn off and her bangs were unraveling, winging out without spray. No wonder Cro-Magnon Cabby didn't recognize her on the ride to the Regency and back downtown. Allie barely recognized herself. She opened her purse wide and shook it. Found a lip gloss and tissue, which she took out to wipe her face. Observed herself in the compact and tried to unwing a curl with a finger. No luck. She wet the finger and tried again. Gave up on that and was about to apply gloss to her lips when she saw a set of eyes to her right staring at her in the compact mirror.

"Hey there, Allie," the voice said.

She veered around and froze.

"Welcome home," said Eddie Ray.

14

The Face
Of God

Mylo Thrump couldn't sleep last night and took a cab before dawn to the Little Prince Book Palace, browsing at the window display. The newspapers already were tacked on the boards, and he could admire them in the light of the overhead street lamps. The latest tabloids used the entire spectrum of ink: violet, blue, indigo, green, yellow, orange, and red. These papers had pizzazz. So did the *Chronicle,* the cheapest thrill in town.

Ask the common Joe and Josephine. You couldn't get Joe to change your windshield wiper or Josephine to pour you a cup of Sanka for four bits, but you could brighten their day for that much with his newspaper. You could also disgrace the likes of the *Herald* or the *New York Times*. He considered those newspapers, the so-called publications of record, stepping to the side so his reflection did not interfere. (Mylo wanted to be objective.) They looked sad, gloomy. Gray as the overcast skies. Then he stepped in front of the *Chronicle* and superimposed his reflection on the page, admiring the palette of pop colors like an avant-garde painter from the Metropolitan Museum of Art.

Last night Mylo went overboard with ink. It was an off day. But you couldn't tell by the bedazzling design. Laurel's reward story was the only banner of merit, along with a pit bull/pizza man filler that Mylo picked off the scanner and composed himself:

The Perils of Pizza
Pit Bull Mauls Delivery Man,
Devours A Medium Pepperoni!

Not bad. The story would have had more appeal if the man's hand had been dismembered, and then reattached, but a hospital spokeswoman said the victim would keep his hand and his job. At any rate, Mylo was grateful for the "brightener." Kimberly had come up empty-handed again, unable to find a telephone listing and address for con man Edward Raymond Bok. Mylo consulted his stolen police directories that cross-listed where residents lived—even ones without telephones—by name and address. In other words, you could look under Edward Raymond Bok to learn where he lived: 346 Union Terrace. Or you could look under that address to see who lived there: Edward Raymond Bok (along with other tenants). He gave Kimberly this address. She left the newsroom to interview Bok, came back late, and informed Mylo that the con man already skipped town.

Mylo didn't want to disappoint his readers. So he ordered the most colorful front page ever. Even in lamplight, the *Chronicle* was more enticing today than the *National Enquirer,* his first mistress. Mylo's mother would hide it on top of the Frigidaire, which he would raid at night with a chair to read the tabloid by the light of the open icebox door. Snacking on baked ham, munching pitless olives, he would memorize the Speck murders or relive the most recent cattle mutilation. Mylo grew up with that newspaper. He grew fat on it. The *National Enquirer* got him into journalism in the first place with exclusives about aliens, Loch Ness and Big Foot sightings, Bolivian preschool pregnancies and Russian geriatric ones—exotica of all sorts and persuasions. Now it was a celebrity gossip rag.

Mylo consoled himself with its racier black-and-white cousin, The Weekly World News, which carried this banner headline:

AIDS Fear Slashes
Vampire Attacks!

Mylo couldn't beat that. Whoever wrote it had seen the face of God.

Mylo liked to play God. He did whenever he sat at his desk or edited the blinking screen of a computer. He created, rewarded, punished. Destroyed. He focused on local celebrities like Luke Effington, waiting for them to make one mistake. When they did, he precipitated their fall. (Lock'em'up would fall within the week.) Mylo had created the image that put the man in office in the first place. Rewarded him initially for his arrest record. Then condemned him for going a Miranda too many. Now he was destroying him as Adam was destroyed, because of his mate: Allie Effington. Mylo loved the headline that he composed for Laurel's story, as alluring as any in the *Enquirer:*

Lock'em'up Offers Fives & Dimes
For Whereabouts of Missing Wife!

Mylo wondered what his own wife Wendy was thinking when she wrote the headline for yesterday's *Herald*:

D.A. Puts Campaign on Hold
To Focus on Case Involving
His Spouse's Disappearance

"Good grief," Mylo said aloud, noticing that Wendy had used *spouse* instead of *wife*. When had she become so politically correct? It mattered. If Wendy had become a feminist *before* she had abandoned him, then he would have an excuse—she had been brainwashed by women at the *Herald*; however, if she had become one *after* she left him, then Wendy had changed as a person and no longer was the woman he loved.

Thinking about Wendy and feminism reminded Mylo of Kimberly. He would have to crack down on her before she betrayed him to Claude Turner, the publisher. He wasn't afraid of a discrimination complaint—only its impact on Wendy. Though he hated to admit it, Mylo harbored a secret hope for reconciliation, and the only way to get it was by getting her pity or attention via tabloid news.

He checked his watch: 6:07 A.M. He had better get to work before his reporters or publisher showed up. Mylo wanted to plan coverage and check the overnight file to see if anything unusual or absurd had occurred in the early hours. He couldn't count on Kimberly anymore to compose sensational bulletins.

The only thing he could count on from her was trouble.

Mylo's intuition proved right. When he entered his office, flicking on the lights, he discovered this memo from Claude Turner propped against the telephone on his desk:

To: Mylo Thrump, Editor
From: Claude Turner, Publisher
Re: Lunch and agenda at the Gentry Club

This is to finalize our lunch date at the Gentry Club Thursday at noon. Be ready to discuss the following topics:

1. *Expenses,* particularly those related to deadlines and overtime.
2. *Coverage,* particularly how the *Chronicle* will deal with the *Herald* if the latter goes tabloid to compete with our product. (For example, how will you treat my running for public office?)
3. *Fair treatment of employees,* particularly Kimberly Spears.

Mylo deciphered the memo. Hans Auerbach had complained to the publisher about deadlines and overtime. That was obvious. Wendy was going to compete directly with the *Chronicle.* That was obvious, too. But the "fair treatment" item explained why Kimberly didn't have a story for the morning paper. Instead of tracking down Edward Raymond Bok at 346 Union Terrace, she was complaining to Claude Turner at the front office.

Mylo started to dial Kimberly's number and then remembered how early it was. He finished dialing anyway and let her answer, a sleepy, "Yeah?" He slammed down the phone, happy to have this small vengeance, even though he knew that she had "caller-id." He had a blocker on his line. Then he filed the memo in the garbage and consulted the overnight. At this hour 1-900 calls had yet to be transcribed, so he logged on to his home page via Netscape. But the system was down. Mylo would have to make do with the wire reports. He scanned them, unimpressed, until coming across this item:

> The curious case of the missing D.A.'s wife has led to a local apartment building at 346 Union Terrace, detectives reported today.
>
> On Monday, Allison Effington, 28, wife of Luke Effington, was seen leaving the Am-Vets Building and taking a cab to that residence while her husband was declaring his candidacy for the City Commission, the police log indicates.
>
> Early reports in local newspapers hinted that Mrs. Effington may have been abducted.
>
> "We're following up on this new lead," said Dt. Nathan Howe who refused to disclose the identity of suspect whom Mrs. Effington may have known.
>
> On Tuesday, at a special press conference called by Luke Effington, the district attorney said. . . .

The rest of the story was old news.

"Could it be?" Mylo whispered, checking his police directory under the name of Edward Raymond Bok: *346 Union Terrace, Apt. 4D*. Mylo knew that building. It contained twenty apartments, five on each floor, mostly marrieds and older or single women. Then he checked another directory that provided a list of tenants in the building:

1. Adusumeli, Numa
2. Bok, Edward R

3. Capone, Jane and George
4. Dias, Lori
5. Edmonds, Jenieva
6. Guthrie, Sarah
7. Gwynn, Mike and Felicia
8. Haemmeroe, Denise and Diane
9. Hernandez, Jorge
10. Metcalf, Walt and Alan
11. Minelli, Anna
12. Root, Tuesdae
13. Schuler, Freida
14. Sengo, Andile
15. Stapleton, NL
16. Underwood, Lor'e and Ishmael
17. Webster, Joette
18. Witmer, Ulysses
19. Xue, Bixiong
20. Zucker, Tobias M. III

Mylo stifled the glee he felt upon scanning those names. He eliminated the female, ethnic, and married ones, leaving "Metcalf, Walt and Alan," "Stapleton, NL," "Witmer, Ulysses," and "Zucker, Tobias M. III"—in addition to "Bok, Edward R." He grabbed a pencil and crossed out "Metcalf" (gay, probably); "Witmer" (elderly, probably); and "Zucker" (too elite-sounding and pretentious for Ms. Effington and this address). That left "Stapleton" and "Bok"—a better than fifty-fifty chance that Kimberly's con man was also Laurel's missing link in solving the mystery of what happened to the D.A.'s wife. In fact, "Stapleton" could be female because she abbreviated her first and last name.

Mylo looked under "Stapleton, NL" in the regular telephone directory and found the listing. He looked at his watch: 6:22 a.m. and dialed.

"Hello?" a woman answered, frightened, as if she were avoiding someone. "Who's calling?"

Mylo hung up the receiver and dialed his reporters, telling Kimberly and Laurel to come to work by 7 A.M. "Breaking story," he announced, anticipating the scoop of his tabloid career.

* * *

"Come in, come in," Mylo told Laurel and Kimberly as soon as they reported to work. The women entered his office and sat down. They looked tired and angry. "I have great news," he told them.

"No news is good news at the *Chronicle*," Kimberly quipped.

"I need my sleep," Laurel said, puffing. She looked at Mylo as if he had disappointed her. "It's going to be one of those mornings, isn't it?"

"Let's dispense with pleasantries," Mylo remarked. He looked at Kimberly. "You know why your con man skipped town?"

"Duh," she replied. "Because the authorities are after him?"

"Lose the attitude. Because," Mylo continued, "you didn't get your butt to his apartment quick enough, Kim."

"Does this concern me?" Laurel asked. "If not, I'd like to leave."

Mylo's spirits sank. Usually Laurel enjoyed his taking down Kimberly a notch or two. Something had gone awry or been struck between the two women. "Yes," he told Laurel. "It concerns you."

"I'm tired of all the backbiting that goes on around here," she said.

"Since when?"

"Look," Kimberly interrupted. "Laurel and I have declared a truce. Even she thinks that you pit us against each other—for your own gain."

"For the newspaper," Mylo corrected. He stood and stared at Laurel, his protégé, the last person he thought would betray him. "Is this true?"

"Maybe."

"Don't back down on me now," Kimberly admonished Laurel.

"I'm a reporter," Laurel said. "I just want to do my job."

Mylo grabbed the overnight file from his desk and thrust it at her. "Then do it. Read the wire report on the last known whereabouts of Allie Effington."

Laurel perked up again. "Fantastic!" she said, showing the file to Kimberly.

Kimberly scanned it. "Unbelievable," she said in a flat voice.

"Touché."

"Don't get so cocky," she told him, holding up a finger to make a point. "I know what you're thinking. What you're planning to write." She held out a hand as if scanning a phantom headline. 'Edward Bok conned the D.A.'s wife.' "

"Good girl."

"Don't call me girl," Kimberly snapped.

"*Woman.*"

"If this continues," Laurel warned, "I'm leaving."

"You'll be leaving without a follow-up story," Mylo noted, pushing Laurel's button.

Kimberly persisted. "At least thirty people live in that building," she told Mylo, trying to put a dent in his theory. "Maybe

Allie is holed up with a girlfriend. Or maybe the entire episode was a hoax."

Mylo sat down. He hadn't considered that possibility. He hated hoaxes. Every now and then some smart aleck would feed him a false story and then deny or retract it, hoping to prove to readers how unreliable the *Chronicle* can be. Once a man even claimed he was pregnant, and his cohort, a local doctor, verified it with an X-ray, provided to Mylo free of charge (that alone should have alerted him). Once a woman claimed to have won the Lotto, vowing to marry the first man who proposed; she even showed Mylo a ticket—obscuring the date with her thumb—that contained the *previous* week's winning numbers. Boy, did he and Laurel fall for that one. But readers loved the retraction the next day—Mylo claimed nobody proposed to the hoaxster upon seeing her photo in the personals—all part of the fun of subscribing to the *Chronicle*. "What proof do you have of a hoax?" he asked Kimberly.

"No proof. Intuition."

"Women's?"

"*No*," Kimberly sneered. "Reporter's."

"I disagree," Laurel said.

Kimberly shook her head, mumbling something under her breath.

"No, really, Kim. I think Mr. Thrump is on to this con man."

"It's absurd!" she replied.

Now Mylo disagreed. "If this guy could dupe Job Service and the Veterans Administration, then he could dupe the D.A.'s wife. What's more, she's a sitting duck in that mansion. She'd make a great mark."

"He's right," Laurel said.

"All right," Kimberly agreed. "I'll keep an open mind."

"I'm glad to see that both of you are getting along so well," Mylo told them, "because I'm putting both of you on this story."

The women looked at each other. "Double by-line?" they asked simultaneously, as if programmed.

"You'll be working alone," Mylo said. "Best version goes directly to the front page."

Kimberly swung around to Laurel. "You see what I mean. He's always using us for his own gain!"

"For the newspaper," Mylo corrected again.

Laurel pouted. "Maybe."

"I won't do it," Kimberly stated. "I won't play along."

"Well, then," Mylo said, his voice trailing off. He peered over Kimberly's shoulders through the glass windows of his office that opened to the newsroom. A few old-timers had arrived already, having coffee, donuts. Reading the *Herald.* Someone put the TV on to watch "Good Morning America." And everything became ominously quiet, except for static on the scanner, as it had Monday night.

Something was going to happen.

Two armed policemen and a detective entered the newsroom.

"What do *they* want?" Mylo asked, dreading the answer.

Kimberly and Laurel turned around, got up, and gawked.

Mylo and the reporters left his office to meet them and find out why the detective was waving a warrant.

"Detective Howe," he said. "Which one of you is Laurel Eby?"

The women didn't answer. Neither did Mylo.

The detective pointed at a desk and told the policemen to rifle it, taking all the files.

"That's *my* desk, not Laurel's!" Kimberly shouted, realizing as soon as she said it that she had betrayed her colleague.

"Nice," Laurel remarked. "I make a truce, and this is how you treat me."

"Sorry. I have important files in my drawer."

The detective asked Laurel to identify herself and her desk. She did.

"You can't do this," Mylo told him.

"Warrant says I can."

"On what grounds?"

"Obstruction." The detective gave Mylo the document and ordered the policemen to proceed.

The entire newsroom gathered round to watch.

One cop rifled the desk, placing each confiscated item on the floor. The other cop tagged and recorded each item as evidence: One astrology guide, Leo; one book, *Women Who Run With the Wolves;* one pamphlet, USDA, *Bovine Reproduction;* one makeup kit; diet pills; one address book; no files.

"No files?" Mylo asked, surprised.

"Well, what did you expect!" Laurel snapped at him, embarrassed. "I invent the news. I don't report it."

"What's this?" the cop asked, pulling out a manila envelope full of letters.

"Fan mail," Laurel answered. "That's private."

The telephone in Mylo's office was ringing, a distraction. Mylo wondered who was calling as the detective paged through Laurel's letters. Maybe it was the publisher's attorney wanting to advise Mylo what to do during a newsroom search. He glanced at Kimberly and whispered for her to take the call.

"I'm not your errand girl," she hissed.

He told her it might be the attorney.

"Oh." Kimberly nodded and slunk away.

"Bingo," a policeman said, displaying Laurel's notebook that contained gossip she had garnered at the Gentry Club about Allie's alleged infidelity.

Detective Howe told the policemen to box up the items. He approached Laurel. "Will you accompany me to the D.A.'s office to tell us all you know about the disappearance of Mrs. Effington?"

Laurel glanced at Mylo for instructions.

"No," he told her.

"No," she said.

The detective read Laurel her rights as one of the policemen handcuffed her and the other hoisted the box.

"Help!" she pleaded as she was escorted out of the newsroom.

One of the old-timers had the sense to take notes during the search, knowing that someone had to write the story for tomorrow's paper.

"Hang in there!" Mylo shouted as Laurel disappeared out the exit and into the hall.

The reporters buzzed. "I knew it, I knew it," one was saying. "What's this paper coming to?" asked another. "Why Laurel Eby, of all people?" The men and women moaned and groaned. Then the pack followed the detective to find out why the moose writer had become the focus of the investigation.

Mylo Thrump sat down at Laurel's empty desk, feeling a wave of sadness wash over him. He was not mourning the loss of his protégé, though. He was thinking about how her arrest was going to postpone the scoop of his life. He hung his head in his arms, welcoming the familiar blackness.

Kimberly burst out of his office and smacked him on the back. "Buck up, mister," she told him.

Mylo snapped to.

Kimberly was gathering her notebook and purse. "Good news," she said.

Mylo let down his guard and raised his hopes. "What? What?"

"Elizabeth Effington just called in with a tip," Kimberly said, hungrier than a piranha. She savored the word—"*murder*"—and added: "Luke's closing in on Allie's killer."

15

Small World

Allie felt dead for lack of sleep on a bunk in Seton Place across from her tormentor Eddie Ray. He had switched bunks with the heckling drunk and taunted her all night, waiting until she dozed off and then slipping off his bunk to hers. He nudged her awake, as she had nudged him yesterday morning in his apartment when she had learned about their plight in the *Chronicle*. "Doesn't feel too good," he told her, "does it, Allie Cat?" Eddie Ray had changed her one first name to two because it suited her new lifestyle, he said, waving another copy of the *Chronicle* that bore Allie's photograph. If she didn't obey him, he threatened, he would expose her as the loose-moraled low life that she was.

That hit home. That was the right button.

Only now, Allie had endured about enough. It was nearly 8:30 A.M. Many of the homeless had left the facility, especially those with children. Only a few dozen older residents were lingering until the checkout hour. Gertrude, the caretaker, had left her station in the gymnasium to tend to business at the front desk. Even the bag lady who had admired Allie's "nice" blouse abandoned the bunk beside her; as soon as the woman waddled toward the exit, Eddie Ray threw his duffel bag on that bunk and flopped down.

Allie put on her heels, preparing to leave.

"What's the rush, Allie Cat?" Eddie Ray asked, sprawling on the sheets, his head propped on the duffel bag like a pillow. "Someplace important to go? Rotary maybe? Dance class?"

"Go to hell."

"Hey, listen. I know I done you wrong, AC." He yawned and needed a shave. "Let bygones be. Forgive and forget. Live and"—

"Shut up."

—"learn."

Allie stood up, making her bed, the polite thing to do.

Eddie Ray laughed at her. "You still think you're home, don't you? Cute."

She tried to ignore him, the anger welling in her empty belly until it seemed ready to burst.

"Sit down," he told her. "You ain't going home. You ain't going anywhere"—

She turned to face him.

—"'cept with me, sugar." He smiled his lopsided smile.

"Try to stop me."

He waved the *Chronicle* as if it were a flag. "Don't make me do it, Allie Cat. Lotta people here could use that ten grand your hubby is offering to anyone that finds you." He crossed his legs and hooted. "Yes, indeed. Heard it yesterday on the radio. Man," Eddie Ray complained, "he's cheap. You're worth more than that, sugar. I know."

Allie stared at him. "Luke knows about *you*. It's only a matter of time until he tracks you down."

"Cheap. Still," Eddie Ray mused, "if I wasn't involved with you, I'd be tracking you down, like a hound"—he hee-hawed—"after an *alley cat*." His lopsided smile waned as he remembered that Allie had not obeyed his command to sit down. "Sit down, bitch," he commanded.

Allie sat down, legs pressed together, arms on her lap over her purse. She was seething.

"That's better."

She surveyed the shelter, seeing if she could make a run for it without anyone noticing her. A few more residents were leaving. If she stalled Eddie Ray a bit longer, contained her rage, only a handful would see her flee. He wouldn't have time to harm or identify her.

"We can make this quick and easy," he cautioned, "or long and hard."

"Give me back my earrings. They're fake," she lied. "Like you."

"Very funny," he said, sitting up on the bunk and swinging his cleated boots menacingly to the floor. "The fake part, I mean. I know gold when I see it. Diamonds, too."

"They have sentimental value."

"Now go and break my heart, Allie Cat. You won't be needing earrings where you're headed. Or sentiment." He stood up. "Quick and easy. You accompany me, real quiet like, out of town," he said, "or give me the rest of your valuables." He stepped toward her. "Open that purse."

"You're robbing me in a homeless shelter," Allie stated. "How pathetic."

"If I'm pathetic," Eddie Ray told her, his eyes narrowing, "what does that make *you?*"

Allie opened her purse.

He hovered over her now as she rummaged inside. "Give me your credit cards," he ordered her, "and the rest of your cash."

Allie explained that she didn't take any money to Rotary Club because she wasn't counting on seeing him Monday night. "Why else would I be here, stupid?" she said, giving him her worthless credit cards and hoping he wouldn't ask her for the MasterCard confiscated by the automated teller. "You think this place takes American Express?"

"No," he replied, glancing at the cards. "But the Hilton and Regency do." He scrutinized her. "Why are you here anyway? What's up?"

"Oh, right," Allie said, feigning disgust. She was improvising as she spoke. "I should've just plunked down my American Express with my name on it, stupid, and let the concierge phone the cops."

"Concierge?"

"Person at the desk, stupid."

"If I'm stupid, what does that make you?" He put the cards in his shirt pocket. "You're turning into a two-first-name individual," he said, "before my very eyes, Allie Cat." He waved her off with his hand. "Go on. Get out of here. Shoo."

Allie slowly rose and clicked toward the front of the shelter, anticipating at any moment that Eddie Ray would strike her from behind. The exit seemed a mile away. She quickened her pace and heard his voice.

"You-all see that lady walking out?" he called to the dozen

or so stragglers in the shelter. "Allie Effington, D.A.'s wife. Gone AWOL. You-all tell that to police, hear? Your meal ticket."

Allie stopped and glanced around, to see if anyone recognized her. Only two or three had looked up from their bunks. No one took the bait. The residents had other, more serious concerns on their mind, like how they were going to eat that day. Find shelter. Stay safe.

"Bitch."

"Is that the only word you know?" Allie called out without looking back, trying to get the last word. "Asshole."

"What does that make you?"

Allie had to protect herself. She would try to find a place to stay in one of the shelters listed on the slip that Gertrude had given her. She checked her purse to see if she still had it.

"Nothing in there, Allie Cat."

Allie found it and closed her purse. The city needed that new homeless shelter, still under construction, but why was it being built on the outskirts of town? How would the people get there with aching feet, carrying their belongings in shopping bags or on their backs?

"There goes Allie Effington, D.A.'s wife," Eddie Ray hooted again behind her. "Good lay, people. Not the best."

"Oh, shut up," an old man said to Eddie Ray. "You're making a spectacle."

"But in her *mind* she's the best," Eddie Ray continued, "and that counts for something."

Allie doubled over, still standing, feeling a combination of fear, anger, hunger. She debated collapsing on the spot, fainting and hoping someone would rescue her. Maybe the old man. But she couldn't yield that easily to Eddie Ray and struggled to regain her consciousness. She fought the urge to vomit and forced herself to breathe.

"Scaredy Cat," Eddie Ray taunted, knowing she was under his control, as if he could get her to obey his every whim.

The room started to blur as Eddie Ray's voice became liquid in the background. Allie mustered all her strength, vowing not to succumb to her wooziness. Eddie Ray probably would take advantage of her situation, and she was worth more than that. The wooziness stopped. *"I'm worth more than that,"* she said aloud, and her head cleared without warning. She felt grounded, as if she belonged in whatever space she was set in. And she belonged here, listening without fear to Eddie Ray's "Allie Cat" taunts. She said the mantra again, and her body became sturdy and erect, responding to her *mind*: a new discovery. She felt compassion surge through her. She was caring about her well-being for the first time, reclaiming the love trapped inside her—not for a man—but for herself. This was a gift, she realized, a valuable commodity in a homeless shelter. Love can make a *home* anywhere, even here.

At that moment Allie experienced a sense of lightness and relief—self-worth—as something divine descended on her and entered her being. She smiled, knowing that Luke would call such a moment a rebirth, although Jesus the miracle worker had little to do with it. But Jesus the social worker just might. The source didn't matter. After years of searching for a cause and losing her identity, she had found both in the least likely of places: Seton Place. However absurd, she could see how events of the past few days had a higher purpose than gossip in the *Chronicle*.

"There's a reward for that woman. Read all about it," Eddie Ray bellowed.

Allie turned around.

He was waving the newspaper, standing by his bunk.

She clicked toward the exit with conviction now, undaunted by his taunts. Nobody had recognized her anyway, it was apparent, in her disheveled state of dress with her winged hair and welted eyes.

Gertrude entered the gymnasium, a look of fear on her face. "Get out of the way, quick," she told Allie.

"Huh?"

"Move!" Gertrude shouted as Allie obeyed, believing, alas, that someone in the shelter did recognize and report her.

Two armed policemen and a detective ambled into the facility.

Allie prepared to surrender, patting her hair down and straightening her wrinkled blouse and skirt. She thought about telling them that she had amnesia, ending up in a homeless shelter, and felt her belly ache again. No. She would tell them the truth and let them and others deal with it. She felt better immediately.

Gertrude stood beside her. "Did he hurt you, honey?"

"Huh?"

The officers rushed past her and headed for Eddie Ray.

Eddie Ray pointed at Allie. "There she is, there she is! Turn around," he pleaded. "*Look!*"

The officers ran toward him now, and Gertrude followed them, leaving her side. As Allie watched her scurry down an aisle of bunks, she noticed that the caretaker was clutching the front page of Monday's *Chronicle* that bore Eddie Ray's photo.

Allie Effington, fallen socialite, no longer looked like herself; but con man Eddie Ray Bok *did.*

"Ahh," Allie said, feeling empowered. Maybe there was a God. Maybe Jesus did descend on you like a security blanket in your moment of need. Maybe, just maybe, Gertrude was an angel. This much was clear: during the night she must have overheard or seen Eddie Ray taunting Allie and had become suspicious. Then she had associated him with the picture in the newspaper. Allie beamed, her spirit about to burst in joy. Gertrude had performed the kind of selfless act that Allie wanted to pass on to others, protecting them from street thugs like Eddie Ray.

"What-all are you doing?" he yelled again as the officers wrestled him to the floor and handcuffed him. "She's the one you want, not me!" Shackled, he could no longer point at Allie as the detective read him his rights. "Damn it!"

She took the final steps out of the facility, savoring his pleas and twangy curses. For the first time since her mother had died in Vermont, Allie said a prayer. She had glimpsed her mission in life and would heed the will of God—or whatever force was fulfilling her now. She had courage. She could meet any challenge. She could accomplish any goal. Of course she didn't know how long the exhilarating feeling would last, but she would ride it out. Let it sweep her in its currents and see where she ended up.

Allie Effington, fallen suburbanite, could go home. But she headed for another shelter to make arrangements for the night.

Someone was going to get a visit.

16

Open/Shut Case

This is how it feels to be important, Eddie Ray thought as the
two policemen escorted him down the long, tunnellike hall
leading to Luke's office. A cop on either side. One black, one
white. Like a Benetton ad in *Cosmo*: United Colors. *Clomp,
clomp.* Eddie Ray tried to keep up with them, difficult to do
handcuffed. So he lifted his legs and let the officers bear his
weight momentarily before falling into step again. *Clomp,
clomp, clomp.* They could be Cotton-Eye Joeing. He wanted to
hum a few bars of "Dixie" but doubted the black cop would be
amused. The white cop reached for the D.A.'s door with his free
hand and opened it without breaking stride. The trio marched

past a secretary in the lobby into an office that had a faint bean-bag smell: vinyl. Eddie Ray lifted his boots once more and clompedy-clomped to attention in front of Luke's desk, along-side which stood a tall, red-headed woman who looked like the Wicked Witch.

Eddie Ray longed for a toke off the recently discarded Lizard of Oz bong.

Lock'em'up was smiling his Ekeziel smile, savoring the moment.

"Howdy."

Luke studied him. "I have a charge here made out against you, Mr. Bok. The question is whether it should be kidnapping, robbery, manslaughter, or murder," he said. "In the first degree."

Eddie Ray balanced his weight on the pointy toes of his boots, adding an inch to his height. He was going to need every bit and more of his five-eight frame. "Ah, you're just angry," he whined. "You got a grudge, is all."

"Maybe so." Luke eased back in his chair. "But my policy, when the facts warrant"—he waved a finger at Eddie Ray—"and they *do* in this case," he assured him, "is to go with the highest charge if the suspect is uncooperative."

"You ain't got no murder"—Eddie Ray mocked—"in the first degree. What you got is a bitchy wife who at this very moment is hiding out at Seton Place."

"I would appreciate it," Luke advised, "being I am the one charging you, Mr. Bok, to refrain from calling my wife 'bitch' and to consider carefully what you say to me, inasmuch as it may be held against you in a court of law." Luke showed him a document and flung it upside-down on his desk. "People versus Edward Raymond Bok, 346 Union Terrace."

"T'aint federal, is it?"

"State."

"Good."

"You're not appreciating your situation," Luke advised him, pointing at the document. "Care to read this? Oh, I forgot"—he made a cross with his wrists—"cuffs."

Before Eddie Ray could reply, a game-show buzzer went off followed by static and a tiny female voice: "Detective Howe is here, sir. Shall I send him in?"

Luke hit the intercom button and said yes. He addressed the Wicked Witch beside him. "Elizabeth, please excuse us. We're about to interrogate the prisoner."

"I'd like to see that," she replied.

"No."

The detective entered, carrying a brown bag. He laid it on the D.A.'s desk.

"I want to stay," the woman said in a louder voice. Maybe she was an assistant D.A.

"Absolutely not."

The woman grabbed a clipboard from his desk.

"Thanks," Luke said to the detective, pointing at the bag. It didn't seem like lunch.

The woman stomped toward the exit.

"I'll talk to you immediately afterward," Luke told her as she left and slammed the door.

Detective Howe bent over and whispered something into Luke's ear. Luke nodded. The detective was tall, gray-haired, athletic, and didn't have a first name (let alone a middle one). Bad news. The interrogator looked at Eddie Ray. "The D.A. has covered the basics, I understand."

"Basics, my ass," Eddie Ray replied. "You-all go ahead and think what you want to think. Doesn't mean it's true."

"Enlighten us," Luke said. He had a baby/blubber face that went sour as milk, the color of his complexion. "Where is Allie?"

"I *told* you. Seton Place. Flophouse."

"I doubt you'd find my wife there," Luke quipped. "You don't know her tastes."

"Yes, I do," Eddie Ray replied.

The D.A.'s face went sourer.

"I told your goons here to get her at Seton Place," Eddie Ray told him, "but instead they arrested *me*."

Luke turned to the detective. "Did you see my wife at the homeless shelter?"

"No."

Luke turned to the officers and asked the same question.

"No," said the black cop. "No," said whitey.

Luke got up, taller than Eddie Ray anticipated. The detective stood beside him. Both were over six feet tall and imposing. "I'll take it from here," the detective said to Lock'em'up. Then he addressed the policemen. "Did you read him his rights?"

"Yes," said the black cop.

"I know my rights," Eddie Ray said, allowing himself a half-smile, knowing the effect of his lazy cheek. It ticked off people. He had been arrested before for misdemeanors in Tulsa and could weasel out of anything. In the end, Eddie Ray had more faith in himself than in a One First Name flunky public defender. "Listen," he told the detective. "His wife is *fine*. She don't want to go home. She's what you might call a 'neglected' spouse married to an 'emotionally vacant workaholic,' " Eddie Ray added, calling on the sub-science of *Cosmo*logy.

Luke went ashen at the words.

Right button.

"Don't push it," the detective replied, as if reading his mind. He grabbed the chair beside Luke's desk and swung it around. "Sit."

Eddie Ray obeyed.

Luke towered over him. "Where is she?" he asked, cutting in on the detective. "You tell us now, mister, or I'm filing that murder charge."

"Luke," the detective said in a compassionate voice. "Let me handle this downstairs at headquarters. It's too important to let feelings get in the way."

"He ain't got no feelings. *Emotionally vacant*," Eddie Ray repeated, as Luke whitened again like a lily awilt in Tulsa sun. "Tell you what I do know," Eddie Ray said to both of them. "You-all can't charge me with murder without her body. T'aint legal. Won't stick."

"Jessie, Dan. Hoist him up. Put him eye level."

"I'm advising against this, Luke," the detective warned.

The cops lifted Eddie Ray off the chair so that only the tips of his boots touched the floor. "One more time," Luke said to him. "*Where is my wife?*"

"No body, no murder," Eddie Ray said. "Open/shut case."

"Put him down," the detective intervened, nudging Luke toward the window. (Eddie Ray would have pushed him through it.) The D.A. returned to his desk and sat down, shaking his head and cursing under his breath. He didn't look all that emotionally vacant at the moment.

The cops eased down Eddie Ray in front of the chair. He got his bearing and stood straight. "Brutality, brutality," he said. "You're violating my constitutional rights."

"Which one, Mr. Bok?" the detective asked.

Eddie Ray shrugged. "I dunno."

"You don't know how much trouble you're in," the detective said. "Fact is, we *could* book you on a murder count and let Mr. Effington decide the charge. Unless, of course, we are mistaken. But you have to help us understand what happened. Otherwise we have no option."

"I said it before and I'll say it again. Allie Effington is at Seton Place."

The detective nodded to Lock'em'up.

The game-show buzz sounded again. "Send in the first witness," Luke said into a gizmo box on his desk.

"You ain't got no witness."

"Turn around," Luke said.

Eddie Ray struggled to do so, trying to shake off each cop holding his arms, and saw Mama "the Cookie Killer" Minelli.

"That ain't no witness. That's my dadburn neighbor"—he cast her a two-cheek smile and readjusted the attitude— "Howdy, ma'am."

She approached him, full of Woe-Is-Mia.

"Tell us, Anna," the detective asked. "What happened Monday night?"

"*Anna?*" This was becoming more serious than Eddie Ray thought. The detective with no first name was on One First Name basis with Mrs. Minelli.

"I don't like to squeal on anybody," she said, turning her head slowly to face Eddie Ray and waving her Piggly/Wiggly hands at him in a karate-chop pattern. "But I'll squeal on you, Edward." She spoke tenderly to Luke. "What he did is so terrible, I feel I cannot say it in your presence, Mr. D.A."

The detective asked Luke if he wanted the interrogation to continue at police headquarters.

"No."

"Okay, sure," Eddie Ray said, trying to throw up his hands in mock submission. But the cuffs prevented that. "I confess. I did it."

Everyone in the room gawked at him. "Wait," the detective said, taking a minitape recorder out of his back pocket and switching it on. "Confession, suspect E.R. Bok. Officers Heyworth and Cooper present, along with D.A."

Eddie Ray wet his lips and let his cheek go limp. "I confess," he said mournfully, "I cross the hall and take her newspaper. And I still have her cookie plate. I'll return it as soon as I wash it."

"Asshole," the white cop whispered.

The others glowered at him.

"You-all look disappointed. You don't believe me. I can tell." Eddie Ray glanced at Mrs. Minelli. "I *will* return that plate."

"Very funny, Mr. Bok," the detective said, shutting off the recorder and stuffing it in his pocket. "Tell us what you heard, Anna."

"He's telling the truth about my plate. I bring him cookies some nights when his lady friend comes to visit," she said. "Believe me, I never would have done so had I known that she was the D.A.'s wife, poor woman."

Luke hung his head.

"What happened to her?" the detective asked.

"She came Monday night"—

"Boy did she ever," Eddie Ray interjected.

"Shut up!" Luke yelled.

"Quiet!" the detective said.

—"as usual, only this time I hear screaming. The lady friend. I hear the two of them fighting in the hall." Mrs. Minelli took a tissue from her red tent dress and wiped her eyes. "I'll never forget what she said, thanks to you," she told Eddie Ray. "Her words will haunt me forever."

"What did she say?" the detective asked softly.

"She said, 'Don't, Eddie Ray, don't!' "

Luke looked up suddenly and asked Mrs. Minelli, "Did she visit him the *same* day each week?"

"Oh, yes. Monday night."

Luke hung his head again.

The detective approached Mrs. Minelli, standing between Eddie Ray and Luke, and put his hand on her shoulder. "Anna," he asked, "why didn't you call the police when you heard the screaming?"

"Yeah," Eddie Ray said. "Why didn't you?"

The black cop nudged him in the ribs with his elbow.

"Ouch."

"I didn't want to believe it," Mrs. Minelli said. "I thought maybe she is not hurt. Maybe she'll go home." She dabbed her eyes with the tissue and then blew her nose in it. "But she stayed. And the next morning I hear screaming again, more fighting, and"—she pointed at Eddie Ray—"I'll never forgive you, God as judge. I hear her struggling on the floor, sobbing, and then nothing. Silence. Then Eddie Ray says"—

"You're making this up, bitch!"

"Shut up!" Luke told Eddie Ray.

—"He says, 'I hope you learned your lesson, *bitch.*' "

"Oops."

Luke and the detective looked grimly at Eddie Ray.

Mrs. Minelli dabbed her eyes and put the tissue in her pocket. "Then he dragged her body into his apartment."

"Now that's a lie!"

"And he has the nerve to take my newspaper!" Mrs. Minelli

added. She put her hand over one of her mammoth breasts, as if taking an oath. "He kills a woman and steals my newspaper? But later I found out why. I went to buy another *Chronicle* and saw the poor woman's picture on the front page. He was hiding evidence."

"You're crazy," Eddie Ray said.

"*He's* crazy," Mrs. Minelli said, stifling a sob. "I think his head got screwed up. In Vietnam."

Luke looked melancholy again, suspecting the worst.

"She's *not* dead," Eddie Ray told him, feeling a twinge of compassion. "She's at Seton Place."

The detective continued the interrogation. "That's right, isn't it, Mr. Bok? You were there."

"Of course I was," Eddie Ray said. "You arrested me."

"*Tet.*"

Man-oh-man.

The detective turned to Luke, who came out of his trance and hit the game-show buzzer again, summoning the next witness.

"Turn around," Luke said.

"Geez."

There was Tim Bert Russell.

"You seem to recognize each other," the detective remarked, motioning to him to stand beside Mrs. Minelli. "Thanks for coming, Timothy."

"I knew it, I knew it!" Eddie Ray said.

"What do you know about Tet?" the detective asked Eddie Ray. "Did you realize that Timothy here fought in that terrible time? Were you planning to con him, too?"

"I dunno."

"Why don't you refresh his memory?" the detective said to Timothy of Tuscaloosa, who of late had changed his two first names to one. But he was still Tim Bert in Eddie Ray's eyes.

"Happy to oblige."

"I'm on to you," Eddie Ray told him.

Tim Bert would not face Eddie Ray but explained how people like him cheat the Unemployment Service, bilking millions each year from the federal budget. "As for Vietnam, as for Tet," Tim Bert said, his face flushing, "I became suspicious when he started bragging on it. If you go to war and see action, heck, you don't have to relive it. It becomes part of you. So I knew he was lying from the get-go and got angry. I'm angry right now."

"Understandable," the detective said.

"You nearly broke my arm, *Timothy*. Hey, hey"—Eddie Ray pleaded with Luke—"That's manhandling. That's a misdemeanor."

Tim Bert nodded. "Maybe if I broke your arm you wouldn't have harmed that woman. Don't think I haven't pondered that." He glanced furtively at Luke and continued telling Detective Howe his story. "I wanted to be sure. So I tracked his social security number back to Tulsa. Got in touch with some of the recruiters there, and they led me to a retired sergeant, Cee Jay Arnold. Turns out Eddie Ray signed up, all right," Tim Bert revealed, "and went AWOL before he even reached boot camp."

"Not surprising," the detective said.

Luke sighed.

Mrs. Minelli made the sign of the cross.

This was a conspiracy. "Cee Jay can prove that I signed up," Eddie Ray said, "but he *can't* prove that I went AWOL. No, sir-ee."

"Let's find out," the detective said, reaching behind him for the telephone on Luke's desk. "Why don't we call up this Cee Jay Arnold and hear what he has to say?"

Luke instructed the detective to hit the console switch on the keyboard so everyone could hear Mr. Arnold.

Static sounded overhead. Eddie Ray noticed ceiling speakers in the corners of the room.

The detective took a slip of paper out of his shirt pocket and dialed, the rotary tone clicking in stereo. Then more static.

"Tap the intercom set on the side," Luke told the detective, who did. The line started ringing.

Cee Jay's voice filled the room. "Eddie Ray? Sure, I know him," the ex-recruiter told the detective, without being asked a question. "Worthless bastard, if you ask me. Coward, too." He paused, uncertain what to say next, as if waiting for a cue. Then added, "When I think of those boys we signed up actually did go to war and never come back, I just plumb hurt all over." He paused again. "That good enough?"

"You-all paying him or *what*?" Eddie Ray asked, yanking on the cuffs so his wrists burned. "He's slime. He'll say anything for a dollar!" Eddie Ray yelled at the ceiling speakers. "Why don't you tell them about those poor boys you signed up and lied to, Cee Jay? They can't testify against you because they're *dead*, man, and you're the one signed *their* warrants."

"Don't you slander me, boy. *You're* the turd in the toilet now!" Cee Jay calmed down and said, "Army'll tell you. I was top recruiter three years running."

"Thank you," Detective Howe said.

"Are you the guy gonna send me that fee like you-all promised?" Cee Jay asked. "I'm on pension and"—

The detective hung up and buzzed the secretary himself this time. The intercom worked. "Send in the next"—

"Aw, come on! Jesus Christ."

The secretary replied, "She's on her way in."

"Turn around," Luke told Eddie Ray.

"Hell."

In strolled The Teach, the woman who had replaced Juanita at Job Service on Monday and helped undercover Eddie Ray's scam.

"She ain't no witness," Eddie Ray said, standing on tiptoe as high as he could. "She's a clerk, damn it." The officers tugged him down. "You-all got *nothing* on me!"

"You're just not understanding the problem here, Mr. Bok," the detective said as The Teach took her position next to Mrs. Minelli and Tim Bert "Timothy" Russell.

The Teach glowered at Eddie Ray as she had at Job Service.

"Tell us what you know about the suspect, Mrs. Watts."

She told the detective that Eddie Ray came to her window "stoned" to collect his unemployment check. "You can smell it on his breath, see it in his eyes. I see it all the time, from where I sit. Disgraceful. Nobody is ever going to hire these men. Junkies. Jail the lot of them, I say." She pointed at Eddie Ray, diagramming his sentence. "This one's on drugs, sure as punch."

"Ah," the detective said, tapping his head as if a light bulb had flicked on in the dark, evil recesses of his cranium. "Motive."

"You ain't got nothing," Eddie Ray said again. "First of all, you ain't got no body. Second, t'aint relevant what Cee Jay said about me and Vietnam. Or Tim Bert, for that matter. Cee Jay's crooked as they come, and Mr. Tet here ain't exactly a public servant. He *man*handled me." Likewise Eddie Ray dismissed Mrs. Minelli's testimony. "She don't know from beans what happened in the hall. Ask her. She never opened her door to see. For all she knows"—he repeated the line she said about "learning a lesson"—"I could have been talking about algebra, not Allie." He sneered at The Teach. "And this one's talking hearsay.

She ain't got no proof about drugs"—he looked at the detective—"no sir-ee, and you ain't got no proof, neither."

"Don't be too sure," Luke said.

"Then show me what you got. Nothing. Am I right? Well," he asked the D.A., "*am* I, Luke 'Ekeziel' Effington?" He half-smiled, enjoying how Lock'em'up shuddered at the sound of his middle name. "Open/shut case."

But Luke was ready for another go-around. He stood up and pointed to the sack that the detective had brought with him on entering the room. "I already have what I need to charge you, so shut your trap."

"As for the drugs," the detective added, "you must have forgotten the marijuana water on your bean bag, plus traces of so many controlled substances, the lab had to work overtime."

Luke opened the sack on his desk, extracting key pieces of evidence. "These are my wife's earrings," he said. "Necklace."

The detective added, "You'll never believe where we found them in his duffel bag. You don't want to know it."

"These are my credit cards," Luke said, lying them on the desk next to the jewelry.

Mrs. Minelli was crying. Tim Bert was restraining himself, ready to pounce upon Eddie Ray. The Teach was nodding, knowing Eddie Ray was as worthless as Cee Jay Arnold had said.

"In addition to the jewelry and the credit cards, Mr. Bok," the detective said, "we found traces of blood on your bed sheets. We'll be sending them to a DNA lab to determine whether it is the same type as Mrs. Effington's." He turned to Luke. "There should be two more items in that sack."

Luke peered inside and took out a baggy containing a pen and another with a slip of paper. "Campaign handout," Luke said, "with her prints on it." He extracted a receipt from Hair Today with a scrawl in Allie's handwriting. "It says 'Help!' "

"Ida May *Help* Me."

Luke closed in on him. "I'm going to ask one more time," he said. "Where is she?"

The detective pointed to Luke. "I'd answer him, Mr. Bok. This man takes no prisoners."

"I ain't saying another word. I want an attorney."

Luke went to the door. "Everybody out except Detective Howe and the officers."

The witnesses filed toward the exit.

"Thanks for coming down on short notice," the detective said.

Mrs. Minelli turned around, tried to say something to Eddie Ray, but then thought better of it and padded away with the rest out the door.

The prisoner and his enemies were alone. "You're violating my rights," Eddie Ray told them.

Luke walked around him, sizing him up. "Of course we are, shit-head."

"Brutality, brutality." Eddie Ray would inform his lawyer about this, he said, "as soon as I get me one."

"Brutal you want, brutal you get."

Eddie Ray struggled against the cuffs and the cops holding his arms tighter. "Easy, man. I'll cooperate."

"Where is my wife, you cock-sucking son-of-a-bitch?"

"Seton Place."

"Jesse, Dan. Hoist him up again," Luke said.

"No!" Eddie Ray yelled as he rose off the floor. "Listen, man. I don't know how-all to tell you this, Mr. Effington. But your wife like *seduced* me"—oops; that was an inappropriate

*Cosmo*logic word—"uh, like came on to me, dig? And I fell for it. So yeah, I slept with her. Sort of. But ĩ didn't mistreat her or nothing. I didn't kill her." He glanced at Jesse and Dan. "I tell you, she's fine."

"You've been telling me she's fine," Luke noted, "but not where she *is*."

"Your wife," Eddie Ray said for the final time, "is at Seton Place."

"Now what would she be doing there with her jewelry in your jock strap," the detective said, "and her credit cards in your pocket?"

"Jock strap?" Luke asked.

"Okay, okay. I see now why you don't believe me," Eddie Ray admitted. The detective turned his back and faced the desk, intentionally, it seemed, returning items of evidence in the bag. Eddie Ray had been trumped. If he confessed to robbing Allie at the homeless shelter, he would get jail time sure enough. But if he kept his mouth shut, he would get beaten or worse: charged with murder in the first degree. "Put me down," he told the cops. "I'll talk to the detective. Not the D.A."

"You're on your own now, Mr. Bok," the detective said without facing Eddie Ray. "You requested an attorney. Far as I'm concerned, I'm not even in the room."

That was a cue.

"Lift him about an inch higher," Luke told the policemen.

Up went Eddie Ray until he was eye level with the prosecutor. "Sorry," he told Luke. "I didn't mean her no harm."

Luke kneed him in the balls so that the kneecap seemed to rise waist level and watched him double over, gagging. "Let him drop."

Eddie Ray collapsed in a fetal heap, which Sigmoid Freud would tell you meant trouble, and knew that The Big "D"—the equalizer—was in his midst. So he moaned and welcomed this last, pitiful, slow-mo video of his life: Luke's Paisley shoes and cheap ball-on polish, whitey cop's nicotine hand over his mouth to stifle pleas, and the strange homey scent of vinyl that permeated the place and reminded him of his bean bag. . . . Then he was lifted and kneed in the groin again, the floor coming up to greet him, along with syrupy spews of cupcake that hadn't quite made it through the intestinal track. This was an embarrassing way to leave the world. He wasn't leaving it yet, it seemed. Because someone was cupping his face, wiping his mouth with a monogram hankie that had "E" on it. Positioning a polyester crotch in front of him. There was a voice, too: "Look at it from my perspective. I got my wife's killer or lover where I want him." The voice asked, "Are you ready to confess?"

Eddie Ray was opening his mouth like a fish out of water.

Detective Howe bent down and thrust his minitape recorder in his face.

"Where is Allie Effington?" Luke asked.

The detective urged, "Make it easy on yourself and talk."

Eddie Ray breathed deeply. He wanted to go out of this world with a memorable last word like "jasmine" or "taffeta," something sophisticated to compensate for the life that he should have led, and so mustered all his strength to make his final pronouncement—surveying the room to ensure witnesses would hear it—only to wheeze: "mothafucka."

Eddie Ray was shoved backward and beheld a hanging Japaneselike lantern on the ceiling and felt himself rising toward the light. He hoped that God would forgive his sins (or Satan be impressed by them). But that was not to be, for it was only the black cop and whitey cop like pallbearers hoisting his body, curled still from the kneeing. And then he heard, before the Jap

lantern flared above and blinked out, not Grandma Bok apolo-
gizing for the beatings and abuse or Mama for running off with
roughneck Richardson or even Daddy zapped by lightning on a
Kerr McGee rig, but some Yankee One First Name Nasal
Twanger, whispering: "I'm going to bust you if it's the last thing
I do. Go ahead, boys. Lock'em'up!"

17

A Kinder, Gentler D.A.

Luke should have felt better. In record time, he had helped arrest the man who lived at 346 Union Terrace. But it was obvious why Allie had taken a cab there Monday night: she had a paramour.

Luke was beginning to suspect as much. From the start, the investigation into her disappearance had been leaning that way. Up until Bok's arrest, however, Luke had dismissed the specter of foul play. Now he wasn't so sure. Pieces of the mosaic were falling into place, as they usually did; one thing always leads to another. In this case, adultery may have led to violence.

Detective Howe would know more when preliminary tests were completed in the police laboratory.

Luke was saddened by his wife's betrayal, yet savvy enough to know that sins of such caliber seldom happen without catalysts. He had to accept some responsibility. The suspect, Edward R. Bok, undoubtedly borrowed the phrase—"emotionally vacant workaholic"—from Allie (along with her jewelry and credit cards). Detective Howe had taken the bag of evidence to headquarters downstairs where Bok and other prisoners—Laurel Eby, among them—were kept temporarily in holding cells.

Luke glanced at his watch: 11:04 A.M. He had worked through the night again, preparing for this morning's events. He yawned, easing back in his chair and taking a document from his desk, rereading it. The trap was set. A judge-friend, who had approved the newsroom search and arrest of Laurel Eby, was waiting in his office, ready to help again. Although Luke disliked playing the role of the bully, he knew Detective Howe needed as much information as possible about Bok, and only one other person had spoken to him recently.

Luke huffed, knowing he would do whatever it took to locate Allie. But regretted abusing Bok. Typically, he ignored complaints about brutality. Sometimes a little pain helped a suspect remember facts that could save a person's life. When detectives roughed up a prisoner, Luke accepted the standard excuse: "resisting arrest." He had never participated in such violence. Now that he had vented his anger, shame replaced it. Clearly, Detective Howe was right: Luke was too close to the case.

Time had come for some hard decisions. First, he would officially end his campaign. (It seemed frivolous in light of

Allie's absence.) Second, he would take an extended leave of absence himself from his prosecutor responsibilities. Maybe even resign. Third, he would have to release his sister as campaign manager and adviser.

That was going to be difficult. Elizabeth was waiting in the lobby to confer with him, but he wanted to delay their meeting awhile longer. Luke needed to focus on the good things that came out of the scandal and gain strength. The next few days promised to be more trying than the first half of the week.

Luke counted his blessings. In losing Allie, he felt a sense of family in the D.A.'s office for the first time in four years. For instance, Nora Jones, his deputy, to whom he delegated duties via his secretary Janice, had taken over the day-to-day chores. Nora, Janice, and the rest of his staff also had pitched in and helped track down Bok. They respected Luke and his tough-on-crime stance. In fact, he was getting support from all corners. The dispatchers downstairs had sent out bulletins on the scanner and extra patrols on the street, following up pronto on all leads. Detective Howe had postponed other important cases to focus on this one. And each potential witness had cooperated fully, discussing their run-ins with the suspect. You couldn't get them to *stop* talking about Bok.

Except for Allie, apparently.

Out of bad came good. Luke believed in this Miltonic message, and though he was crushed by Allie's affair with Bok, he was not threatened by it. Instead Luke worried about Allie's mental state and physical condition. He recalled how strangely his wife was behaving during Rotary—an anxiety attack, no doubt—and probably had left during his speech about family values because of guilt. She must have gone to Bok's apartment, trying to end their liaison, whereupon Bok had become violent.

Luke shuddered. The specter of losing Allie had terrified him, emphasizing her worth, and he wanted desperately another chance to make amends and save their marriage.

In the end, Luke knew, he really believed in family values. Some politicians and fundamentalists used the term to promote their agendas, but he embraced values as a D.A. embraces the penal code. Luke would accept the consequences, not place the blame.

The question now was, would Elizabeth?

He leaned forward in his chair and buzzed his secretary. Today even the intercom was cooperating. "Any messages?" Luke asked.

Janice replied, "The only one you need to be aware of are several by Kimberly Spears of the *Chronicle*. She called fifteen minutes ago—for the sixth time—and is investigating the Bok case downstairs at headquarters. She wants an interview."

Before Luke could reply, he heard Elizabeth's voice in the background, stating, "Not on her life." Luke sighed and told Janice to summon Kimberly to his office. "Then send in Elizabeth," he said.

Elizabeth burst in the office. "What's the meaning of giving an interview to Kimberly Spears? She's the same reporter who gave you the nickname Lock'em'up," Elizabeth said, taking her usual position in the chair next to Luke. She clutched her clipboard over her heart like a shield.

"We have to talk," Luke said softly.

"Yes, we do." Elizabeth scanned the notes she had made in the pad on the clipboard. "It's time to undo what you did at the last press conference. I want you to reaffirm that you're a serious candidate for City Commission."

"Elizabeth. . . ."

She ignored him, sensing what was coming. "I can tell you that Claude Turner, your probable challenger, is a homosexual," Elizabeth said. She paused and studied Luke. "The people of this city will not support a gay candidate. This is not San Francisco."

""I don't believe he's gay, and even if he was, I would not care. I do about this, though," he told her. "Why are you opposed to homosexuals?"

"The Bible says"—

"No," Luke interrupted. "I don't want to hear a passage. I want to hear my sister."

"The Bible says so."

"What do *you* say?"

Elizabeth reddened. On the one hand, she seemed to welcome Luke's interest in her opinion, and on the other, she seemed not to have an opinion. "Well," she began, "in Romans"—

"*Your* opinion."

"You're putting me on the spot. What I think is not important," Elizabeth said, her eyes welling up for the first time in years. "How many times did our father tell me that? Why are you doing this to me?" she yelled, as if on the bring of a breakdown or, perhaps, acceptance. Then she steadied herself, breathed deeply, and said, "I agree with the Bible." She quoted the passage: "And the men, in a similar fashion, giving up normal relations with women, are consumed with passion for each other, men doing shameful things with men and receiving in themselves due reward for their perversion."

"I see." Luke always thought the verses dealt with the consequences of lust, but he lacked the energy to debate Elizabeth.

"I'm not alone in my convictions. If we 'out' Claude Turner," she said carefully, "which we can do without fear of libel—he's a public figure, after all—we will win the primary and probably run unopposed in the general election."

"You realize by now," Luke replied, "that my wife was having an affair with the man we arrested."

Elizabeth reddened again. She told him that God would provide, "as He provided for Job."

Luke understood the allusion. "So you think my wife is dead and that God will provide me with a new one. Comforting. Thanks."

"It was Allie's fault. She has to accept the consequences of her acts, like all of us."

"I'm glad you feel that way," Luke replied, planning to use that statement against Elizabeth momentarily. He swung around in his chair toward the window, waiting for her to finish the sermon.

"Allie got involved with the wrong type of person. You can't do a thing about it but go on with your career, including the campaign." Elizabeth seemed to have struck a chord of inspiration. "Do you know what Paul would say to her?"

He swung around. "Paul? Who's Paul?"

"Corinthians." Elizabeth rolled her eyes and recited: "It is good for a man not to touch a woman. Nevertheless, to avoid fornication, let every man have his own wife, and let every woman have her own husband." She spoke in a somber, tolerant tone. "Allie sinned. She fell, and fell hard. But you have not sinned. God," Elizabeth asserted, "will provide."

"You're not the only one in this family who believes in God," Luke told her, angry now. "You're not the only one who prays." He confided that he had prayed for guidance and now believed that he should not only end his campaign but also fire her and take an extended leave of absence. "Maybe even resign as D.A."

Elizabeth clutched the clipboard over her heart again. "That's Satan talking. Not my brother."

"Satan works in strange ways, Elizabeth. Did it ever occur to you that he is working through *you*, encouraging you to hate, as you hate homosexuals? Getting you to condemn my wife, even bury her, before you know what happened to her? For all you know," Luke added, "Allie could be afraid to come home, because she has lost faith. Not faith in God." His eyes watered. "Faith in *me*."

Elizabeth quoted another Bible passage, changing the gender: "If you do not warn someone wicked to renounce evil and so save her life, it is the wicked person who will die for the guilt, but I shall hold you responsible for her death."

"Ezekiel," Luke told her.

"I'm impressed. I didn't think you'd get that one."

"Well, it goes right to the heart of the matter, doesn't it, this passage?" Luke said, reminding Elizabeth that he had a moral obligation to make amends with Allie. "So that I, too, may save my life"—*and my marriage*, he thought.

"You're changing the meaning of these passages."

"Here's one for you. Matthew, chapter seven, first verse." Luke didn't have to recite it to Elizabeth: *Do not judge and you will not be judged.*

"Oh, *that*."

"Well, you're right about accepting consequences," Luke said. "When your wife is having an affair, you can't solicit votes from conservatives with a 'family values' theme. If we 'out' Claude, as you put it, he will play hardball and focus on Allie and me. I don't want to wage a dirty fight. That hurts the party."

Elizabeth was quiet, sullen.

Luke stood up and wandered to the window, overlooking the city, and wondered where Allie was, praying she was all right. A sense of security descended on him, which he knew meant that he was on the right track. The inner voice upon which he had come to rely spoke again, stating: *Fire Elizabeth.*

"Then we won't use Claude's gayness against him," she said. "We'll imply it."

He faced her. "This is what we will do. We will schedule a press conference for 8 A.M. tomorrow. Call up the local media."

She jotted this down in her clipboard.

"At which time," Luke continued, "I will withdraw officially as a candidate and then resign as D.A."

Elizabeth glanced up. "No," she said. "I won't let you."

"I'm accepting consequences, and so should you."

"Accept other ones. Accept the fact you have to fight dirty to beat Claude Turner."

"Elizabeth," Luke told her, "you're fired."

She stood up and came at him with the clipboard. At first he put out his arm to block the blow, but his sister hugged him, breaking down. "Please. I've put my life on hold. First for father. Now for you. I don't know what I would do without you. You need me," she said, a tear slipping down her cheek. "I *need* to be needed by somebody in the family."

Luke took her in his arms and consoled her. "Don't you see, Elizabeth? This is exactly how Allie must feel," he said. "I'm to blame. I put my interests ahead of the women I love and who love me. I have to resign. It's the right thing to do."

She pulled away from him. Her eyes had turned hard again. "Satan is making you do this. Admit it."

The intercom buzzed. "Kimberly Spears has arrived," Janice informed Luke.

He went to his desk and tapped the intercom set, though there was no static. "Elizabeth is just leaving. Send in Ms. Spears as soon as she does."

Elizabeth composed herself, wiping the stray tear from her cheek. "All right," she said. "I'll schedule the press conference." She glared at him with hate or fear. (Luke couldn't tell.) Before she left, she told him, "The last thing I do for you."

Elizabeth exited and Kimberly entered.

"She seems a bit flustered," the reporter noted.

"Her usual state."

Kimberly was not quite convinced. "I'd like to set up an interview with her afterward."

Luke smiled, still standing. "I don't think so."

"Ah," Kimberly replied, sitting in the chair alongside his desk and waiting for Luke to sit as well. He didn't. She looked up and quipped, "You still haven't forgiven me for your nickname, have you?"

Luke returned to his desk and sat, picking up the warrant. "Let's just say that I have forgiven you. But not forgotten."

"Good," she replied, taking out her pen and pad. "Now about my colleague, Laurel"—

"Excuse me." Luke buzzed his secretary. "No calls. Tell Detective Howe that I'm ready whenever he is." He turned his attention again to Kimberly. "You were saying?"

"Do you have an appointment with Howe, the detective in charge of the Bok case?"

Luke nodded.

"May I stay here and observe?"

Luke nodded.

"Why so 'nice' all of a sudden? Have you really forgiven me?"

Luke leaned forward. "You know, you really messed up things for me with that nickname, 'Lock'em'up.' It stuck."

"You earned it."

"Do you know why I locked up that battered wife?"

"You wanted her to testify against her husband. When she refused, you put her behind bars. Obstruction."

"Her husband had threatened to kill her."

"All the more reason to treat her compassionately."

"She had a history of returning to him. We knew the woman's husband and how violent he was. If I didn't charge and jail her, I couldn't have guaranteed her safety."

"That's cruel. Only a man thinks like that."

The intercom buzzed and Janice told Luke that the detective and his officers were in the lobby. "Send them in," he told her.

Kimberly jotted down a few notes. "Surely there were better ways to deal with the situation," she countered. "Like arresting her husband. He's the one who belonged in jail."

The detective and officers walked in the room.

"I agree. But we needed the woman's help. She spent the night in a holding cell and agreed to testify against her husband. Maybe it was cruel," Luke said, "but she's alive and he's in prison."

"Let's get down to business," Kimberly said, annoyed.

"Okay." Luke handed her the warrant ordering Kimberly to divulge all she knew about Edward Raymond Bok, under pain of imprisonment.

"What?"

Luke informed her that a newsroom search was occurring at the *Chronicle.*

"Mylo would have alerted me," she said haltingly, unsure.

"We already have your files"—Luke glanced at the detective, who nodded—"but now we need you to cooperate with us in person."

Detective Howe introduced himself. "I wouldn't mess with this man, Ms. Spears. You of all people should know that."

"Everything Bok told me was 'off the record,' " Kimberly said, standing up. "I honor anonymity. Moreover, there's a shield law in this state. You can't touch me. Or Laurel Eby for that matter."

Luke knew about shield laws protecting reporters from divulging *anonymous* information. "Laurel Eby tried to bribe me, trading information about my wife. You can't do that to a district attorney. As for the shield law," he added, "it doesn't apply in your case when you identify your source on the front page."

Kimberly became flustered. "My editor rewrote my story. He's the one who inserted the name."

Luke rifled his desk for a copy of Tuesday's *Chronicle*. He pointed at the Bok story about the scuffle with Timothy Russell at Job Service. "The by-line says 'Kimberly Spears.' It does not say 'Mylo Thrump.' "

Kimberly put the warrant in her mouth, biting down so she could free her hands and put her pen and pad in her purse. She took the document out of her mouth, scanned it again, and stated: "According to the code of professional journalists, I don't have to tell you anything confided to me off the record." She threw the warrant back on Luke's desk. "Shield law applies."

The detective said, "Your word against his. In either case, a judge will work it out."

"Let's go see that judge," Kimberly said.

Luke pointed to her by-line again. "Let me depose you now," he said, offering her a quick on-the-record interrogation.

"If you cooperate," the detective added, "maybe we can book this creep Bok. Then the D.A. can file a charge that will stick."

Kimberly was weakening. "I asked him one or two questions in the newspaper lobby. I also talked to Tim Bert at the Job Service. That's all. Nothing important happened."

The detective said, "Let us decide that, Ms. Spears."

The officers took out their cuffs.

Luke said he had something to tell Kimberly "off the record."

She took the bait, hoping that he would confide information that would get her off the hook.

"Judge Kaminski is a friend of mine," Luke said. "He knows and cares about my wife. Right now he is on the fourth floor, in his office, ready to jail you, Kimberly, if you refuse my request." Luke stood in front of her, trying to appear tough. In truth, though, he was heartsick, wishing he were home with Allie. As soon as Luke thought about his wife, he became resolute. "Will you tell us what you know about Edward Raymond Bok?" he asked.

"No," Kimberly replied, instinctively putting her arms behind her back.

"Go ahead, boys," Luke said, living up to the nickname that Kimberly had given him, locking her up.

18

The Sub-Sub-Science Of "Free E. R. Bok"

Eddie Ray inhaled deeply and yelled, "Let Me Out Of Here!" He looked down the cell block, holding the bars with one hand and his gonads with the other. "Jailer! Guard! Jell-O Belly! Get your butterballs back here!" He put his face against the grates. "Are you listening?"

"*I* am," the woman said in the holding cell across from his. "I want to hear your side of the story."

"Shut up, punk." Eddie Ray told her. He called for the jailer. "Let Me Out Of Here!"

"How'd you meet her?" the woman asked for the umpteenth time, trying to get the goods on him and Allie.

221

Eddie Ray glared at her. "I ain't talking."

"Get it off your chest. Feel better."

"Shut up, nark." She was an informant, sure as he had two first names.

"I'm a reporter."

"I know who you are, nark. Think I haven't done time before?"

"Well, I haven't," she said. "This is a first for me."

Eddie Ray studied her. Foxy, heavy-metalist chick. "You're a druggie. You got busted—or your *man* got busted—and now you're trying to get me to brag. *Confide,* so you can plea bargain with the D.A."

"D.A. doesn't like me."

"Join the club."

The steel retaining door cranked open down the corridor.

Eddie Ray pressed his face on the bars and looked down the cell block. He could hear two sets of shoes.

"Kimberly!" the informant across the aisle exclaimed.

The dumb jailer, whom Eddie Ray had named "Jell-O Belly," was escorting a big-boned woman to the cell. Her frizzy ponytail was held in place with a rubber band and trailed halfway down her broad back. Eddie Ray couldn't see her face as the jailer unlocked her cuffs and then put her in the cell holding the other woman.

"Hello, Laurel," she said to her.

"Finally," the informant replied, gathering her few belongings. Pen, pad. "Can't wait to get out of here."

Kimberly entered the cell and the jailer slammed and locked it.

Eddie Ray recognized the new woman at once. It was the reporter from the *Chronicle* who had interviewed him in the newspaper lobby.

Laurel gasped. "What's going on?"

Kimberly told her that Lock'em'up had arrested her. "The guy's on a tear."

"Oh."

"Hey, bitch reporter," Eddie Ray called.

Both women looked at him.

"You used my name in the paper," he told Kimberly, "and you told me you wouldn't. You lied."

Kimberly gasped upon seeing Eddie Ray. She turned to Laurel as if to verify what she saw.

"*Edward Raymond Bok*," Laurel said, introducing him. Then pointed an upturned palm at the other woman and announced, "Ms. Kimberly Spears."

The jailer waddled down the corridor.

"I ain't through with you," Eddie Ray told Kimberly and pressed his face on the bars, calling after the jailer. "Dumbo! Jell-O Belly! Come back here!" The retaining door cranked shut. "Damn." Eddie Ray pointed at Kimberly. "Dead meat."

Both women gawked at him as if he were an endangered zoo tiger. He pointed at Laurel now. "Informant. Dead meat, too."

"He won't talk to me," Laurel told Kimberly. "He thinks I'm a druggie or a nark."

Eddie Ray limped back to his bunk, still holding his crotch with a cupped hand, as if his balls would drop to the tile floor if he didn't. "No good Lock'em'up."

"Let me help you," Laurel whined.

"Fuck you."

She turned to Kimberly. "Tell him I'm a reporter."

"I don't think he would be impressed by that."

"Fuck you, too." Eddie Ray put a pillow over his eyes, preparing to eavesdrop on their conversation. Maybe he would hear something that he could use against them at a later date. Kimberly filled in Laurel on charges pending against Eddie Ray. Nothing new there. Then they complained about newsroom searches—validity of state "shield laws"—attorney talk that he didn't understand. Finally they started babbling about the district attorney and Eddie Ray perked up under the pillowcase. "He's doing this to get back at us," Laurel was saying. "He knows where we are and who is across from us. He knows we can't file the biggest stories of our lives."

Kimberly commiserated. "Only a man thinks like that."

"Tell me about it," Laurel replied.

Silence.

Time elapsed, and Eddie Ray almost fell asleep. Then he heard Laurel's voice saying, "I wish he would talk to me. Maybe you'll have better luck."

Eddie Ray pulled the pillow from his eyes and pointed at the reporters. "Dead meat," he told them. "Go write some O-Bitch-You-Aries."

"I think not," Laurel said.

Kimberly was smug. "In this state," she said, "you don't want to get charged with murder." She made an injection motion with her thumb and first two fingers. "I'll be at the chamber when they stick you, creep."

The Big "D." Eddie Ray pulled the pillow back over his eyes and shivered, waiting until the women lost their interest in him. He listened as they griped about the *Chronicle*. Kimberly told Laurel she was on the verge of quitting the newspaper—"especially after today"—and joining the *Herald*. "They're revamping," Laurel replied. "I've been approached, too." They each agreed it would be more pleasant working for a woman. "She's divorcing him, you know," Laurel said. Kimberly replied,

"About time. What did a woman like her ever see in a pig like him?" Then they jabbered about the general no-goodness of men, and Eddie Ray incorporated their comments into the sub-science of *Cosmo*logy. "We should both quit," one woman said. "Serve him right," said the other.

Eddie Ray fought the urge to sleep. Each time he dozed on the bunk, he'd turn and his swollen balls would ache miserably. This was some kind of revenge.

The retaining door cranked open again and Eddie Ray jumped off the bed—"awwww!"—keeling over. He fought the urge to puke. Embarrassing, embarrassing. He picked himself off the floor and limped to the grates again.

The jailer was escorting a man down the corridor.

"Guess who's here?" Kimberly hissed to Laurel.

"I was giving up on him."

The man put his fingers over his mouth in a say-no-evil motion. Then glanced at Eddie Ray. "They bothering you, son?" he asked.

The jailer opened Eddie Ray's door. "Visitor," he announced.

"What's he doing?" Laurel whined.

Kimberly let go a sorry laugh. "Scooping us," she said.

Both women were holding the bars of their cells and watch-ing the man extend a hand to Eddie Ray. The jailer stood out-side the locked cell, hand on his holster. "Ten minutes, mister," he said to the visitor.

"You my lawyer?" Eddie Ray asked, shaking the man's sweaty palm. The man looked like a public defender, dressed in a brown tweed jacket and green slacks. "I want to cut a deal."

"So do I," the visitor said, taking out a pad from his back pocket and a pen from inside his jacket.

Eddie Ray wiped a hand on his baggy orange prison pants that hung loose and easy on his gonads. "I want to cop a plea," he said. "I'll admit to robbery if they drop the murder charge."

The man wrote this down. Then walked to the bunk. Sat.

"I'm being set up," Eddie Ray said, charging police brutality. "Luke kicks like a goddamn Rockette."

The man wrote that down, too. "Good quote."

"Unbelievable!" Laurel cried from her cell.

"Unethical!" Kimberly heckled.

The man on the bunk put his fingers over his mouth. "Shhhh."

The jailer turned to face the women. "Keep quiet," he said.

"Shut up!" Eddie Ray mimicked.

The jailer pointed at him. "One more outburst and no more visits, Bok."

"You my lawyer?" Eddie Ray asked the man in the suit.

"I want to make one thing clear," he replied. "I won't be representing you."

Eddie Ray narrowed his eyes. "Why, then, are you here?"

"I'm an advocate."

"That's *like* a lawyer, right?"

"In a substantial way. Sure."

"He's misrepresenting himself," Laurel accused from across the aisle.

"Unethical!" Kimberly called again.

The jailer turned to them and pointed. "Final warning. Keep quiet, or you're here through the weekend," he said. "I do the paperwork."

The advocate humphed at them. "What I represent," he told Eddie Ray, "is the chance for you to exercise your rights."

Eddie Ray was interested now, nodding. "Uh-huh, uh-huh."

"You need to know the law, Mr. Bok, or else the police take advantage of you." He patted the mattress, inviting Eddie Ray to sit beside him. "Everybody has them. Constitutional rights."

"Which one?" he asked as Detective Howe had done to him earlier in the day.

"The most important one, of course. The first."

Eddie Ray limped to the bunk. "Keep talking."

"Constitution protects you. You can speak out against the D.A. or anyone else, for that matter," the man advised.

Eddie Ray liked the way he thought. He could see why he was an advocate and didn't realize the government here provided them along with attorneys—one of them Yankee pluses. He eased himself on the mattress, ready to exercise some rights. Make some amendments. "Fire away," Eddie Ray said. "Fall back."

The man rose and stood with his arms crossed, gaining an edge. But said nothing. Weird. Eddie Ray didn't completely trust him yet and didn't want to make a first or false move. You let others do that. "Who's bluffing who?" Eddie Ray asked him.

"*Whom.* Direct object."

Eddie Ray hated grammar more than smart-mouthed women like the two eavesdropping on him in the opposite cell. He stood up, trying to square his legs and hold his ground but had to hold his legs together, along with his gonads, lest they drop. "Who *are* you? Who's bluffing"—he got it right—"*whom?* Direct object."

"They say you slew Mrs. Effington, but I don't believe it."

"Slough?" Eddie Ray was puzzled. Slough was a marsh where buzzards roost by stockyards. "Slough? Slough who?"

"*Whom,*" Thrump said. "Direct object."

Eddie Ray stood in front of the man and poked him in the lapel. "Listen, buddy. I ain't got no comment."

"*Have* no comment"—he brushed where Eddie Ray touched—"Double negative."

"Damn straight."

"Don't you understand?" the advocate asked Eddie Ray in a compassionate voice. "I'm your ticket out of here." He put the notebook and pen in his suit pocket. "You're going to cooperate one way or the other. With me or Lock'em'up."

The nickname stung. "I'm the desperado," Eddie Ray replied. "The question is, who are *you?*"

"I take questions seriously," the man said. "I also take your rights seriously." He peered into Eddie Ray's eyes as if searching for a weak spot or an opening. "Those who fought and died in Vietnam did so for Americans like you. They gave their lives so you could exercise your rights."

Eddie Ray glanced away, ashamed.

"Free country. Free speech"—the man sidled to the cell door, planning to leave—"Free E.R. Bok."

"Three minutes," the jailer told him.

The women across the aisle were whispering in each other's ear. Both had their notebooks out.

The advocate turned around and saw them. "Put those notebooks and pads away!" he yelled at them, defending Eddie Ray. It seemed like this stranger was a guardian angel, a defender sent by God in a dire moment of need.

The women obeyed.

This man was important.

Eddie Ray knew instinctively that he could use him to gain what was rightfully his, and what rightfully wasn't: namely, freedom. He lifted a leg off the mattress, easing the pressure—"Uh-huh," he said, "I can see it"—and half-smiled: "Free E.R. Bok." It had a nice ring to it. The type that opened a retaining door.

"All right. This here's the real story. Get it right." He lay back on the bunk, draping his legs over the side. "I was desperate," he began. "I needed a lady, see? I mean, she came on her own and all." Eddie Ray glanced at the man. He was not writing this down. He had not taken out his precious notebook. "Okay, okay," he said apologetically. "Forget what I said. This here's the story. She ain't dead—repeat—*ain't* dead. She walked out on me. Vanished."

Now the advocate perked up—"Vanished?"—and seemed startled, offended maybe, as if Eddie Ray had yelled "rape!" or "nark!" or " *Vietnam.*"

"I say something wrong?"

"No, no." The man whipped out his pad. "Vanished?" he asked. "No trace?"

"Yep."

"Thin air?"

"Yep."

"First you see her, then you"—

"Hey, man. Like she was *gone,* okay?"

"Mr. Bok," the advocate replied, dead serious. "Let's talk man to man. I'm going to ask this only once, and I warn you"—he aimed his pen at him—"I'm an expert in these matters. Don't lie."

Eddie Ray eased off the bunk and stood up as straight as his gonads allowed. "I won't lie," he replied. "I can dig it."

"Did you see a UFO?"

" *What?*"

"I am ready to believe you."

Eddie Ray was confused. "Glad someone does," he said warily, deciding to forget the UFO bit and deploy the developing sub-sub-science called "Free E.R. Bok." He would start from the beginning. "Okay," he said. "This here's the truth. Whole, nothing but. I met her last year. Hit it off fine. *Real* fine, if you know what I mean. But her hubby got wise to us. That's all I can figure. Luke lost his manhood, man"—was that another double negative?—"and is going to keep me here," Eddie Ray said, "till I lose mine."

"Or worse," Kimberly taunted, making the injection motion again.

Laurel snickered.

"Pay no attention to them," the man said, consoling Eddie Ray. "You can confide in me. I know about these things."

"Great."

"When you were sleeping that night, did you hear any whirring noises? Did you see, you know, any strange flashing lights," the man said, lowering his voice—"lights that beamed and somehow could, well, *abduct* a woman?"

"Lights?"

"UFO ones."

"Crazy, man."

The man winked.

"Crazy, man," Eddie Ray said again.

The man winked again.

Eddie Ray tried to cipher what this meant.

The man shrugged, glancing at his watch as if he had important business to tend to and would be leaving soon. "Of course," he said, "you have the right to remain silent. But you know that already, don't you? The people who put you here explained all that to you, didn't they? Unlike me," he reminded him, "they don't want to cooperate with you, do they? In fact, as I understand it, you have yet to be assigned an attorney, have you? But enough. I respect silence, as I do all rights. It is, after all, last on the totem. Last rights."

Eddie Ray smiled now in recognition. This was the guy who gave you free subscriptions if you said you saw an alien. "I know who you are," he told the man, connecting the sound of his voice to a face. "You tricked me."

"Two minutes," the jailer announced.

The man extended his hand. "Mylo Thrump, the *Chronicle*."

Eddie Ray refused to shake it. "What did I ever do to you?"

"Not to worry," Mylo whispered, explaining that he had no interest in learning what really happened to Allie Effington. "My readers made up their minds by midweek. What I need now is something sensational to keep their interest."

"Your readers think I'm innocent?"

"They hate your guts. They think you're a slacker, Bok. They think you slew her."

"What the fuck is"—

"*Killed* Mrs. Effington."

—"Oh." Eddie Ray sighed. "I didn't, you know."

Mylo motioned for him to step closer, so his own reporter Kimberly and the informant Laurel couldn't hear. "I've covered courts for years," he whispered. "Tell the jury a good UFO story, and they'll think you're bats."

Eddie Ray and Mylo Thrump understood each other. There was agreement here. Brotherhood.

"I am ready to believe you."

Eddie Ray was being hip-moed, but he didn't care. His face went slack. "Maybe I did see some lights. Maybe the whole room was awhir with them. Flashing lights. Big old *beaming* ones"—he gasped, as if remembering something—"Elvis on board, too. Puffed up, you know. Sequins and pills—little green ones called E.T. pharmaceuticals."

Mylo was getting this word for word.

"Vanished," Eddie Ray said. "Up she went with Elvis, waving nighty-night in a porthole by the stern"—he furrowed his brow—"I believe that's what you call it—the back of the ship. Yeah," he said. "Stern. As in *Howard*."

Mylo put the notebook and pen in his pocket. "We're talking close encounter. We talking free subscription."

"Crazy," Eddie Ray reminded him.

"When you go free, you can thank the First Amendment."

"Cool."

"Time's up," the jailer said, opening the cell door. "He has another visitor."

"That wouldn't be, by chance, another reporter?" Mylo asked. "Wendy Thrump?"

"I really don't know," the jailer said. "But you have to leave. One visitor at a time. Jail rules."

Mylo stepped out of the cell.

"What about us?" Laurel whined.

The jailer closed and locked Eddie Ray's cell.

"Where are you going?" Kimberly asked.

The jailer accompanied Mylo down the corridor.

The women banged on the grates—"Don't leave us!" Laurel said; "Release us!" Kimberly yelled—but Mylo kept walking. The women called him more one- and two-first names than Eddie Ray could ever decode through his mother science.

The retaining door cranked shut again.

"Shut up," he told the women.

They glared at him.

Eddie Ray lumbered back to his bunk and lay down, putting the pillow over his eyes. For the first time since leaving the South, Eddie Ray missed his native land. Right now he ought to be lounging with some two-first-name Betty Lou on a waterbed in a trailer, she tending to his privates with soft warm rags. Just his luck to be paired with Allie Effington. He could see that now. There were incredible strokes of good *and* bad luck. He had encountered the second kind when he had hooked up with a D.A.'s wife. Yes, indeed. No matter how you cut it, no matter who you blamed, his misfortunes all came back to one woman: Allie.

He daydreamed under the pillow, imagining payback.

The retaining door cranked open again. In came another visitor, a real attorney, Eddie Ray hoped. He could hear shoes of the jailer and little clickety taps like heels: *Cosmo*-ite footwear. Fuck Me/Rape Me maracas. "Juanita," he mumbled into the pillowcase. Somebody cared about him, after all. Too bad she had to catch him like this, in wimpy prison oranges with tender Rockette-ed balls.

It was very Id-deflating.

"This way," he heard the jailer say. Eddie Ray kept the pillow on his head, half out of embarrassment and half out of self-pity to play upon her codependent Puerto Rican heart. "Ten minutes, Ida May," the jailer told the person.

Ida May? Eddie Ray flung off the pillow and whipped out of the bunk—"Awwwww!"—he groaned and fell fetally on the floor, holding his own. He dry-heaved and then blacked out momentarily.

"I'll just stand in front of the bars," the woman was saying to the jailer—he recognized her voice—"He's just faking an attack. He'll come around."

"Be right here if you need me."

"I might," the voice said.

Eddie Ray swiveled around on the floor and glimpsed up the woman's skirt. He recognized those legs. He got up on his knees and looked at the tattered, stained blouse and the torn skirt.

It did not appear by her slovenly manner that the sub-science of *Cosmo*logy would apply. He stood up, doubling over, and smelled a musky sour odor; then glanced at her dirty blonde hair plastered on her head like paint on a mannequin. He eyed her, head to toe. The shoes that made little clicks on the floor were mud-caked and peeling, as if she had trod through a slough. He cocked his head. She was doggone familiar. He pulled up the lazy cheek. Observed the way she stood there with a hand on her hip, a shapely hip . . . the way she swayed there with her legs about to tango, *long* legs . . . the way she huffed and puffed at him, nostrils flared, as if in the throes. But she was not in the throes. Nor was it Juanita. It was his she-frog, his nighty-night, his habeas corpus. Allie Effington, in the flesh.

"What's wrong, darling?"

"Guard! Jell-O Belly!"

The jailer was in his usual trance, as if he had heard one too many cell-block conversations. "Eight minutes," he said.

Laurel and Kimberly across the aisle were gripping the bars, watching the spectacle.

"Is that who I think it is?" Laurel asked.

"Maybe," Kimberly said. "*Yes.*"

The visitor had her back to them. "Didn't you recognize me?" she whined, addressing Eddie Ray, holding the flares of her skirt and twirling like a prima ballerina. "New look."

Eddie Ray was speechless.

She pretended to be disappointed. "So you're not pleased to see me, sweetie. Honey-angel."

Eddie Ray swiped at Allie through the grates. She stepped back, afraid. Then started twirling again. The women across the aisle were scribbling frantically in their notebooks, recording the scene. *Think, boy, think,* Eddie Ray thought as the jailer announced: "Seven minutes." Maybe, to keep her here, he should engage Allie in a conversation, ask her how she was doing, other than muddy. "Come closer," he told her in a half-tender/half-tempered manner, planning to grasp her by the throat and force the jailer to listen as he identified her. She took another step backward. "Damn, damn!" Eddie Ray said. This was stupid. He banged his head on the grates to get the jailer's attention. "This is Allie Effington, asshole," he told him.

"That's it. No visitors," the jailer replied, focusing on the word "asshole" instead of "Allie." "I don't have to put up with this crap."

"Stay Right Where You Are, Bitch."

"That's it, lady," the jailer said. "He gets belligerent, visitors gotta go."

"Good rule," Allie said, sounding like a D.A.'s wife.

"Can she talk to us?" Kimberly asked the jailer.

"Please?" Laurel asked.

Allie turned around and noticed Laurel for the first time.

"Oops."

"Remember me?" Laurel said. "We spoke at Rotary."

"I really should be going," she said, clicking toward the retaining door.

The jailer turned to Eddie Ray and said, "You can do better, bub. She gotta have a shower." Then he ambled down the corridor.

The door cranked open and closed.

A silence descended.

Eddie Ray and the women were dumbstruck.

This was an incredible stroke of bad luck. Allie had escaped, defying the science of One First Name/Two First Names, along with the sub-science of *Cosmo*logy and the evolving sub-sub one of "Free E.R. Bok."

He glanced across the aisle at the reporters.

There was no more posturing. No more vying for interviews. No more intimidation, either. These ladies were beyond threats. Laurel gave him the finger. Kimberly made the lethal injection hand-motion again.

They were pissed.

"We're going to write you up proper," Kimberly said in mocking drawl.

"Double byline," Laurel said.

"That like a double negative?" he asked, trying to befriend them by using reporter-talk.

"Dead meat," Kimberly told him.

"Road kill," Laurel said.

Bitches. Eddie Ray hated One First Name women too proud to know when they were had. "Double byline, huh?" he asked, pressing his face against the bars and pretending to look down the corridor. "I don't see nobody."

Kimberly glanced at Laurel. "What's he talking about?"

Eddie Ray cupped his ear. "I don't hear nobody."

Laurel hung her head and pouted, realizing what he was saying.

"Get comfy, girls," Eddie Ray told them, knowing Mylo Thrump was going to leave them in the slammer a spell while he wrote the front-page story. He told the women that.

"He wouldn't dare," Kimberly said.

"He would," Laurel whined.

They looked at each other, hesitated, and then started banging the grates and calling for the jailer. Eddie Ray returned to his bunk, put a pillow over his eyes, and savored each crying out—helpless, ornery—women begging men to hear and heed their pleas. Futile, futile. He put a hand on his aching balls and listened to the duet like a lullaby.

Eddie Ray lapsed, mercifully, into sleep.

19

Possible Questions, Probable Replies

"I'll open with a statement and then take a few questions," Luke announced, debating whether to proceed without Elizabeth. "Testing. One, two."

It had come to this. He was going to end his campaign and resign as D.A. Then he was going to wait at home until he knew what happened to Allie.

"Start soon," a reporter said. "We're ten minutes late."

"I got a deadline," said Wendy Thrump of the *Herald*. Her newspaper came out at 3 P.M. so her story had to be filed by noon.

"Give me a minute," Luke said, gathering his thoughts. He surveyed the mob in the conference room at what promised to be his last public appearance. He felt a little like Richard Nixon, although there would be no helicopter or loyal staff awaiting him in the wings to bid a maudlin good-bye. Even Nora Jones, his deputy, and all the assistant D.A.s and staff workers were not present. Or invited. Elizabeth's idea, no doubt; his sister would spare him the humiliation without thinking that he needed support. Luke was being courageous, following his moral code—family values—even though his sister didn't share them.

Luke was alone among his enemies in the media. He tried to find a friendly face and focused on Wendy again in the front row. "Have you seen my sister Elizabeth?" he asked nonchalantly, trying to mask his concern.

Wendy shook her head and checked her watch.

The TV crews shone their lights on him, another cue.

Luke was uncomfortable without his sister near the podium. The lights seemed to illuminate his guilt about Allie and worry about Elizabeth. Worse, the tangle of microphones were pointing at him menacingly. He felt like a suspect in his conference room. He was going to be interrogated by the very people he loathed, responsible for the miniseries that changed his life in one week.

"Why are we waiting?" a radio announcer inquired.

"Is something wrong?" asked the magazine writer who had posed the tricky question at the last press conference. She had known all along that Allie had a paramour and was observing Luke, focusing her intelligence and intuition on him, peering inside his being for the truth.

"You'd make a great district attorney," Luke told her, trying to lighten the mood.

"Will we need a new one?" the writer asked.

Ouch. He pretended to ignore her. The regulars were jock-eying for position near the podium—local broadcast personali-ties, wire and print people—but no one from the *Chronicle*.

That was strange. Laurel and Kimberly were released this morning, thanks to the efforts of the state Press Association, which Luke assumed Claude Turner had engaged. An attorney had struck a compromise. The reporters would share with authorities but not publicize in the *Chronicle* information about the case. Luke speculated that the reporters missed the press conference because they were at the newspaper now, writing about their twenty-four hours or so in jail.

"This better be good," a radio talk-show host was saying. "I missed my morning show because of this gig."

"Testing"—there was no amplification—"Oh," Luke noted, realizing once more that he had mistaken microphones meant to record him for ones that would reverberate his voice. Would he ever get the hang of this? He sighed in relief, surer about his deci-sions, knowing that he would never need to worry about stage fright again after he had dropped out of the public eye. No more campaigns, banquets. No more constituents to woo or speeches to memorize. No more reporters, either. That suited him fine.

"Is anything wrong?" the magazine writer asked again.

Luke snapped to attention. The reporters in the room were staring at him now, debating whether to swarm him like a mob. He would have to begin without Elizabeth. He drummed the podium lightly with his fingertips. "I guess it's about time," he said, unfolding a piece of paper with a statement that he had to compose himself.

Luke faced the reporters again and made eye contact. "I hope that you won't make this any tougher on me than usual," he told the reporters. "This has been a colossal week." He scanned the statement and began. "The good news is that we have arrested a suspect. Some of you know that already through your sources in the police department. But I cannot release his name because I have yet to charge him. I should make a decision about that before tomorrow at 10 A.M."—he swallowed—"at which time I will resign as D.A."

The reporters glanced up from their pads. They had not anticipated this.

He liked catching them off-guard. "Nora Jones, my deputy, will assume my duties as acting D.A. In addition," Luke noted, "I am withdrawing officially from the primary and am no longer a candidate for City Commission. Simply, it's improper for me to run for public office while my wife Allie is still missing." He folded the statement and tucked it back in his shirt pocket. "Basically, I called you here to tell you these decisions, not to take questions about the case."

"Have you located the whereabouts of your wife?" a TV anchorwoman asked, breaking the rule that Luke had just announced.

"No comment."

The anchorwoman followed up. "Word has it that police no longer believe she was abducted."

"No comment."

Some reporters groaned, realizing that Luke was going to stonewall any questions about the suspect in custody or his wife. But a few journalists also knew that Luke's resignation and withdrawal from the campaign were newsworthy and temporarily would bump the abduction story from headlines and TV bulletins. One of these was the wire-service reporter whom Luke pointed to, taking the next question.

"Will you be returning then to your business, Values, Inc.?"

Luke glanced again at the door, searching for Elizabeth. As a board member of the family-owned department-store chain, she had a right to know his plans before they were announced publicly. He had tried to phone her at home last night, but there had been no answer, only a Bible recording on her answering machine—a curious passage out of Numbers—"And Moses sent messengers from Kadesh to the king of Edom. So says your brother Israel. You know all the trouble that has befallen us." Luke knew that *messengers* were reporters and *brother* was he and *trouble that has befallen us* alluded to his recent decisions. Or maybe he was reading too much into the verse, as fundamentalists sometimes do when they needed answers to simplify their lives.

The reporters needed answers.

"What was the question?" Luke asked the wire service guy.

He repeated it.

Luke replied, "It would be improper for me to answer that inasmuch as I have yet to speak to individual board members, including my sister."

All reporters in the room groaned. One said, "You won't talk about the case. And now you won't even talk about your business."

"I'm sorry," Luke said. "I *can* tell you that there will be some changes at Values, Inc. But I can't discuss them right now. No comment."

Wendy Thrump was waving her hand and Luke called on her, an ethical but tough journalist whom he admired.

"Why did you conduct newsroom searches at the *Chronicle* and jail two reporters, Laurel Eby and Kimberly Spears?" she asked. "Why didn't the shield laws protect them?"

Why was Wendy Thrump, the editor of a rival newspaper, so interested in reporters for the *Chronicle*? Luke asked her that.

She blushed, as if hiding something confidential that would interest others in the room. "I ask questions. You answer them."

"Right," Luke noted.

"On what grounds did you decide to jail the reporters and take their files," Wendy asked as if she had seen those files.

"Are you covering this for the *Herald* or the *Chronicle*?"

"I ask the questions."

"I answer them," Luke said.

Wendy smiled. "Right."

He huffed. He could not discuss the case because Eddie Ray had yet to be charged officially. Neither could Luke discuss his plans for the future because they concerned Elizabeth. Finally he could not discuss why he locked up the reporters because that would complicate the investigation, leading in a vicious circle back to Eddie Ray. The media would focus on Laurel being one of the last people to see Allie at Rotary, and that eventually would lead them to the cab driver that drove her to 346 Union Terrace. The media would focus on Kimberly being one of the last people to talk to Eddie Ray; either way, the press would uncover the identity of the suspect. "I'm sorry," he told Wendy. "This, too, involves the case about which I may"—

"Oh, come on," Wendy complained.

—"not speak." Luke apologized again but said: "No comment."

"You jailed two young women who were doing their jobs. Why?"

Luke surveyed the room for his next question.

A few of the reporters were leaving, eager to get to phones to report the breaking news about Luke's resignation.

The magazine writer was waving her hand, and he called on her.

"Where's Elizabeth?" the writer asked.

Uh-oh.

"I've been observing you two for years now. She'd never miss a press conference," the writer stated. "Where could she possibly be?"

Luke broke out in a cold sweat. If he indicated that Elizabeth was missing, the media would pounce on that angle like cats on prey. He had learned his lesson in the aftermath of Allie's disappearance and didn't want to precipitate a second family scandal. Fact was, Luke worried about Allie's *and* Elizabeth's mental state and felt, given the delicate nature of the situation, that his only response could be: "no comment."

The remaining reporters walked out without Luke ending the session. He stood at the podium, watching them exit and leer at him, leaving him in an empty room so that the only one he could call on was the inner voice that guided him through tense times.

The voice said: *No comment.*

Luke headed back to his office. Janice was not at her desk in the lobby. Luke opened the door and saw her inside, putting his files in a box marked "personal belongings."

"So soon?" she asked, turning around.

He nodded.

Janice told him she was boxing up files that he might need one day, should he decide to run again as district attorney.

"You'd have me back?" As soon as he asked the question, he thought about Allie.

Janice remarked, "You're the best D.A. I've ever worked with. For the first time, we put the victim before the interests of the criminal. Your successor has a tough act to follow, *Lock-'em'up.*" His secretary was teasing him, trying to ease the awkwardness of his departure.

Luke took her comment in good humor. "That reminds me," he said. "Tell Nora to call me at home if she needs me. I'll be hiding out there, at least until Friday. Then I'll be out of the country for several days. But I'll call in on occasion."

"A vacation?"

"Business."

"Of course."

Janice helped Luke gather the rest of his belongings from the desk drawers. He had nothing "personal" to put in that box. He asked his secretary if she wanted him to leave the intercom, the wall clock, and the hanging ceiling lantern—compliments of Values, Inc.

"Leave the intercom," Janice said, giving him a quick hug. "Sentimental value."

"I'm going to miss you," he told her.

"Go home," she said.

When he got there he ignored the three rolled copies of the *Chronicle* on the portico and pushed the key in the lock. The door of the minimansion swung open on its own. Odd. He had locked it. "Oh no," he groaned. He should have suspected as much, with all the recent publicity: thieves struck when people were at weddings or wakes or, in his case, working all hours at the D.A.'s office. Criminals knew when houses were empty. No relatives. No neighbors. No witnesses.

Luke slipped inside and saw scuff marks on the high-gloss tile. This was a burglary in progress. He had a pistol, but it was in the top drawer of the nightstand in the bedroom. He would have to get there first. Unclip the lock. Make his day. Make *headlines.* He buckled and nearly fell. Then tiptoed into the living room and saw a trail of mud and clothes—*Allie's* clothes—the ones she had worn that night at Rotary. He buckled again and bent down, inspecting the blouse. It was spattered and stained but not with blood. Luke didn't know what to think. He had been through too much to think. He slumped to the floor, feeling nauseous.

Then he smelled the Folger's.

There were sounds, small hints—the sputtering of Mr. Coffee, the shower not far from where he knelt in the hall—indications that someone he knew, or thought he knew, had come home. He stood. The coffee maker completed its cycle. He inched down the hall toward the bathroom and put his ear on the door, which also was unlocked and swung open.

"Oh, my God!"

Luke jumped back.

"You could have knocked!" She wrapped a towel around herself. "You scared me half to death."

He was in the preliminary stages of shock and thus could not fully express his surprise.

Allie reached for her robe and slippers and put them on. "Hello," she said, undoing the towel around her waist and bending to wrap it around her hair. She flung her head back and shimmied past him. "I didn't hear you come in."

He watched her pad to the kitchen and staggered after her, holding the wall for support. "*You didn't hear me come in?*"—she wasn't acknowledging the situation—"You've been missing," he said, "presumed *dead,* for Pete's sake, and all you have to say is, 'Hello? I didn't hear you come in?' "

"Well, I didn't." She entered the kitchen and tightened the belt of her robe. "I wasn't expecting you. I thought you'd be at the office." She went to the counter. "Want coffee? Fresh pot?" She poured herself a cup. Allie sighed. "Play along, will you?" she said. "This is difficult."

"I can't believe you're home," he said, noticing the redness across her eye where her purse strap had struck her at Eddie Ray's apartment. "Did he hurt you?"

Allie was not wearing makeup. "It's nothing, really."

"Because if he did"—

"Please," she said.

—"I'll, I'll. . . ." Fact was, Luke already had vented his anger on Eddie Ray. So he didn't finish his threat.

Allie took his hand and led him to a chair in the kitchen. He remained standing. She poured him a cup of coffee at the counter and opened the refrigerator, looking for milk. He had not gone grocery shopping. She put his coffee on the table.

Luke understood now why Allie was underplaying her homecoming. If he played along, as she put it, pretending nothing had happened, it would be easier to reconcile and forgive each other.

"I'm glad I'm home," she said tentatively.

Luke forced a smile. "Look," he said. "I need to telephone the office. The whole city has been looking for you." Luke thought about the extra hours that Detective Howe and others had put in, postponing bonafide cases. He told Allie it was imperative that he inform the police and his secretary Janice.

"But not the media," Allie begged. She told Luke she didn't want to make headlines again unless she deserved the recognition. "I've changed," she confided, "or am in the process of changing." She mumbled something about the plight of the homeless. "There's a whole world that I never knew existed. Men, women. Children."

Luke was confused. Why was she talking about the homeless instead of them and their marriage?

Allie explained that one of the conditions upon which she would insist, if they were going to reconcile, was her involvement in this cause. "I'm going to make a difference. I can feel it."

His wife had come home and already was talking about getting out of the house.

"Where's your sister?" Allie asked, concerned.

Luke said he didn't know. "She's had a tough week."

Allie nodded. "I need to apologize to Elizabeth."

Luke felt a pang at the mention of his sister's name. He knew that he couldn't confide his worst suspicions—that she was having a breakdown—while he and Allie were coming to terms.

"I have some conditions, too. Actually, just one," Luke said. She turned her head, as if he were going to discuss Eddie Ray. He would hold off on that awhile longer as well. Luke gently took her chin so that he could look her in the eyes, make contact, a skill he was still learning, though this time he got it right. "We've hurt each other, Allie. I'm not trying to place the blame. I'm trying to take responsibility."

"You're a stand-up guy. I always liked that about you."

He liked that part of himself, too. It had earned him his reputation as a hard-nosed prosecutor who would jail himself if the facts warranted. And the facts of his marriage had become more obvious to him with each passing hour without his wife. He told Allie that. He also told her that he had announced his resignation as D.A. and dropped out of the City Commission race.

Allie pulled away from him. "How can we save our marriage? You'll spend the rest of your life hating me for ruining your career."

He laughed at the irony.

"Don't laugh at me," Allie said.

Luke took her hand. It was important that he hold on to her in some way, as if she could vanish. "I've changed, too. Or like you am in the process of changing. For the better," he remarked. He explained that they seemed to have switched lives this week. She wanted to be Civic Servant of the Year, helping the homeless, and he wanted to spend more time with his spouse. "Strange life," he said.

"I don't think Rotary Club will give me that award."

"I don't think you want me to redecorate the house."

She squeezed his hand. "You said you had some conditions," she reminded him. "One actually."

"That there are *no* conditions."

Allie seemed disappointed. "So you really don't want me to get involved with the shelters?"

"That's a condition."

"I see."

"No, Allie. You misunderstood." He explained that any kind of limitation was *conditional* and can harm a marriage. So his "condition," simply, was that they would place no limitations on their relationship. "This way we can learn to forgive each other when we make mistakes."

She still looked confused. "You mean we should have an 'open' marriage?" she asked.

Uh-oh. He didn't intend to imply that. Luke felt his stomach tighten as he thought about Eddie Ray Bok and decided, perhaps, that he ought to mention his position on extramarital affairs. "We shouldn't allow anyone to come between us, Allie. That part of a marriage goes without saying."

Allie frowned. "I knew we'd come around to this."

Luke told her that she should tell the truth. "I can handle it," he assured her. "It might hurt me now but will help in the long run." He released her hand and stepped back, dreading what she might disclose. But asked anyway. "What happened Monday when you left in the middle of my speech?"

Her eyes darted and refocused on him again, as if she knew suddenly how to proceed. Luke noted that her pupils even opened to let in more light. He was studying his wife so intensely that he saw his face reflected in her eyes, and this comforted him. She spoke softly, apologetically. "You were talking about values," she began, "and I had what they call some kind of a panic attack. I went to see him and"—she slumped forward, into his arms—"I can't do this, Luke." She regained her composure and stood up. "I wanted to end it. He turned on me," she said. "You have no idea."

He reached to dry her tears, but there weren't any. So he lifted her chin and stared at her again without any suspicion. The final scenario with Bok was just as Luke had imagined it. If it wasn't, his wife was sparing him the pain. They both seemed to know that they were in this together and would have to ask hard questions but also accept easy alibis. *No* conditions.

"That's the truth," she said. "That's what happened."

"Okay," he replied.

"You don't believe me."

"I have to telephone the police and my office, Allie. They're spending public money to look for you."

"No media."

He said he would tell that to the authorities. "But I need to know what you want me to do about Bok." He touched her face. "It's obvious he hurt you. It's also obvious that you were robbed."

"In a homeless shelter, no less."

Luke flushed. So Eddie Ray was telling the truth about Allie spending the night at Seton Place. He didn't want to interrogate her about what she was doing there with him.

"He tracked me down," she said, reading his mind or realizing the implications of what she had said. Allie started weeping now and embraced him. "He took my earrings, you know, and credit cards." She dried her eyes. "Except the MasterCard," she said, frowning again. "The automatic teller ate it when you reported it missing."

"Did he force you to use it? To withdraw any money?"

"Yes. I mean no. I mean sometimes." Allie fanned herself with her hand, trying to catch her breath. She was flustered. "It's complicated."

Luke said he could make it simple. Eddie Ray was found with her credit cards and jewelry. "Do you want me to charge him with robbery or theft?"

"Did you recover the earrings?"

Luke nodded.

"Why do I have to decide now?"

"Because," Luke told her, "he's in jail and people need to know."

Allie shook her head. "I don't want anything else about me in the newspaper."

"Good," he replied. Luke knew that Detective Howe would not pursue state charges now against Bok but would recommend federal ones concerning the con job at Job Service. Someone else would handle it. "That's settled."

"We need a vacation," Allie said.

Luke told her that he would be traveling to Japan on business tomorrow and that she should accompany him.

"Fantastic," she said, sighing in relief. She needed to get out of town and the limelight.

Now all Luke had to do was notify authorities about Allie and request that they wait until tomorrow before releasing any information. Then he would try to locate Elizabeth. He turned to use the phone when Allie reached out and kissed him on the cheek. The worst was over now, though some problems remained. For the moment, all he had to do was hold her, bury his face into her hair that smelled sweetly of Prell, and enjoy the feel of her. He hadn't lost everything, after all. Luke had found himself. "Allie, Allie," he whispered and returned her kiss passionately, intimately, as the cuckoo clock in the background went off, marking high noon.

20

Scooped
And Duped

It had been awhile since Claude Turner had invited Mylo Thrump to the Gentry, once a monastery and now a barbed-wire enclosed palatial estate. It was quarter past noon. Mylo was late because of the midday rush. Worse, the cabby—a Third World refugee of some sort, maybe Pango Pango—had yet to master U.S. traffic, swerving back and forth and nearly colliding with other vehicles. Finally the taxi turned from the access road to the mile-long bumpy gravel one leading to the country club.

Mylo was queasy enough, dreading the meeting. He became more so because he tried to read the *Chronicle* in the backseat. He had brought a copy of the morning edition to impress

Claude, if, as Mylo suspected, the publisher was going to discipline him for overtime and other expenses. There was also a new wrinkle—the jailing and release of Kimberly and Laurel. Mylo had returned to the holding cell last night after filing his story only to learn from the guard that the reporters had been freed. Neither one had checked in with him at the newsroom or had come to work this morning. If the publisher demanded an explanation, Mylo planned to tell him tht he had decided to prioritize, making sure the newspaper got out before the girls did.

The taxi was halfway to the entrance. The closer it came, the more Mylo tensed. So he opened the *Chronicle* again to admire the headline—

E.R. Bok Claims D.A.'s
Wife Abducted By UFOs!

along with the adjacent sidebar—

Suspect Sights "Elvis"
As Allie Beams Aboard!

and felt better.

With any luck, the edition would sell out and offset expenses for the week. Mylo was proud of his work, the best fabrications of his tabloid career. They were bound to get Wendy's attention, especially since the *Herald* would be copycatting his concept. *Bring on the competition,* Mylo thought. Wendy would be out of her league and maybe, just maybe, back in their house.

He folded and tucked the newspaper under his arm as the cab continued its crawl toward the club entrance. He hoped

Claude already had read the stories whose bizarre aspects were balanced with facts and quotes. Mylo had called up a dozen 1-900 psychics, paying for interviews. Laurel's psychic who did police work on occasion had told Mylo that Allie was fine and would return home within forty-eight hours, but he had omitted this from the published version. His readers may or may not believe in UFOs or Elvis, but they were certain the D.A.'s wife had been slain. Mylo planned to reinforce that notion without actually stating it outright. In the end, he knew, that was why they read the *Chronicle*. He would explain this to Claude. Then he would broach the delicate subject of the missing reporters who, for all Mylo knew, had been abducted by the same aliens that had beamed up Allie.

Mylo dug into his pocket for the fare as the cab pulled up at the entrance. He opened his wallet and extracted a crisp ten. The fare was $9.25. "I need a receipt," Mylo told the driver.

The valet outside opened the cab door.

The cabby muttered something in Pango Pangoese. He inspected the ornate architecture of the Gentry, giving Mylo a blank receipt. "Reech get reecher," he said.

Mylo took the receipt and stuffed it into his pocket—he would fill in $15.75 later as a business expense—and told the driver to keep the change.

"Reech get reecher," the cabby said again.

The valet stuck his head inside. "Coming sir?"

Mylo stepped out of the cab, the valet slammed the door, and the cabby pulled away with his arm out, as if to signal a right turn. He gave the "reech" the finger, a gesture that spoke without an accent and had universal meaning.

Armed with the *Chronicle*, Mylo climbed the triple-tier steps of The Gentry, opened the oaken doors, and headed for the dining room.

The maitre d', bearded, in black—resembling a professor at the reservation desk—blocked Mylo's path. "Follow me, please," he said, as if he recognized the editor or had been given a detailed description. "Mr. Turner is waiting."

"Lead the way," Mylo replied, undoing the knot of his tie. He was nervous, sensing some kind of trap as the maitre d' escorted him toward the far corner of the room where Claude had a private table. Mylo and the maitre d' passed a bank of stained-glass bay windows and imagined the original ones of the monastery, magi or halos; the ones now featured scenes of yawls, surreys, hearths, zeppelins—water, earth, fire, air—symbolizing what the membership owned. *Reech get reecher*, Mylo thought, imagining a story that would appeal to the city's large immigrant population.

Mylo eased his apprehension by identifying patrons at each table. People who appeared regularly on the social page or in club news. Mylo wished that he could decipher the murmur, the scandalous indiscretions and backstabbing. The luxurious lies. He could assign stories simply by noting who sat with whom: city manager and comptroller; senator and archbishop; banker and aerobics instructor; Margaret Hopkins, Wendy Thrump, Laurel Eby, and Kimberly Spears.

Mylo stopped—"I'll be damned"—and stared at the happy quartet. "The *Sappho Gazette*."

"Sir," the maitre d' said, putting his arm around Mylo as if they were close friends and leading him to Claude's table two tables down from where his wife sat with her boss and his protégés. Mylo let the maitre d' guide him, pull out a chair, and seat him across from his publisher.

"You're twenty minutes late," Claude said.

Mylo was still looking at the other table. Wendy noticed him, cocked her head, and blinked both eyes, an eerie acknowledgment.

Then she smiled and nudged Laurel, who saw Mylo and nudged Kimberly, a chain reaction of betrayal. Margaret Hopkins's thin sloping shoulders bobbed up and down, as if the old woman were giggling, but she did not turn around: bad form.

When Mylo did, his publisher was fuming.

Claude was bibbed for lunch, but his food, trout and rice pilaf, was untouched on his plate. The trout with its glazed head and open gills looked more dead than delicacy. "I took the liberty of beginning without you," the publisher told him.

A tuxedoed waiter came to the table and asked Claude whether he should show his guest a menu.

"No," Claude replied.

The waiter scurried off and stood guard in the corner of the room, smart enough to know that when a member was angry, you kept within sight but not within earshot.

"I haven't eaten lunch," Mylo told him.

"What you have eaten," Claude replied, "are my profits. Or, shall I say, *I* have eaten them. Losses." He pushed his plate aside and displayed his ledger, multicolored arrows on laser-printed glossy paper. "Let's start with this arrow—overtime—and make our way toward phone and print-shop expenditures."

While Claude was explaining what the arrows meant, Mylo glanced at Wendy's table again, noticing that Kimberly was holding a copy of the *Chronicle* while Laurel pointed at the headline. The reporters giggled. Margaret's dainty shoulders bobbed. Wendy laughed and then covered her mouth.

"Mr. Thrump!" Claude scolded. "Pay attention to me. You can pay them a visit later." He coughed. "You'll be leaving momentarily."

Mylo forced himself to look at the ledger. "What were you saying?"

Frustrated, Claude picked up the ledger and placed it on an adjacent chair. "It doesn't matter at this point."

Mylo used the opportunity to plop down the *Chronicle* beside Claude's plate so that the publisher could read it as he ate. The dead trout looked even deader alongside a newspaper. "Don't worry about profits," he told Claude. "This'll sell out."

"Take the paper away at once!" Claude hissed, and the waiter, observing in the corner, strode toward the table and asked if he should take away the plate. The publisher blushed. "No, Wayne."

The waiter returned to the corner like an obedient sentry.

"Excuse me a moment," Mylo said, leaving the newspaper on the table and approaching Wendy and her cohorts.

"Look who's here," Kimberly said to Laurel.

"Oh."

Wendy told him, "Knot your tie."

Mylo addressed the reporters. "Why didn't you come to work last night or at least call in? Where were you this morning? What are you doing here?"

"Sir," Margaret Hopkins interrupted. "You are making a scene."

"I think it's all very obvious," Laurel, his ex-ally, noted.

Margaret said, "This is a private celebration."

"What are you celebrating?" he asked Wendy, knotting his tie.

"That's obvious, too," Kimberly replied, smug as ever.

Mylo noticed that they were drinking champagne from long tubular glasses.

Kimberly raised hers and Laurel clinked it.

"Please leave," Wendy told Mylo. "I'll talk to you later. Promise."

Mylo felt gentle hands around his shoulders as the vigilant waiter guided him back but did not seat him again at Claude's table. The place setting, newspaper, and the publisher's lunch had been taken away. This time the waiter did not return to the corner of the room.

"You're fired," Claude said to Mylo.

"I quit," Mylo replied.

"Did you hear him, Wayne?" the publisher asked the waiter.

"Yes."

"Good," Claude said. "I accept your resignation, Mr. Thrump."

Mylo winced. The publisher was weaseling out of benefits. "I take that back. I'm fired."

"Too late."

"Why?"

Mylo wanted to know why it was too late to be fired but the publisher misunderstood and said, "You cost me thousands of dollars in expenses. My switchboard tells me someone has been making 1-900 calls, at your behest. You failed to inform me about my political adversary, Luke, conducting newsroom searches in *my* building and imprisoning my reporters. Worse, your treatment of our women yesterday will affirm allegations that Ms. Spears has made against you in a suit that she has filed, or so my attorney counsels. And if that is not enough, dear man," Claude said, unbibbing himself and whipping the cloth to the table, "then please look again at the table where your wife is seated with Mrs. Hopkins. She is rubbing this in my face before my friends and associates"—

"Mine, too."

—"on the eve of my announcing as a candidate for City Commission."

"Bad timing."

The waiter brought Claude a covered plate and left quickly during the lull. Claude lifted the lid and took out a steaming cloth, washing his hands of the matter like Pilot. "Despite what you may think," he told Mylo, "this is, decidedly, not personal. The *Herald* has adopted our format, I am told. In light of all you have done in recent days, what choice do I have?"

"Keep me. We scooped the *Herald* today and we'll scoop 'em tomorrow."

"How?" Claude asked, whipping the cloth on the table as he had done his bib. "By allowing a suspect who may have slain the wife of one of my club members to use my newspaper as a vehicle of shame and embarrassment?"

"So you read my story about E.R. Bok?" Mylo folded his arms and defended it. "I interviewed a man in jail. He told me that Allie Effington was abducted by UFOs. If he's guilty, the jury will say so. If he's crazy, the jury won't. But in either case," Mylo said, "it's not our responsibility."

"That may have worked with your former reporters," Claude said, "but that won't wash with me." He folded his hands so the knuckles whitened. A few guests at other tables turned to witness what was transpiring at Claude's. He coughed, swallowed, and breathed deeply. His knuckles returned to healthy pink.

Mylo was enjoying all this. "You were saying?"

"This story will stay in people's minds," Claude said. "They will clip it and put it in memory books and link my name thereto when they vote. Moreover, my opponents in the primary will run ads about it and wage a miserable campaign, harkening this inane"—he paused, stifling a cough—"this *inhumane* UFO story. My character is at stake. My reputation as a serious businessman. Thus," he concluded, "I have no choice now but to return to the old format and assign one of our senior employees to reestablish our credibility."

So, Mylo thought, the old-timers were going to be celebrating his firing, too, as the women were across the way, clinking goblets.

The waiter used the lull to remove Claude's washcloth from the table. Before he could leave, the publisher told him, "Please escort Mr. Thrump out of the dining hall."

The waiter put his hand on Mylo's arm, and he batted it away.

"I can find my own way out."

"Make sure you do so without stopping at Margaret's table," Claude said. He motioned to the waiter. "See that he does."

Mylo stopped at Margaret's table.

The waiter rushed to him and grasped him by the arm, pulling Mylo toward the exit.

"Old woman," Mylo said, as Margaret and the rest of the guests watched with embarrassment and interest. He pushed the waiter aside and pointed at Claude. "He's afraid of you. Good show."

Margaret pretended not to listen.

Mylo ambled outside to the steps of the country club and stopped, welcoming the fresh air. As he did he heard his wife call behind him, "Wait up, will you?" Wendy had followed him outside. Mylo felt happy that she cared enough to console him. He had feelings for her. In a perverse way, he admired how she had snared Laurel and Kimberly while he was working on his story, scoring a coup with an exclusive interview with E.R. Bok. This afternoon, on the display rack of the Little Prince Book Store, the *Chronicle* would go out in a blaze of red ink, Elvis, and UFOs, while the *Herald*—due out in two hours—would pale as usual alongside it. He was going to tell this to Wendy when he noticed she was holding some documents.

"I have something for you," she said.

"Look, Wendy. I just got sacked. Can't this wait?

She seemed genuinely concerned. "I'm sorry, Mylo."

They were standing toe to toe. Her dark hair, streaked with little gray, was blowing off her shoulders. "You're not going to serve me with divorce papers now, are you?" he asked.

"Soon."

"Good," Mylo said. He had another divorce to deal with today, his marriage to the *Chronicle*.

"It's been fun competing with you," Wendy said, asking him if he had any plans.

"Any openings at the *Herald*?"

"You'd be working for me, buster."

"Put me on rewrite. I know how to edit those girls."

"I edit better."

"Old times," he said, thinking about the early days of their marriage. Anything he could do, Wendy thought she could do better. They should've played the song—"Anything You Can Do"—at their wedding instead of the bridal march. Mylo couldn't resist one last dig before he asked the valet to summon a taxi for him so he could return to the *Chronicle*, to clear out his office. "Did you read my stories in the paper this morning?"

Wendy smiled weakly. "That's why I wanted to speak to you. But now since you've been fired"—she tucked the papers under her arm—"let go, I mean. Well," she said, "no need."

Mylo thrust out his hand. "Let me read what you have there," he said. Maybe Wendy was going to ask his advice.

"No."

"Come on."

"Oh, sure," she said, weakening a wee too soon for his liking. She gave him printouts of two front-page *Herald* stories. One carried a double by-line—Laurel Eby *and* Kimberly Spears—claiming that Allie Effington was alive and well and had visited Mr. Bok yesterday in jail. "She never was abducted, you know," Wendy said, "by Elvis or anyone else. In fact, I know how she feels." Wendy hesitated, and for a moment, Mylo thought that she would embrace him. "I know how it hurts to leave your husband because," she said, "you can't face him anymore in the morning."

"Geez, Wendy. Thanks."

"Sometimes you leave to make a point."

"You're making one now, I take it," Mylo said. He read the *Herald* story, seething inside. He remembered the disheveled-looking woman in the lobby by the retaining door of the cell block, dismissing her as the junkie girlfriend of another inmate. "I think that I am going to be ill," he whispered, admiring the headline—

D.A.'s Wife Is Safe & Sound, Roaming City Underground

—the damn thing even rhymed!

"A bit too 'tab' for my taste," Wendy said, "but that's what the public wants."

Mylo scanned the second printout containing Wendy's story—

D.A. Quits, Drops Out Of Race, Awaiting Return Of His Spouse

—and looked up. "When did that happen?" he asked.

"This morning. I didn't see you or anyone from the *Chronicle* at the press conference," she said. "I knew I did some damage but I followed you out here to say it wasn't personal."

"It sure feels personal," Mylo said, acknowledging that he had been scooped and duped by his soon-to-be ex-wife. In sum, the story of his career had turned out to be his editorial obituary.

"Don't take it personally even it feels that way." Wendy looked smugger than Kimberly and Laurel ever were in his newsroom. She was savoring her own moment. "I never thought I would see it," she said.

Mylo Thrump had been trumped.

21

The Untold Story

It was Friday morning. Allie had already had her fix of coffee at the kitchen table. The thump of the *Chronicle* and cluck of the cuckoo had tolled, setting off flurries inside her. She had plugged in the telephones because Luke was at the office, signing Eddie Ray's release—ironically, his last act as D.A. She needed to keep an open line but still screen calls through her answering machine. Luke was due back any moment. The sooner, the better. Their flight for Japan left in less than two hours, and nobody in the media knew that she was home.

But they would as soon as Eddie Ray was released.

Allie was having second thoughts. In the past week her moods had swung like a tetherball around a pole. Now that she was home, the minimansion seemed different, as did her marriage and outlook on life. It was not all bad. For instance, the middle-class taste of her husband seemed less pretentious now rather than gaudy, as if he didn't require high-ticket items to remind him of his wealth. Allie had begun to see Luke for what he *was* rather than for what he wasn't, and she discovered she had wed a committed moral man trying his best to employ his God-given talents in helpful ways. Allie knew other rich men who didn't run for public office; profit was their sole pursuit. In his place, these men would have dumped Allie and excluded her in divorce settlements. Luke wanted her back, and she worried that she would not live up to his expectations.

Allie sighed. There had been only one awkward moment concerning Eddie Ray when Luke had felt obliged to ask if they had practiced safe sex. Fair question, she told him. But still experienced shame and guilt. Luke reassured her immediately that he only was being practical and took her in his arms, showing her a tenderness that she never knew existed: love, with no bounds or conditions. And yet, despite all the changes, her newfound essence, her revitalized marriage, her deeper spiritual yearnings—despite her better judgment—Allie, for some reason, felt the old depression rise and damper her goals.

She tried to rationalize these feelings. It had been a rollercoaster week that had begun with a tryst and mystery abduction and ended in the *Chronicle* with Elvis and UFOs. She had clipped that front-page story and put it in her memory book in the bedroom. She had enjoyed all the attention as an alcoholic enjoys a drink, sating some inner destructive craving. Alone now in her kitchen with the portable telephone alongside her empty coffee cup, in case she needed her husband—Allie was the one who had requested this—she felt dependent again and lonely. She wished she could tap that sense of reborn faith and confidence she had experienced in her moment of need at Seton Place; but it, too, had escaped her like air from a punctured balloon.

Allie swirled the black liquid in her coffee cup. Then watched it settle and smooth on the bottom. Perhaps, she thought, the trip to Japan had brought on the bout of doom and gloom, for the only fate worse than being a D.A.'s wife was being a VIP one accompanying a husband on a buying spree for a cut-rate department-store chain.

"Get with it," Allie said to herself. She went upstairs to the bedroom and entered the walk-in closet, pulling out the set of alligator luggage from the bottom rack. She ran a hand over the merchandise—it reminded her of Eddie Ray's snakeskin boots—and felt sorry for reptiles that lost their skin because humans had clothes and feet. Maybe the airline would lose the baggage.

Allie was morose. She put the suitcases on the unmade bed and opened a valise, inhaling the musky scent. It reeked of the past. The not-so-good old days. She closed her eyes and tried to forget the years of boredom with a man on the cutting edge of synthetic. She had to remind herself that people change and Luke *had* changed but wondered whether people also reverted back to their bad habits. Already her desire to help the homeless seemed like a tremendous commitment now, one that potentially could disappoint hundreds of deserving individuals.

Allie lapsed into a daze and grabbed a handful of magazines from the rack by her side of the bed, throwing them in the valise. She noticed what she was doing and tried to read meaning into her absentmindedness. After personal upheaval, some people sought the company of new friends, but Allie read new magazines. She could even chart the changes in her life by the publications she kept, going from *Teen Beat* to *Young Miss* in her adolescent mall stage and then to a steady progression of women's magazines, *Seventeen* to *Glamour* to *Cosmo* to *Vogue* to *Harper's Bazaar* and finally to *Elle*, whose cover models she most resembled, beautiful but slightly off-kilter. Was there life after *Elle*? And if so, did it mean *Redbook*, *McCall's*, and *Good House-keeping*? A progression that could lead, if you weren't careful, to Rotary Ann-dom? She dismissed the thoughts and fetched her designer wardrobe—A to Z—-Alain to Zena, even the evening wear. Then packed Luke's clothes—polyester suits, matching belts, knee-high socks, retro ties—100 percent "virgin" rayon shirts. These were clothes that would melt instead of burn if she tossed them into the fireplace.

Perhaps Allie could help Luke select a new line in Tokyo. *No*, Allie thought. *Absolutely not.* She would not latch onto Luke's life, as Elizabeth had done, to give meaning to her own. She finished packing, disgusted with herself. Then remembered she had a mission: putting a little *home* into homeless shelters. She had a role model: Gertrude, the caretaker at Seton Place. She had a life: a rich one. Somehow she would use the wealth that was part hers as Luke's wife to remodel facilities throughout the city. As for the new shelter on the outskirts, maybe she could devise a transportation system—a bus or taxi service—stopping at points downtown to pick up residents. "Yes," Allie said as she hauled the suitcases to the front door. Now her mood swung the other way, from depression to contentment.

The mood of the house seemed to sway with her. The telephone was ringing in the kitchen and Luke's Firebird was cherry-bombing down the street. He was home so there was no need to answer the call. Instead she returned to the kitchen and listened to the machine click on the fourth ring. After the announcement—Luke stating that he was unable to get to the phone, Elizabeth said, in her usual tone: "Pick it up."

Allie did. Before her sister-in-law could respond, Allie apologized to her for duping her Monday night in the restroom at Rotary Club. The admission was met with silence. "Elizabeth? Are you there?" Allie called into the receiver.

"You're home," her sister-in-law said in a deadpan voice.

"Where are *you*?"

"Tulsa."

Now Allie was speechless, assuming this had to do with Eddie Ray. Elizabeth's nosiness could complicate matters just as Allie had been working out solutions.

"My prayers are answered," Elizabeth said, explaining that she had arrived yesterday in Oklahoma to visit Oral Roberts. "Praise the Lord," she said. "You're safe."

Luke announced in the hall that he was home.

"You prayed for *me*?" Allie asked, almost ready to share her own reborn experience at Seton Place. She had not yet confided that to Luke. "I didn't know that you had any feelings for me. Good ones, I mean."

"I don't," Elizabeth replied. "But I'm smart enough to know that if my brother loses you, then I lose him. I lose everything."

Luke entered the kitchen. "There you are," he said.

"Why don't you tell him that yourself, Elizabeth"—

"Is she all right?" he asked.

—"He's right here." She gave him the phone and sat at the table, feeling depressed again. The mood swings were driving her crazy! Not only would Allie have to rebuild her life with

Luke, she would have to deal with Elizabeth, who intended to hang on to her husband.

Luke filled in Elizabeth about what had transpired since the press conference during which he had resigned and dropped out of the race. He paused, listening to her. Allie could hear the tinny voice lash out at him. "That's not how it's going to be," he informed her. "You have your own life. Better yet," he said, glancing at Allie apologetically, "you have a career. Hold on." He put his hand on the receiver and whispered to Allie that he had wanted to tell her this in private, but that she should listen in on his conversation with Elizabeth. "It's important."

"Huh?"

Luke removed his hand from the receiver and told his sister, "It's important, Liz." He disclosed why he was traveling to Japan. "I'm transferring to you controlling interest in Values, Inc. and selling my remaining shares to a business concern. Congratulations. You're the new CEO." He listened for her reaction. "Yes, you will." He paused. "No, you won't." He paused. "Well," he said, "you're wrong. You're the new head. You'll get the hang of it." Luke hung up and turned to Allie.

She was beaming. Her dreams were coming true. Allie and Luke would have to redefine and renew their lives and purposes in life *together.* She embraced and kissed him. "I'm proud of you, honey," she told him.

"How about a second honeymoon after Tokyo?" he asked Allie. "Then you can come home and take on the world."

Allie stroked his hair with sudden concern. She was excited by his offer of a vacation but put that momentarily out of her mind. She knew how idleness could destroy basic values and didn't want her husband to experience what she had at home. "What will you do, Luke?" she asked.

"I have no idea," he replied. "Not an inkling."

She pulled away from him. "That's not good." She explained how it feels to live in a house as large as theirs with nothing to do. "Can't you see?" Allie implored. "We're switching lives. I'm becoming active in the community and you're dropping out of it. That's not the solution."

He reached for her again. "Do I have to tell you, at this precise moment, what I'll be doing for the rest of my life?"

"No."

He held her close. "We'll have plenty of time during the trip to discuss this," he said. Luke told her that he had faith in his decisions because he was in contact with an inner voice. "I think it's God or the Spirit guiding me. Or maybe my conscience." He shook his head. "But you don't want to hear that, I know."

"I've changed," Allie said, beginning to appreciate a man who believed in a power greater than his own. Men could be such power jerks. Maybe if more believed in a deity, they would be nicer to women, knowing they would be held accountable. Allie confided a few details of her moment of peace and security that occurred while she was at Seton Place. "I don't know why it's so hard to share with you, Luke. It's so *private*." In fact, telling him about it now seemed like another betrayal.

"Like I said, we'll have plenty of time to discuss that, too, on our trip," Luke reminded her. "Now, where would you like to go?"

"Maui."

The phone rang.

"That's Elizabeth," Luke said. "She doesn't want to be CEO. But she'll have to or sell the family business." He smiled, proud of himself. "I'm forcing her to make that choice." He reached to pick up the phone.

"No," Allie said, stopping him.

"I really should talk to her," Luke replied.

"Let me." Allie didn't want Elizabeth throwing a wrench in their plans with some new ploy, feigning illness or a breakdown at Oral Roberts. On the other hand, that wasn't a bad place to get sick, with healers and hospital beds by the hundreds there. "I need to assert myself," Allie told him. "You're my husband. She has to respect that."

Allie picked up the phone. "Hello?"

"Who's this?" the voice said.

"Allie," she replied on impulse, confused because it wasn't Elizabeth.

"So you're home," the voice said. "Just as I figured."

Oops.

"Who's on the line?" Luke asked.

"Who *is* this?" Allie inquired.

"Mylo Thrump."

"Mylo Thrump," Allie repeated in a flat tone. Then she lapsed, once more, into another of her infamous dazes. *Flash* went the trip to Japan. *Flash* went the second honeymoon to Maui. *Flash flash* went the discussions about Luke's future and Allie's faith.

"Hang up," Luke told her.

Thrump said, "I'm on assignment for the *National Enquirer*. My readers have inquiring minds like your own, Mrs. Effington."

"Hang up the phone, Allie!" Luke took it from her and said, "No comment."

Allie took the phone away from him.

"What are you doing?" Luke asked.

"Asserting myself," she replied, and told Thrump to phone Elvis or E.T. if he wanted an interview.

"Good quote," Mylo told her. "I'll be right over."

Allie hung up and told Luke, "Quick. Rev up the Firebird.

"I'll get the bags," he said.

"I'll lock the house."

Luke ran for the front door.

The phone rang again and Allie, on impulse, looked for the cord to rip out of the wall as she had seen so many times on television. But this was a portable phone so she unscrewed the antenna. That didn't work. The message on the answering machine ended and a new voice said, "This is Wendy Thrump from the *Herald*. I understand you're safe at home. Please pick up the phone, Mrs. Effington." Allie banged the phone on the kitchen table, committing an act of phone-a-cide. The receiver fell apart. But the answering machine was in the living room and needed to be unplugged. The twenty-second message time ran out for Wendy Thrump as the cherry bombs of the Firebird fired in the driveway.

"Come on!" Luke called to Allie at the front door. "The bags are in the trunk! Let's go!"

The phone rang again. Allie ran to the open door—Luke was already in the driver's seat, motioning to her—as Eddie Ray's voice resounded like a ghost throughout house. "I'm free, bitch. Thought you-all'd like to know." Allie froze as the call clicked off and his words resonated through her being. She felt faint. She felt her hopes sink as if her feelings were as heavy as lead in her body. Her moods had swung this way and that so many times this morning that Allie was ready to acquiesce and collapse. Or have a bonafide breakdown. Then it happened again. The warmth entered where the pain ached most inside her and emanated out, soothing her. You didn't need another person to rescue you, if you knew where to look within for the answers. This time Allie heard an inner voice telling her: *Everything is going to be all right.*

The phone rang again.

Allie flicked on the security system locking the doors and windows throughout the minimansion and reporting any break-ins to police headquarters, where her former-D.A. husband had plenty of friends. She ran to open the passenger door and got in the car.

"Hit it," she said as the Firebird with the eagle emblem on the hood blasted out of the drive and into the street, as if it would take wing and ascend into the white puffs of cloud that awaited them on high.

"Praise the Lord," Luke said.

Allie eased back in her bucket seat and closed her eyes, welcoming the rumble of the engine, louder than one on a jet. "You can say that again."

Luke did.

Allie knew that he would.

They were on a journey together, realizing that marriage was about two spirits uniting as one, not two bodies. Like millions of Americans, Luke and Allie were trying to rekindle faith—in God and each other—a happy-ending story that no tabloid would touch, in this day and age.